Murder on the Last Frontier

MURDER ON THE LAST FRONTIER

CATHY PEGAU

KENSINGTON BOOKS
www.kensingtonbooks.com

To the extent that the image or images on the cover of this book depict a person or persons, such person or persons are merely models, and are not intended to portray any character or characters featured in the book.

This book is a work of fiction. Names, characters, places, and incidents either are products of the author's imagination or are used fictitiously. Any resemblance to actual persons, living or dead, events, or locales is entirely coincidental.

KENSINGTON BOOKS are published by

Kensington Publishing Corp.
119 West 40th Street
New York, NY 10018

All Kensington titles, imprints, and distributed lines are available at special quantity discounts for bulk purchases for sales promotion, premiums, fund-raising, educational, or institutional use.

Special book excerpts or customized printings can also be created to fit specific needs. For details, write or phone the office of the Kensington Sales Manager: Kensington Publishing Corp., 119 West 40th Street, New York, NY 10018. Attn. Sales Department. Phone: 1-800-221-2647.

eISBN-13: 978-1-4967-0055-1
eISBN-10: 1-4967-0055-4
First Kensington Electronic Edition: December 2015

ISBN-13: 978-1-4967-0054-4
ISBN-10: 1-4967-0054-6
First Kensington Trade Paperback Printing: December 2015

10 9 8 7 6 5 4 3 2 1

Printed in the United States of America

Acknowledgments

Many thanks to . . .

Marv Van Den Broek for inspiration from a story he told as my family and I explored a nearly forgotten graveyard.

Michele Harvey, beta reader extraordinaire, for catching glitches and asking all the right questions.

Author friends Alyssa Linn Palmer and Sharron Camaratta for reading/critiquing/plot help. You both keep me on track, tell it like it is, and make me a better writer.

Cathy Sherman, Nancy Bird, Mimi Briggs, and Denis Keogh at the Cordova Museum for letting me scour files and pick their brains. Paula Payne, Miriam Dunbar, Sally Campbell, and Anna Hernandez from the Cordova Public Library for support and pointing me to the right drawers and shelves.

Lovely agent Natalie Lakosil for sticking with me even when I'm freaking out.

Editor John Scognamiglio for liking Charlotte as much as I do and giving her a chance to get out in the world.

Extra special thanks to my friends and family for support and love. I couldn't do this without you!

Author's Notes

This is a work of fiction, just like it says in the disclaimer. No real persons, past or present, are depicted in these pages. The murder itself is loosely based on an incident I was told happened in Cordova, Alaska, in the 1930s or 1940s. I didn't pursue researching that crime and don't know any details of it. And to be honest, I didn't really want to know. Why? Because I didn't want to be influenced by the facts of a real case. If there are any similarities beyond the occupation of the victim, it is truly a coincidence. But now that the book is done, I'm going to look for that information!

A few real people involved in the history of Cordova and elsewhere are mentioned, but not portrayed here. Historic facts are presented with as much accuracy as I could muster, and if I missed or messed up anything, it's all on me. Cordova is, of course, a real place, though I will admit to scooting a few buildings here and there, changing the layout of the town a little, and tweaking names of establishments. That's artistic license for you.

Chapter 1

Cordova, Alaska Territory, 1919

The stench of rotting fish, salt, and tar rose from the dock and the water surrounding the *S.S. Snow Queen*, nearly making Charlotte Brody gag. Even if she'd had a free hand, she would have refused to press her handkerchief to her nose. She was in Alaska now, and Alaskan women were made of sterner stuff. They also probably breathed through their mouths to preserve their senses.

The midnight arrival had infused the steamship with bustling energy. The crew dashed about, doing whatever tasks were necessary when they made port. Disembarking passengers followed the signs and lanterns on the deck to the gangplank.

Clutching her satchel against her side to keep thieving hands from its contents, Charlotte grasped the rain-slick rail and made her way down the incline. The chest-to-back press of her fellow travelers was a situation calling for the protection of a scented handkerchief if there ever was one. Most of the passengers, herself included, hadn't seen a real tub in the seven days since leaving Seattle. There had been facilities for a washup each morning, but a long soak in a hot bath was definitely in order, and soon.

A gust of icy, wet wind blew in from the bay, plastering stray hairs to her cheek and sending a chill through her. Three weeks ago, Charlotte had been wilting in the heat and humidity of Yonkers. Now, she was shivering. Late August in Alaska was nothing like the summer days back East.

The *Snow Queen* bobbed against the pier, rocking the gangplank. Charlotte tightened her grip on the rail, taking care not to run into the sack slung over the shoulder of the man in front of her. If it weren't for the rain, the angle wouldn't have been nearly so treacherous. She shuffled along, grateful that current fashion put the hem of her skirt well above her ankles so it wouldn't catch on the rough planks or under her heels.

Michael was down there somewhere. The *Snow Queen*'s late arrival due to storm delays wasn't unusual, and the good-sized crowd on the dock attested to Cordovans' patience.

"Alaskans are used to things getting here when they get here," the captain had said during dinner one night.

Well, I'm here now.

A shimmer of anticipation skittered across Charlotte's skin and tickled her stomach. Her parents had tried to talk her out of going, but she was determined. Sidestepping the real reason she needed a change, she'd barely managed to keep her argument even-toned under their disapproval.

Eventually, they'd conceded, but only because Michael would be there. Not that their parents could have stopped her. At least the dark cloud of discontent had been lifted between the three of them.

Just a week's travel by train from Yonkers to Seattle, then the steamer to Alaska, and here she was. The Last Frontier.

The scenery on the way up the coast had been breathtaking. Glorious mountains, stretches of blue-white glaciers, even a number of small icebergs that made a few passengers fret. The *Titanic* disaster was still quite fresh in people's minds.

Charlotte hadn't been concerned. The extended daylight hours so far north meant hazards were easier to avoid. She often stayed out on deck, bundled against the chill and unaware of the time, watching porpoises swimming in front of the bow, sea otters floating on their backs as they bobbed on the waves, and large brown bears ambling along the not-so-distant beaches. She was familiar with the gulls that followed the boat, but the sight of bald eagles soaring overhead was a first for her. One time, a great leviathan had breached off the port side, close enough to see barnacles clinging to its lower jaw. Charlotte thought her heart had stopped as the beast threw itself up into the air and crashed to the surface, spraying water onto the lower deck.

"Charlotte, over here!" Michael's familiar voice called up to her over the crowd.

Her gaze darted among the upturned faces illuminated by the pier lights. Michael waved his fur cap, his blond hair fluttering in the sea breeze and a grand smile on his moustached lip.

A moustache? Her brother sporting a moustache? Mother would have had a say about that.

But Mother and Father were thousands of miles away.

Charlotte smiled, as happy to see Michael as she was relieved to leave the past back East, and released the rail to wave back. Her boot caught on the edge of the next plank, and she stumbled. Strong hands grabbed her long, wool coat from behind to keep her from falling into the man in front of her.

"Easy, miss," the gravelly voice behind her said, not unkindly, as she was set back on her feet. "No call for ye flyin' into the drink."

She glanced over her shoulder at the burly man who had saved her. "Thank you, no."

He touched his hand to his wide-brimmed hat and grinned. Or she assumed he grinned. The corners of his blue eyes creased and the tangle of graying brown facial hair moved in that manner.

Charlotte resumed her grip on the rail and safely made it to the bottom of the gangplank. Passengers veered off into the crowd waiting beyond the low wooden safety barrier. Michael shouldered his way to the front. The green mackinaw over his black suit was dotted with rain. She hurried over, dropped her bag, and threw herself into his arms.

Michael laughed and lifted her off her feet in a tight hug. He might have swung her around, but there were too many people within kicking range for such a thing. The town doctor shouldn't create patients.

"God, I've missed you, Charlie," he said, setting her on her feet.

Charlotte slapped his chest playfully. "I've missed you too, but not so much that you can call me by that nickname."

She was an adult now. Charlotte Mae Brody had made it to Alaska on her own and could take care of herself.

Michael rubbed his chest, still chuckling. "Fair enough." He hefted her satchel and gave an exaggerated grunt. "Goodness, what do you have in here? Bricks?"

Charlotte slipped her hand around his other arm. "Books. Be glad I packed my typewriter in my trunk."

They both glanced up at the block-and-tackle winch conveying pallets of cargo from the ship's hold. Longshoremen swung the heavy load expertly to the dock where workers sorted passenger bags onto open horse-drawn carts.

"Sullivan's rooming house has a storage shed," Michael said. "Your things should be there later. They'll be safe until morning when we can get them to your room."

Michael had told Charlotte he'd secure her a room as soon as she announced her intention to come to Alaska. Living at Sullivan's, he'd explained, would be more comfortable, as his own home, with its attached office and exam room, would be too small for the two of them.

"That's fine. I packed the necessities in my satchel."

"Yes, along with the bricks." They laughed again, and Michael guided her away from the ship. "There isn't much in the way of transportation to town. You up for a midnight stroll?"

A lone motorcar idled in front of the steamship company's office. Several people argued or haggled with the driver—and each other—for a ride in the six-passenger Model T. Even if there had been plenty of taxicabs, Charlotte would have refused a ride, as she felt quite awake and energized.

"I'm not in the least tired." She started toward the road, following the majority of folks who had disembarked. If Alaskans walked to town at midnight in the rain, so would she. "How far is it?"

"Half a mile or so."

The packed-dirt road was slick with mud. Michael drew his flashlight from the deep pocket of his coat to navigate around puddles. Walkers ahead and behind them had kerosene lanterns or flashlights as well. The chatter of conversation and the occasional burst of laughter accompanied them as Charlotte brought Michael up-to-date on family and friends.

The road followed the shoreline, curving in and out of patches of spruce trees to provide glimpses of the town ahead. Vague outlines of buildings and several streets lit with electric or gas lamps indicated it was larger than she had assumed.

"How many people live here?"

"One thousand or so, including the Natives who mostly live along the lake and homesteaders who live outside of town but use its services." He narrowed his gaze as if evaluating Cordova from a distance. "Things are a little different in these parts, Sis. It takes some getting used to."

"You know I've never been afraid of a challenge, Michael. I want to know what it's really like." She pulled him closer. "Not what you prettied up for Mother and Father, or what you glossed over for me. I want the real story of living here."

Michael stiffened, staring straight ahead, and said nothing for several moments. "I tried to keep some of the more shocking events out of my letters. Folks looking to leave civilization behind can be rough, and boys returning from war can have some troubles not suitable for correspondence with your little sister."

He hadn't been on the front himself, due to childhood bouts with bronchitis, but he'd worked at several stateside hospitals. He'd treated shell-shocked soldiers back East, and she had watched him lose sleep and weight throughout his tenure, due to his concerns for the men.

Before the war ended a year ago, Michael had responded to an advertisement for doctors in the Alaska Territory. As grim as he made it out to be, he'd regained weight and lost the haunted look he'd had before leaving New York. Alaska agreed with him, erasing the years of turmoil he'd endured on behalf of his patients. She hoped it would do the same for her.

"You could have told me." She hugged his arm tighter. "I'm not so delicate—or so little—that I can't lend an ear or a shoulder, you know."

He patted her arm. "Thank you, but I'm fine." Then he gave her a startled look. "Is that what brought you up here? You wanted to see what I *wasn't* telling you?"

Charlotte let out a laugh that masked her knee-jerk inclination to tell him the truth of it. A couple ahead of them turned around. She clamped her hand over her mouth, cheeks burning. The couple resumed their own quiet conversation.

"Something like that," she said at a more ladylike volume. "I've already started my first article to Kit. As soon as I can, I'll unpack and post it. She'll be tickled to get something postmarked from Alaska."

Kit, her best friend since their primary-school days, worked as an assistant editor at *The Modern Woman Review*. She'd been positively giddy over Charlotte's proposal for a series of articles written by a woman in the wild Alaska frontier. Kit's boss, Mr. Malone, had approved the assignment after he learned Charlotte would be paying her own way and giving them editorial latitude. She trusted Kit not to change her writing too much, and Charlotte would keep carbon copies of her work for reference. If necessary, she could compare her original stories to what was printed in *Modern Woman*.

The series would be less controversial than Charlotte's typical writings about the suffragette movement, as well as her more recent work on the potential effects of the soon-to-be-voted-upon national Volstead Act. Those articles had produced heated responses from all sides, something many journalists aspired to. What was the point of having your words in print if they weren't going to stir up emotion?

She wasn't one to back down, but after threatening letters to the papers and broken windows at her parents' home, she'd realized she needed to let things cool off before someone got hurt. Alaska, with its potential for adventure and an opportunity to make peace with herself, was the perfect solution.

"You can go after lunch tomorrow," Michael said. "The post office is in the federal building across from my office. Your little stories will find their way to the ladies back home in a month or so, depending on the weather. I'm sure they'll be a fine source of conversation for you and your friends when you return."

Charlotte drew him to a stop, her boots slipping in the mud, and hurt and anger squeezing her chest. "My little stories? Is that what you think of them? That they're just a lark, a fancy to pass the time here before I head home to . . . what? The ladies' sewing circle and Wednesday luncheons?"

He blinked down at her, his brow wrinkled. "That's not what I meant."

"No? Then what did you mean?" She released his arm and crossed her arms over her chest. She had sent him copies of her earlier articles in which she'd described the often dangerous and sometimes deadly struggles for equality and the potential ramifications of national Prohibition. Did he think those were frivolous too?

Michael shifted the flashlight to his other hand, then ran his fingers through his hair, catching his cap before it fell to the ground. He gave a heavy sigh, looking so much like Father—but with hair—that Charlotte had to steel herself against the inclination to agree with Michael, just to keep the peace.

"I meant your visit here will make a great read back home. You wrote that your friends were constantly asking about my life in Alaska. Now you can give them a taste of it. And yes, over luncheon. What's wrong with that?"

"What's wrong, aside from your belittling attitude, is that I may not go back." Charlotte resumed walking toward town, the heat of indignation keeping the chilled air at bay. Why had she said such a thing? The trip up the coast had been exciting, and she looked forward to the experience of Alaska, but to stay longer than April, as she'd planned?

Maybe. She wasn't sure yet. Living here would certainly keep her mind off the past twelve months.

She managed three or four steps before Michael grabbed her arm and spun her toward him. His face was contorted with confusion. "What? That's insane. You can't stay. I can't look out for you."

"I'm not asking you to. I'm an adult and quite capable of taking care of myself." Her anger diminished a smidgen at the concern in his eyes. Charlotte grasped his hand, loosening it from her arm, and squeezed his fingers. "Please, let's not argue about this, not now."

He leaned closer, his voice low so passersby couldn't hear. "This is no place for you, Charlotte. Unmarried women here are not treated as they are back home."

She knew exactly how some women were treated at home by family and society. By lovers. "You mean like possessions or playthings? Your letters suggested women here enjoyed more freedoms, not less."

"Married women, yes. Unmarried women are looked upon as a challenge to be wedded or bedded." His voice had taken on a low, growling quality that was quite unlike him. "There are few men here worthy of the former, and I'll be damned if anyone tries the latter."

Despite his brotherly protectiveness and the sentiment, she nearly laughed in his face. She was twenty-six years old. Did he truly believe she was so innocent? Now was probably not the time to horrify him with her indiscretions. "I'll be sure to consult you if anyone approaches with either proposition."

Even in the poor illumination of his flashlight, she saw his face darken at her flippant remark. Charlotte took his arm again and urged him onward, forestalling a lecture. The taxicab rumbled up from behind them, making it impossible to hear any response he might have had.

Good. She wasn't in the mood to argue. Not when the desire to be truthful with him, as they had been with each other until recent years, had put her within a hair's breadth of telling him everything.

Alaska had tamed his demons. Maybe it could tame hers as well.

The indistinct jangle of a distant piano became a jaunty tune as Charlotte and Michael stepped up onto the wooden boardwalk marking the start of the town proper. Faint, muddy footprints faded along the worn slats; shopkeepers were probably kept busy sweeping. Tall power poles lined both sides of the street. For some reason, the idea that Cordova had electricity, telegraph, and telephone lines amused Charlotte. Michael's descriptions in his letters notwithstanding, she'd expected something more rustic. Backwards even.

Michael flicked off his flashlight and returned it to his pocket. Electric streetlamps illuminated the buildings, all closed at the late hour. Nothing on the other side of the street seemed to be open either.

"Where's the music coming from?" she asked.

Michael gestured ahead and farther into town with his chin. "Probably the Tidewater Club. It stayed open late for the ship's arrival. No alcohol is served, supposedly, but they offer food and entertainment."

Several men veered off the boardwalk and up an alley between two dark buildings. A woman's laughter echoed back to the main street. There hadn't been a woman with them, which meant she'd been in the alley.

Charlotte caught Michael's eye. His cheeks flushed, and he looked away. Her own face heated. She knew about ladies of the evening, but that probably wasn't what he'd meant about entertainment, nor was it something a brother wished to discuss with his sister.

"Here's Sullivan's." He released her arm and dug into his trouser pocket.

The rooming house looked like many of the buildings along the row. The front windows, curtained for the night, were smaller than those of the general store across the street. A faint light glowed behind them.

Two quick gunshots rang out, close to where Michael had indicated the Tidewater was located. Charlotte's heart jumped into her throat, and she instinctively ducked. Michael covered her hunched form with his body. Pulse pounding, she heard no other reports and straightened. Michael peered up the road, into the darkness. When nothing further happened, he lowered his arm.

"Probably just celebrating," he said. "If not, I'll be patching someone up or performing an autopsy come morning."

She scanned the street, but no one so much as poked his or her head out a door or window to investigate. "Does that happen often?"

"The celebratory shooting? Once in a while."

"What about the autopsies?"

He shrugged. "Too often for my liking, but it's part of the job."

His acceptance of the possibility surprised Charlotte. While she'd expected Alaska to be untamed, shootings in the street weren't something she'd anticipated. Gun-toting cowboys, like the ones in the Buffalo Bill Cody's Wild West Show she'd seen as a child, were supposed to be reminiscent of days gone by. Maybe those days weren't quite gone here.

Michael removed a set of two keys on a brass fob from his pocket and fit the larger key to the lock. The door opened to a quaint parlor with two upholstered chairs and a round table with both a lamp and a black candlestick telephone on it. To the right, narrow stairs disappeared into darkness above. The air was damp, with a mustiness tinged with linseed oil. A poster on the wall listed the house rules. At the very top, written in bold script, were the visiting hours and a reminder that the front door was locked at nine p.m.

Michael gently closed the door behind them. "Ladies are on this floor," he whispered. "Mrs. Sullivan is in the first rooms on the left. She doesn't like visitors so late, but said I could show you to your room since you're my sister and all."

The stairs creaked, the sound followed by soft footfalls. Michael motioned for Charlotte to hurry down the hall. Before she could, a young woman came into sight, her sable hair in a loose pile atop her head. She stopped three steps from the bottom, her kohl-darkened eyes widened in surprise, and her hand pressed to her breast. Her low-cut green dress showed considerably more cleavage than Charlotte's square-collared blouse, and its narrow fit defined the woman's curves. After a moment, the woman relaxed and smiled, bringing her finger to her ruby lips. She minced down the last steps in glossy black buckled shoes.

"Mum's the word," she whispered, and winked at Charlotte in a conspiratorial manner. At the bottom of the stairs, she startled when she caught sight of Michael, but her grin quickly returned. "Hey there, Doc." She glanced between him and Charlotte, the grin broadening. "I won't tell if you won't."

Michael's cheeks reddened. "This is my sister Charlotte. I met her at the ship this evening."

The woman nodded. "That's right, I remember your mentioning she'd be visiting." How would she know Michael's personal business? She smiled at Charlotte, her hand extended. "I'm Marie. Welcome to Alaska."

Charlotte took her hand. From the corner of her eye, she saw her brother grimace. "Nice to meet you."

"The pleasure's mine." Marie turned back to Michael. "Before I forget, Doc. Darcy needs to see you. She's been feeling poorly the last week or so."

"I told her—" He had started to speak in a normal tone, then caught himself. The conversation had been carried on in whispers to prevent disturbing the landlady or other tenants. He lowered his voice. "I told her to come to my office last week for an exam."

Marie's expression became earnest. "Can't you come over tomorrow? Brigit's been giving her grief about slacking. More than usual, anyways. I know it's not your regular time and all, but Darcy's been sleeping all she can."

Charlotte cocked an eyebrow in query. Regular time?

Michael set down Charlotte's satchel and strode forward. Taking Marie's upper arm, he guided her to the front door. "Tell her I'll come by in the next couple of days. Meanwhile, she needs fluids—not alcohol—and as much rest as she can get."

"I'll tell her, but I don't know if Brigit will let her get all that much rest." Marie gave a chuckle, then glanced over her shoulder at Charlotte. "Nice meeting you."

Charlotte waved as Michael ushered Marie out the door and locked it behind her.

"When *is* your regular time to visit Darcy?" Charlotte asked, unable to keep the grin off her face.

He shook his head, realizing she wasn't about to let this particular subject drop. "Every other Thursday. I tend the whores at Miss Brigit's house, all right? Hastings, the other doctor, won't lower himself to see them. The U.S. marshal and the residents mostly pretend they don't exist as long as no one gets robbed and the girls get regular health exams."

Charlotte shrugged. "It seems like it's worked out for the best, under the circumstances."

"You approve of prostitution? I'd have thought a feminist like you would rail against such a thing." Michael crossed his arms and tilted his head, his standard posture for catching someone—particularly Charlotte—in a falsehood.

"I rail against the exploitation and abuse of anyone." She mimicked his stance. "Are the women willing participants, or is this Miss Brigit forcing them to solicit men?"

His shoulders dropped. "Willing, as far as I know."

Charlotte picked up her bag. "They're adults who have chosen what to do with their bodies. As long as they're being treated well, I have no issue with it if they don't."

A good number of her suffragette and feminist friends argued that it was exploitation either way, but Charlotte knew painting the entire sex trade with one stroke was wrong. Every situation was different. She was often in the minority with that thinking and wondered how the people of Cordova felt. Were they the "live and let live" sort of folks one would associate with a frontier community?

Michael gestured for her to continue down the hall. The floor beneath the worn runner squeaked under their weight. Another small lamp burned at the far end. The first door on the right was the water closet. Two more doors on the right and three on the left had black numbers neatly painted on their white surfaces. If the same configuration held upstairs, Mrs. Sullivan's ten dollars a month rent for each room earned her quite the income, depending on occupancy.

Michael stopped at the last door on the right and fit the second key to the lock. The door opened silently. He reached in and turned the knob on the wall. A lamp in the corner glowed with a soft light as the electric bulb warmed. Stepping into the room, Charlotte set her satchel on the square table. A wooden chair beside the table, a single narrow bed made up with a flowered quilt, and a wardrobe were all the furnishings. A radiator in the corner ticked, emitting heat. The double-hung window's curtains were drawn against the night. It wasn't much larger than her room back home, but it would suffice.

This is home, she reminded herself. *At least for now.*

"I'm guessing Mother and Father wouldn't exactly see the girls and Brigit the same way you do," he said solemnly, continuing the conversation now that they wouldn't disturb her new neighbors.

Charlotte unbuttoned her coat and draped it over the back of the chair. "If they did, brother dear, you would have told them you treat whores in your letters. You seem rather comfortable with the idea."

"They need medical attention, and it's my duty to keep them and the town healthy," he said.

"And no one's bothered that they're doing a brisk business here?" More interesting tidbits for her articles took root.

Michael handed her the keys, his lips pressed tight beneath his trim moustache. "Depends on who you talk to. I have patients first thing in the morning. I expect you'll want to sleep later than normal, considering the hour."

She gave herself a point for making him change the subject. "You know I'm not much of a morning person to begin with. I'll get acquainted with some of the town and come by your office for lunch."

"Farther down the road here, on the right. Can't miss it."

Charlotte rose on her toes to peck him on the cheek. "Thank you. I hope you're as glad to have me here as I am to be here."

He sighed like Father again. "I am, but you must understand, it's a different world here. I just want you to be safe." He chucked her under the chin. "I'm your big brother. It's my right to be overprotective."

They both smiled. No matter their disagreements, Charlotte

knew they'd be able to work things out eventually. She chalked up his protectiveness as natural concern, but she'd show him soon enough that there was no need for him to worry.

"Come lock the front door behind me, or Mrs. Sullivan will have my hide."

She followed him out to the parlor and bid him good night. After locking the door, Charlotte returned to her room and opened the valve on the radiator. She sat on the bed. Springs creaked, but nothing poked out from beneath the covers. Someone coughed in the room beside hers. Scraping and squeaking sounds from overhead suggested the man above her had shifted in bed.

Or there was another late-night visitor like Marie.

Pulling her satchel to her, she withdrew her journal, pen, and inkpot. She was now too weary to stay up for long, but wanted to get the initial emotion and images of landing in Cordova down before losing them to sleep.

Adventures on the Last Frontier, she wrote.

She couldn't wait.

Chapter 2

Bam-bam-bam.

Her head pounded. She covered it with the pillow, but that didn't help.

Bam-bam-bam.

"Deputy Marshal. Open up in there!"

Charlotte bolted upright, headache forgotten, and flung the blankets off. Heart racing, she hurried to the door and opened it. "What's wrong? Is there a fire?"

A man in a wide-brimmed hat filled the doorway, his fist raised. Black eyebrows met over a nose that might have been broken once or twice. Glacier-blue eyes burned into hers as he lowered his hand. "You're not Martha Griggs."

He sounded somewhat disappointed.

His gaze traveled from Charlotte's face to her body. She was suddenly aware of her state. She wore her thin nightclothes, her hair was loose about her shoulders, and the chill of the morning had caused his eyes to linger on her chest for a reason. She crossed her free arm over her breasts and held onto the edge of the door.

"No, I'm not."

Before she could give her name, he stepped forward. When she refused to give way, he peered into the room over her head as if this Martha person was hiding within. This close, Charlotte noted his mackinaw had seen better days, as had the brown wool shirt beneath it, though he smelled clean enough.

"Where is she?" he asked with more than a little frustration in his voice. There was a hint of some accent, but she couldn't place it.

"I don't know. I've only been here since last night."

He glared down at her, backing up a step. "Not a working girl, are you?"

Heat rose through Charlotte's chest, neck, and face. "No, I'm not."

She must have blushed mightily, because his stern expression became a wry grin. "You seem flustered."

"Of course I am. Pounding on the door at such an ungodly hour would fluster anyone."

"It's nearly ten, ma'am. Hardly ungodly. At least for the God-fearin'."

Charlotte's fingers pressed into the wood door. "It isn't God you need to fear, Deputy."

The man's eyes narrowed. "Are you threatening a federal marshal?"

Oh, Lord. She had, hadn't she? But the glint in his eyes and the smile threatening to break his frown assured her he was teasing. Nonetheless, she'd tread carefully from now on.

"What's your name?" he asked.

She swallowed hard, then licked her dry lips. "Charlotte Brody."

He gave her another quick perusal and backed up a step. "The doctor's sister."

It made sense that the townspeople knew Michael, but did everyone know she'd be visiting? With only one thousand souls, it was likely.

"Yes."

The deputy swept his hat off his head. Of course, now he'd be polite, knowing who her brother was. A lock of dark hair tumbled over his forehead. He smoothed it out of the way. "Sorry, ma'am. Sullivan's is a reputable place, but now and again a new woman tries to set up shop here. We had word Martha moved in from another location."

"I haven't seen anyone of the sort." The lie came easily. She had no proof Marie's visit last night was anything but innocent. No proof at all.

He set the hat on his head and tugged the brim. "Sorry to bother you, Miss Brody. If you see or hear of any of the ladies moving in, I'd be obliged if you let me know. Marshal's office is right across from your brother's place, in the federal building."

"Are you the only one there, Deputy . . . ?"

His smile revealed a small dimple in his left cheek. "Eddington. James Eddington. And no, I'm not. My superior is Thomas Blaine. Either of us can take your statement."

"Thank you, Deputy Eddington."

He touched the hat brim again. "Ma'am."

Eddington turned on his heel with almost military precision. He strode down the hall as if he owned the place, tall leather boots thudding on the carpet. Charlotte watched until he disappeared around the corner into the parlor and she heard the front door close.

Retreating into her room, she pushed her door closed and leaned her forehead against the cool wood. Not even twenty-four hours in town and she'd twice been mistaken for a sporting woman. A wry laugh escaped her throat. Surely that was some sort of record.

Charlotte dressed in her clothes from the day before and met briefly with Mrs. Sullivan to arrange retrieving her trunks from the shed. The older woman assured her they would remain safe until she was ready to have them delivered to her room. Charlotte insisted she could get them herself, but Mrs. Sullivan was equally adamant that hauling trunks was no work for a proper young lady. And according to Mrs. Sullivan, Cordova needed more proper young ladies. Her two sons, she said, could damn well earn their keep.

Charlotte thanked Mrs. Sullivan, barely managing to refrain from laughing, then went in search of a cup of coffee before meeting Michael for lunch. As she made her way to the café two muddy blocks away, she was able to take in the whole of Cordova in daylight.

The buildings and residents seemed typical of any small town, not much different from many she'd visited, but the setting rivaled any other. Charlotte stared up—way up—at the surrounding green and brown mountains disappearing into low clouds. This was the closest she'd ever been to such huge formations, other than when the Seattle-bound train had whisked by the Rockies. To the west, beyond the weathered warehouse structures of the clam canneries, Orca Inlet was flat gray, with islands that would block the brunt of storms coming in from Prince William Sound.

A gust of salty, fishy wind blew up from the bay, as if in response to her observations. If the current weather was muted by islands, Charlotte could hardly imagine what living here would be like without such protection.

Access to Cordova, Michael had said in his letters, was seasonal via the railroad through a mountain pass, though year-round by ship. You had to want to come here. But limited accessibility hadn't prevented a surprising number of establishments from setting up shop. In the short distance between Sullivan's and the café, there was a laundry, a pharmacy, a jewelry store, and even a bathhouse, among other businesses. She stopped in the bathhouse to make an appointment for later. The prospect of stretching out for a long soak appealed to her. A luxury, perhaps, considering Sullivan's had a tub and running water, but it wouldn't hurt to indulge now and again.

Besides, businesses needed local support to make a go of it, especially ones so far from civilization. Charlotte was definitely a local now. At least for the time being.

The sun peeked from behind thick white clouds, attempting to take the chill off the damp day. August back in New York could be unbearably hot and humid. Despite its nearness to the sea, Cordova wasn't humid at all, but it was wet. Michael had described how it could rain for days on end, and last winter's ten feet of snow had been considered mild for the season.

He'd also warned her that the wind could be the worst part of the weather, cutting through material like an icy knife. She'd felt some of that chill last night, and Charlotte mentally inventoried the winter clothes she had brought. Perhaps she'd need to purchase more substantial garments and boots.

The clatter of cars on rails and the bite of coal fires told her the train yard was nearby. In his letters, Michael had described the area as "Old Town," where Cordova had originally been established on the south shore of Eyak Lake. The Copper River and Northwestern Railway now provided the port town a way to accommodate national and international interests in the copper and fishing industries, and business was booming.

New buildings were going up all the time along the main streets, and beyond. There wasn't much else down near the yard anymore, Michael had said, except an old cemetery and a patch of woods called Nirvana Park.

Here on Main Street, storefront windows glinted in weathered but well-kept buildings. Ladies, in more up-to-date fashions than Charlotte would have expected, passed her on the wooden boardwalk and smiled in greeting. Men, whether dressed in suits or the rough clothing of laborers, touched the brims of their hats as she passed.

On a closer look, however, some of the men strutting along the walkway were actually women. No one gave their trousered legs a second glance, let alone a comment. That certainly wouldn't have been the case in most places.

Homesteaders, Charlotte figured. Or women who'd found

their way here and liked the live-and-let-live lifestyle. Those were the sorts of women she wanted to interview for her articles.

But otherwise, Cordova seemed like any of the small villages she'd visited back East. There had to be something more exciting about living on the frontier than the occasional shooting or women in pants, or her articles would be lining canary cages.

Charlotte opened the door of the café, the bell above tinkling with her arrival. The aroma of coffee and cooked bacon hung in the air. Two of the half dozen tables were occupied, one by an older couple perusing the menu and the other by a lone man with bloodshot eyes and a greenish tint to his skin who nursed a cup of coffee. And perhaps a hangover. To the left stood a long counter with six empty padded stools. A tall and lanky young man—boy, really, probably no older than fifteen—came out through a pair of swinging doors at the far end of the room. Beyond the doors was the clatter and clang of a kitchen at work.

The boy flipped a small white towel over his shoulder. "Sit anywhere you'd like, miss. Can I get you a menu?"

Charlotte sat on the end stool. "Just coffee, please."

He grabbed a white cup and saucer off an artfully arranged stack, then carefully poured out a cup from the large aluminum pot on the stove behind him and slid it in front of her.

"Cream and sugar?"

"Please."

A covered bowl of sugar with a silver spoon sticking out was followed by a small ceramic pitcher the boy retrieved from the icebox under the counter.

"Anything else?" His brown eyes were bright and eager.

Charlotte smiled at him. "No, thank you."

"You just call if you need anything." He snatched the pot up and came around the counter to refill cups and take the couple's order without writing it down, then hurried back to the kitchen calling out their request for soup.

Charlotte spooned a bit of sugar into the cup and added a

dollop of cream. While she sipped the potent brew, she turned her attention to the scenery outside the window. The gap between the clothier and the tailor shop showed the blue-gray waters of Prince William Sound.

A pair of women passed the window. One glanced in, catching Charlotte's gaze. Marie, the woman from last night, stopped, said a word or two to her companion, and entered the café. The door chime sounded.

"Miss Brody," she said breathlessly, "I'm sorry to disturb your refreshment."

Charlotte set her cup down. "No, it's quite all right. Will you join me?"

Marie stepped closer, shaking her head. She was dressed in a modest skirt and blouse, her coat hem falling past her hips. Sturdy boots covered her feet, very unlike the shoes she'd worn last night. "No, thanks. I just wondered if you'd do me a small favor. I know we've just met and all, and you have no cause to, but it's not for me."

The girl—for in the light of day and with her face unpainted, she seemed hardly more than that—wrung her hands together. Worry lined her smooth brow.

"It's your friend, Darcy, isn't it?" Charlotte surmised. "Has she gotten worse?"

The waiter pushed through the doors. "Hey, Marie. You having a bite?"

She waved him off. "Not today, Henry. I'm just talking to Miss Brody for a second." Henry shrugged and returned to the kitchen. "Please," Marie said to Charlotte, "could you ask your brother to come today? Darcy was barely able to get up this morning, she was so sick. Brigit's madder than a wet hen at being short a girl, especially on weekends."

Charlotte was no doctor, but whatever was ailing the poor girl sounded serious. Why was Michael reluctant to check on her? "I'm going to see him shortly and will make sure he goes. I'll drag him there myself if I have to."

Marie clutched Charlotte's sleeve, her relief clear. "Oh, thank you so much, Miss Brody. I'm obliged."

"Happy to help, and please, call me Charlotte."

The girl's face broke into a smile, making her look even younger. "Charlotte. I have to get back to my errands. Thank you."

She darted back out to join the other woman who had stayed on the walk.

Henry came out of the kitchen again, carrying two bowls of soup. He served the couple, then came over to Charlotte. "Refill, miss? They're free."

Charlotte finished her coffee, then slid the cup and saucer away. "No, thank you."

She dug a dime and a nickel out of her purse and laid them beside the dishware.

Henry's eyes widened. "That's way too much, miss. Coffee's only a dime."

She stood, smiling at him. "The coffee was quite good, and the service impeccable. Thank you, Henry."

The boy's cheeks pinked. "Thank you, Miss Brody."

Charlotte left the café, sure she'd be able to talk to Henry about real life on the frontier and the people who inhabited it. Finding sources of information was hard enough, but being new in town meant she'd need all the help she could get. People tended to talk around servers and those in similar humble positions, forgetting they had ears. And mouths.

A salt-and-coal-tinged breeze blew in from the south, accompanied by the rumble of a steam engine. The black trail of smoke puffed westward, toward the docks. She caught a glimpse of freight cars between the buildings and through the trees, carrying ore from the copper mines far north of Cordova. The train carried passengers as well, and Charlotte made a mental note to book passage to view the glaciers along the route.

She turned east, toward Michael's home and office. There

was his sign, MICHAEL C. BRODY, MD, at the end of the street across from the three-story federal building that held the post office and the U.S. marshal's office. Charlotte wondered if Deputy Eddington was inside. Remembering the rude awakening that morning, she felt heat rise on her cheeks. She hoped the deputy would forget seeing her in only a cotton nightgown during that introduction.

Charlotte climbed the stone step to Michael's front door. A window on the right showed a narrow view of his office through floral curtains; the one on the left was covered by a heavy shutter. She opened the door and stepped inside. A battered desk and bookshelves were tucked into the far right corner along with a plain wooden chair. Two more chairs sat on the opposite side of the desk. Cabinets along the walls held bottles and medical supplies. The interior door across from the outer door was slightly ajar. Voices murmured from beyond it.

Not wishing to disturb Michael and his patient, Charlotte closed the door and sat in one of the wooden chairs. She couldn't understand what they were saying, and she wasn't trying to be nosy, but the person talking to him sounded like a woman. Occupational hazard of being a journalist, eavesdropping on conversations. Charlotte picked up a thick book on the desk and skimmed pages as a distraction from the voices in the other room.

After a few moments, the inner door swung open. Charlotte looked up, meeting the eye of a petite blonde adjusting her hat. The other woman smiled and strode toward her with purpose.

"You must be Charlotte. You look just like your picture. Michael's told me all about you." She stuck out her gloved hand. "I'm Ruth."

Charlotte rose and grasped Ruth's hand. She glanced at Michael, who stood behind her. He winced, apologetic. Obviously Ruth was aware of Charlotte, but he'd never mentioned Ruth in his letters home.

"So very nice to finally meet you," Charlotte said. She'd covered for her brother more than once. "Michael's writings didn't do you justice."

Ruth blushed and looked over her shoulder at him, beaming. "He's such a dear." She returned her gaze to Charlotte. "We must get to know each other now that you're here. Oh! Do say you'll be at the mayor's dinner tomorrow night. It'll be the party of the year."

Michael laid his hands on her shoulders. "Charlotte's only just arrived and likely hasn't unpacked. She may be too—"

"I'd love to," Charlotte said, grinning as widely as Ruth, but not for the same reason. Michael narrowed his gaze, knowing Charlotte had accepted the invitation just to irritate him. "I'll see what I have to wear."

Ruth squeezed Charlotte's fingers and gave a small squeal of delight. "Wonderful. If you need to borrow something, just let me know. The Windsor is such a lovely venue when it's done up." She released Charlotte's hand and pecked Michael on the cheek. Charlotte barely managed to stifle her surprise. Who was this young woman kissing her brother? "I'll let you two have your lunch. Mother and Father are expecting me back shortly."

Ruth pulled on leather gloves as she strode to the door, waved, still smiling, and left.

Michael sighed and slumped into his chair behind the desk. "You just had to accept the invitation, didn't you?"

"Well, you obviously weren't going to tell me about it, let alone invite me, so yes." Charlotte took her seat again. "Who is she?"

He avoided Charlotte's gaze for a while, rearranging the items on the desk. Charlotte settled back into the uncomfortable chair and crossed her arms. She wasn't so hungry that she couldn't wait him out. Finally, he looked up at her and rolled his eyes in resignation.

"Her name is Ruth Bartlett. Her father is the Reverend Samuel Bartlett, pastor of the Lutheran church."

Charlotte stared at him. "And?"

She was sure there was an "and" in that statement.

Michael fidgeted. He straightened his straight tie and slicked back his neat hair. "And she is to be my wife."

Shock brought Charlotte to her feet. "Your wife? You never mentioned anything about her. Not a word. When were you going to tell Mother and Father? When were you going to tell me?"

It hurt that he'd kept such an important part of his life from the family. From her. When had things gone awry? While Michael was in medical school? During his disturbing tenure at the hospital? Since her own life had taken a path she'd been too ashamed to discuss with him?

Charlotte winced, mourning the loss of their childhood relationship, of their innocence.

Michael stood and began pacing the small space. "I was trying to find the proper way to explain it. It's happened rather suddenly. And I'm telling you now."

"Only because I stumbled in on you. This sort of thing is to be shared and celebrated, not hidden away." That was how more upsetting incidents were to be handled. Her train of thought went directly to that conclusion. "Is she pregnant?"

Michael's mouth dropped open, as if he were shocked she even knew the word. "What? No, of course not. She's a good girl."

Charlotte's chest tightened, and her stomach knotted. A good girl. Of course she was.

"I wanted to tell you," he continued, "but I knew Mother and Father would have a fit if I told them I was engaged before they could investigate her family."

True enough. The Brodys were progressives, to a point. They'd been incensed with Charlotte's decision to become a journalist who wrote about feminism, equality, and unfair labor practices. Not because they didn't support the ideas, but because of the negative—and potentially dangerous—focus on

Charlotte and the family. To appease them, Charlotte sometimes used a pseudonym for her more controversial articles. But anything that threatened Claxton Brody's business enterprises or punched holes in the moral fiber Frances Brody had woven was to be avoided.

Both she and Michael knew the ramifications of displeasing their parents. The elder Brodys, particularly Father, had a long memory for slights and insults. Marrying the "wrong person," or other indiscretions, qualified as such.

"You won't tell them, will you?" The worry in his eyes, the fear she'd tattle, hurt her worse than his keeping Ruth a secret. Neither of them had been saints, and they'd protected each other from parental wrath on many occasions. This time would be no different.

She came around the desk and grasped his cold hands. "It's not my place to tell them, and I'd never go behind your back like that."

Michael's cheeks pinked. "I'm sorry. I should trust that you'd keep it to yourself." He gave her a wry grin. "And force me to hold my own feet to the fire."

They both laughed.

"Come on," Charlotte said, tugging his hand. "I want to hear all about this woman who's joining the family."

Michael grabbed his mackinaw off the coatrack behind the door. "She really is a great girl. I think you'll like her."

Charlotte gave his arm a squeeze and smiled at him. "I'm sure I will. By the way, I haven't had breakfast, so be prepared to lavish me at luncheon."

On their way out of the restaurant, Charlotte took Michael's arm. "Thank you. That was the most delicious salmon I've ever had. Do you always eat that well?"

The afternoon had cleared somewhat, with patches of pale blue peeking through the clouds, though it wasn't quite warm enough to leave their coats open. A "sucker hole," she'd heard another lunch patron call it—a temporary break in the foul weather that made you think it was over.

Michael's eyes were half closed, his face angled toward the sun. "I wish. No, I figured I'd treat you to a decent first meal. After this, you're on your own."

"I can cook for both of us, you know."

He gave her a sideways, dubious look. "When did you learn to cook?"

"Mrs. Cameron taught me at the end of last summer, when I stayed with Kit." The moment she said it, Charlotte tensed. Kit's mother had given her tips and lessons, keeping Charlotte's mind off her "love woes," as Kit had referred to them in the presence of her parents. Mrs. Cameron hadn't pressed for details, but Charlotte suspected the older woman knew the real reason behind her extended visit.

She hadn't meant to bring up last summer to Michael. Skimming over reality and creating details for letters was one thing. If he asked her about it, she'd have to lie some more.

"So I'm guessing you can now boil water and fry an egg?" he asked.

Charlotte laughed, covering her slip of the tongue. "Funny, but I'll have you know I'm quite the cook. It'll save us both money, and you won't have to worry about dinner or lunch during your hectic days."

"The selection here is somewhat limited."

She shrugged. "So it won't be exciting food. We won't starve."

"And I often trade services for game or fish." His eyebrow quirked upward. "Can you manage that?"

"Not a problem." Charlotte wasn't quite sure what sort of "managing" would be required, but she wouldn't balk now. "What do you say? You provide the food, and I'll prepare it."

After a moment's hesitation, he grinned and gave a nod. "All right. We can work out a list for McGruder's later."

They walked on, and Charlotte breathed in the salty, low-tide-scented air. In the distance, a steam whistle announced the train's approach to town from the north. A pleasant late summer day, for the far north.

"I stopped in at the café before coming to your office," she said as they turned the corner toward the rooming house.

"Decent place. Don't eat the soup on Fridays."

"Thanks for the warning. I spoke to Marie while I had my coffee."

His eyebrows drew together. "She asked about Darcy again, didn't she?"

Charlotte moved aside to allow two racing boys to thunder past them on the boardwalk. "She's worried. I told her I'd talk to you. Will you please go see Darcy today?"

"Yes, I will," he said after a moment. "I'm sure the girl is merely suffering from some minor affliction. Perhaps a cold or a touch of exhaustion. They tend to overdo it, staying up during the longer days of summer, and not realizing how late it is."

Charlotte had little issue with ladies of the evening plying their trade, but that didn't mean she wanted to dwell on what "overdoing it" meant. "Thank you. I'm sure it's nothing, but Marie was very agitated earlier."

"Marie is a kind soul, and she and Darcy are close."

They stepped onto the Main Street walk and came face-to-face with Deputy Eddington. The three of them stopped just short of bumping into each other, surprised expressions all around.

Eddington was the first to recover. He touched the brim of his hat and nodded to them. "Excuse me, Doctor. Miss Brody."

Michael glanced at Charlotte, then back to the lawman. "Deputy. Fine day we're having."

"For the moment, anyway." Eddington replied to Michael, but his blue eyes held Charlotte's. The scruff of beard on his chin hadn't been so obvious earlier that morning. It gave him a dark, dangerous look. "How's your first day in the wilds, Miss Brody?"

She smiled. "Much more civilized than I'd anticipated. Nary a rampaging beast to be had."

Eddington laughed. "It's early yet. Rampaging doesn't start 'til evening around here," he said with a wink. Touching his hat again, he stepped aside to allow them to pass. "Good seeing you again, Miss Brody. Afternoon, Doctor."

The deputy strode up the side street the way Charlotte and Michael had come.

Michael resumed walking, and Charlotte had to pay attention to her footing rather than the retreating figure or trip her way down the street.

"How does Eddington know you?"

Heat suffused her cheeks as she recalled standing in her nightgown in front of the deputy earlier that morning. Would she ever get over that encounter? "He came to the rooming house looking for someone and questioned me."

Michael grunted in reply.

"What do you think of him?" she asked. She was gathering information for her article, she told herself.

"Eddington?" He shrugged. "A decent sort. I don't know him well, but he seems like a fair fellow."

They crossed the street to Sullivan's. Michael opened the front door and stepped aside to allow Charlotte in.

Mrs. Sullivan bustled out of her room. Her white hair was in a neat bun, her long-sleeved, high-collared, navy-blue dress appropriate for her matronly figure. "Doctor, I'm glad you're here."

"Is someone ill?" he asked.

A scowl added more wrinkles to Mrs. Sullivan's face. "No, but my boys may need your services for cracked heads when I get to them. They were supposed to bring your sister's trunks in from the shed, but instead they snuck out and went duck hunting for the weekend."

Charlotte and Michael grinned as they exchanged glances. Mrs. Sullivan held up a key, an expectant look in her bright eyes.

"Not a problem," he said, taking the key. "I'll go get them."

"I'll help." Charlotte hurried after him, ignoring Mrs. Sullivan's protest that a lady shouldn't be hauling heavy bags.

The path around the back of the house was, unsurprisingly, muddy. Michael's heavy boots protected his feet, but Charlotte's thinner leather shoes were soon soaked.

"You'll need real boots around here," Michael said as they reached the shed. It was a solid, roughly twelve-by-twelve-foot square building, painted the same white as the rooming house.

"I have winter gear in my trunk. I paid attention to your list of what to bring."

Another path, beaten into the swath of land between the building on the street and several outbuildings, paralleled the main road. It seemed to lead into a copse of spruce closer to Michael's office and, in the opposite direction, down a slight embankment to the railroad tracks that led to the docks half a mile away.

Michael worked the key into the lock, popping the hasp open, and yanked on the door. Inside, Charlotte's two trunks sat near the entrance. Old luggage, a rusty bicycle, and a wheelbarrow cluttered the rough wood floor. Shelves held dusty canning jars and several large claw traps, among other things shoved into the shadows.

Charlotte and Michael each took an end of one trunk and hauled it into the rooming house. They assured Mrs. Sullivan that Charlotte was fine, if a little muddy, and was quite capable of getting the other one. After setting both trunks in her room, Michael pecked Charlotte on the cheek in farewell.

"Don't forget to go see Darcy," she reminded him.

"On my way now." While he wasn't enthusiastic, she was sure he'd do as promised. Michael was a considerate man, and a good doctor. He wouldn't let poor Darcy suffer if she was truly ill. "I'm going to be out for supper tonight. Boring dealings with the city council, or I'd invite you. Will you be all right on your own?"

She waved off his concern. "I'll be fine. I'll unpack and see what I have to wear for tomorrow night."

"Right. I'll see you tomorrow, Sis."

Charlotte shut the door behind him and got to work.

After she had organized what she could in her room, Charlotte took her bath at the Northern Delight bathhouse. She decided against a walk to Nirvana Park, as the rain and wind had picked up again, making the half-mile walk less attractive. Soaking in the steaming tub nearly put her to sleep. If the attendant hadn't called out, Charlotte was sure she would have sunk into the comfortable depths and drowned.

Back in her room, she transcribed the notes she'd taken during the steamer journey. She carefully pulled the latest sheet from her typewriter and set it on top of the other finished pages. A dwindling packet of paper and carbons sat beside the Royal. Was there a stationery store in town? She hadn't seen one in her brief wanderings today. It was possible McGruder's or one of the other merchants sold paper and carbon. She'd have to ask.

A quiet knock interrupted her feeding a sandwich of paper and carbon around the smooth, black platen of the typewriter. She gave the knob a turn to secure the sheets, then answered the door.

Mrs. Sullivan smiled up at her. "Good evening, dear. I don't mean to intrude, but I was wondering if you had plans for supper? I made a beef roast and potatoes."

Charlotte glanced at her typewriter and notebook on the table. She needed to write, but she'd been at it for a couple of hours already. Her aching back and rumbling stomach made the decision for her. "I'd be delighted," she said, returning a smile.

During a hearty meal followed by after-dinner sherry, Mrs. Sullivan entertained Charlotte with stories of her own girlhood in Canada and her travels west. She was exactly the kind of woman Charlotte wanted to feature in her articles.

"Plenty of opportunities for a woman to make her way

here," Mrs. Sullivan said, refilling their delicate sherry glasses. Charlotte had lost count of the number of drinks they'd consumed, but the contents of the crystal decanter were significantly decreased in volume. "Be that as it may, a lady should always remain a lady."

"Of course," Charlotte agreed, more out of politeness than anything else. The sweet liquor went down easily, and her head swam.

What time was it? She squinted at the cuckoo clock on the wall. After eleven! How had that happened?

"I really must be going." She stood on wobbly legs and set her glass on the tray. "Thank you for a lovely time."

"It was a pleasure, dear girl." Mrs. Sullivan rose as well and tottered to the door. Her gaze became misty as she raised a trembling hand to Charlotte's cheek. "With your fair coloring and blue eyes, you remind me of my Margaret, God rest her soul. She was a beauty like you."

Sympathy twinged in Charlotte's chest. Mrs. Sullivan's daughter had died during the Spanish flu pandemic the year before. Charlotte took the older woman's hand and gently squeezed her frail fingers. "Thank you, Mrs. Sullivan. I'll see you in the morning."

"Good night, dear. And thank you for indulging an old woman."

Charlotte bade her good night, made a quick stop at the bathroom, then headed to her room, grateful it was a short walk and that the light was on at the end of the hall. The room was dark, and she fumbled to find the light switch on the wall. Charlotte shut and locked her door, then closed the curtains. She changed into her nightgown, gave her teeth a quick brushing from water in the pitcher—promising herself to dump the basin in the morning—and turned out the light.

She settled into bed. The room wasn't spinning, exactly, but there was a slight swaying motion. Ignoring it, Charlotte eased into sleep.

A solid thud against the outside wall startled her from that twilight between wakefulness and sleep. She sat up. Had she imagined it, or was someone trying to get in? An urgent voice sounded through the wall, loud enough to be heard, but it was hard to tell if it was a man or a woman. Another thump, right near the head of her bed, shot her to her feet.

Charlotte went to the window. Should she look? She was half afraid to move the curtain aside. What if some ruffian stared back at her? But she couldn't just stand there waiting for him to break the glass.

She quickly dumped the remaining water in the pitcher into the basin and returned to the window. Taking a deep breath, she raised the ceramic ware and shoved the curtain aside.

Nothing. No beetle-browed thief attempting to gain entrance. Just darkness.

Charlotte pressed her forehead to the cool glass and scanned the alley to either side. She didn't dare open the window, so it was difficult to see much of anything. No one lurked within her sight.

Perhaps it was just a pair of drunks wandering home. An unsteady gait and slippery mud could account for the collision with the wall.

That must be it, she assured herself. *Nothing to worry about.*

Charlotte set the pitcher down and went back to bed. She listened for a long while, hearing the creak of the settling house or the occasional bark of a dog or the howl of a wind gust, but nothing else. Finally, her eyes too achy and tired to stay open, she fell asleep.

Loud pounding on her door roused her after what seemed like no more than a few minutes. But watery morning light through the curtains told her she'd slept at least a few hours. The white face of her alarm clock showed it was almost nine.

Bam-bam-bam.

The knock sounded all too familiar.

Damn it all. Now what?

Charlotte stumbled from the bed and threw open the door. As expected, Deputy Marshal James Eddington filled the doorway, his dark brows drawn in a scowl.

"I told you, Deputy, I don't know any Martha Griggs. If you continue to harass me—"

"How about Darcy Dugan?" he growled.

Charlotte blinked at him. "Darcy? You mean the—one of Brigit's girls?"

"So you know her." He stepped closer, blue eyes boring into hers. "When did you see her last?"

"I never have." She swallowed hard when he narrowed his gaze, obviously not believing her. "I've heard her name, but that's all. Her friend Marie asked Michael to go see Darcy."

Eddington didn't budge. "Did you see or hear anything unusual last night?"

The interruption as she'd tried to fall asleep came back to her immediately. "Yes, someone, maybe two people, in the alley behind the house."

"When?"

"It was after eleven, close to midnight, I think."

"But you didn't see anything?"

She shook her head. "No. By the time I looked out the window, they were gone."

He heaved a sigh and ran a large hand over the stubble of his beard. "Damn it. Excuse my language, Miss Brody. Good morning."

Charlotte touched his arm, stopping him before he turned away. "What happened, Deputy?"

Sadness tinged the anger in his eyes. "Darcy Dugan was found near the railroad tracks just below here. She was beaten to death."

Chapter 3

Ice prickled along Charlotte's spine. "Beaten to death? Who did it? And why?"

Anger made Eddington's blue eyes glacial. "If I knew that, Miss Brody, I wouldn't be here. It looks like they went down the slope just west of here to the tracks. The path out back is churned up. Lots of footprints."

Her entire body tensed. "Oh, my God, they were right outside my window."

"Probably so." He glanced down to where her hand gripped his coat, then met her gaze again.

Charlotte's palm—and cheeks—grew warm. She released the deputy's arm, as if it would burn her if she held on too long. "Sorry. Does Michael know?" she asked, her voice much steadier than she expected.

"I sent a message that I need him at the site. He'll be doing the autopsy." Eddington cocked his head. "Why do you ask?"

Charlotte wrapped her arms around herself, the chill returning to her body. "He was supposed to go see Darcy yesterday afternoon. She'd been feeling poorly for a while."

"I'll ask the doctor if he noticed anything unusual." Thoughtful determination lined Eddington's face. "Thank you, Miss Brody."

She expected him to head back down the hallway, but he didn't move for a few moments. He stared at her, and Charlotte waited for his next question. It never came. Finally, he tugged the brim of his hat and strode away.

She shut the door and slumped down onto the wooden chair. "That poor girl."

If she'd only looked out the window sooner, Charlotte might have seen something. She racked her brain, but couldn't recall the voice she'd heard. Not that it had been clear through the wall, and not that she had many to compare it to, having only met a handful of people so far. Still, anything she could remember might help.

Charlotte carried the full basin to the water closet and dumped it down the drain in the sink. She used the facilities, then washed up. There was only a cold-water tap, and the covered bucket of heated water hadn't been refilled yet this morning. Back in her room, the radiator was finally putting out reluctant heat, but the chill ensured she hurry to get dressed.

The foggy mirror attached to the inside of the wardrobe door showed the shadows under her eyes. Not enough sleep since she'd arrived in Cordova. Charlotte pinned up her hair, taking care to smooth the flyaway tendrils back from her face. The simple blouse and skirt she wore could use a pressing. She wondered if Mrs. Sullivan had an iron, or if the laundry down the street charged reasonable rates.

The dark burgundy gown hanging in the back of the wardrobe reminded her of tonight's party. She doubted such a gala would be canceled in light of the death of a prostitute.

Thoughts of the girl spurred Charlotte to want to speak to Michael as soon as possible. She moved the curtain aside to assess the weather. Rain splattered against the panes. Low, gray clouds and the churned-up mud path made for a sobering scene. Poor Darcy had likely spent her last minutes trying to escape her attacker right outside the window. Beaten to death.

"If only I'd woken and checked sooner." A wave of sadness made Charlotte feel heavy.

Did Marie know yet? Deputy Eddington would probably question Miss Brigit and the others soon enough.

Charlotte donned her coat and the wide-brimmed felt hat she'd purchased for the Alaska weather. Michael had said winter here was sometimes like a bothersome houseguest who comes earlier than expected and stays later than appreciated.

She left the rooming house, turning up her collar against the chill wind, and walked to Michael's office. Few people she passed smiled, or even greeted her. Had the weather affected their moods, or was the pang in the air due to the murder? Charlotte glanced at the café across the street. She hadn't had breakfast yet, but her stomach churned at the thought of coffee, let alone food.

Michael's office door opened just as she reached out to twist the knob. Startled, Charlotte stepped back and slipped off the lower step. Her brother dashed forward, grabbing her arm before she landed poorly or fell on the muddy path.

"This isn't a good time, Sis." He pulled the door closed. Deep lines creased his forehead. His coat was open, the suit beneath it rumpled and his tie askew.

"Are you going down to the tracks?" she asked.

The frown deepened. "You've heard?"

Charlotte nodded. "Deputy Eddington was at the rooming house. He believes Darcy and her killer came along the alley, right past my window." She shivered as sorrow and guilt wound their way through her. Why hadn't she looked out sooner?

His fair cheeks paled. "Are you all right? Did you see anything?"

"I'm fine, but I think I heard them last night." She clutched his arm. "In fact, I'm certain of it. Who would have done such a thing? And why?"

Michael slid her hand up under his arm and guided her toward the walk. "For all the good times and parties, these girls live in a dangerous world, Charlotte. The men they do business with aren't always just looking for a bit of fun. Some have problems. And not all of the girls are honest."

"Did she steal from them?"

Michael shrugged. "I don't know. Nothing that required the police, I think. But men are often vulnerable under the wiles of a young woman lavishing them with attention, even if they are paying for it. They tend to forget to be cautious. It may be she tried something and the man became angry."

"Angry enough to chase her through town and kill her?" It didn't ring right to Charlotte, but then again, she'd never dealt with that sort of man.

"A few drinks, a bad day. This isn't Yonkers. Men come to Alaska to leave behind the niceties of society." He escorted her across the street to the café. "Stay here while I do my preliminary investigation for Eddington."

He tried to remove her hand from his arm, but Charlotte gripped harder. "Let me come with you."

She wasn't quite sure why she'd said it, but once she did, Charlotte felt the same rush and tingle of anxiousness as she had with every story she'd ever written.

"No." Michael shook his head and peeled her fingers from his coat. She opened her mouth to protest, but he held his palm up, stopping her. "I'm sure Eddington has the area secured from gawkers—"

"I'm no gawker." Indignation heated her, chest to cheeks.

"No, you're a journalist."

Now he decided her vocation was worth noting? Figured.

She crossed her arms, trying desperately to not look like a petulant girl. He was being professional, maintaining the integrity of the crime scene and the privacy—such as it could be in a small town like Cordova—of the deceased.

She was a professional too. She had felt obligated to tell the suffragettes' stories, to make people see the important work they were willing to sacrifice for. The pains and trials they went through for equality could become dangerous, and women had died for their beliefs. Darcy was likely nothing to the people here, but someone had killed her for a reason.

"All right," she capitulated. "But will you pass along information for me to use in an article for the local paper? It's possible other girls could be in danger."

Michael narrowed his gaze at her, lips pressed tight beneath the dark blond of his moustache. "You'll only pester me if I say no, won't you?"

Charlotte couldn't help her smile. "You know me well."

He grunted in acknowledgment. "Fine. I'll give you what I can, if I think it'll help keep others safe."

Which, in protective big brother parlance, probably meant a whitewashing of details. But Charlotte didn't push it. Not yet, anyway.

"Thank you." She gave him a kiss on the cheek. "I'll wait here for you, or back at your place, if that's okay. I can get started on lunch."

He leaned closer and lowered his voice. The earnestness in his eyes worried her. "Don't talk to anyone about it, Charlotte. Understand?"

"Of course not."

Michael turned on his heel and strode down the boardwalk, his knee-high boots thudding with controlled urgency.

Charlotte lingered over her coffee, glancing out the window with the hope of catching Michael on his way back. After more than half an hour of ignoring the toast she'd ordered, despite not being hungry, and letting her coffee grow cold, she decided to go on to his office. It was a little early to have lunch, but she could see what he had on his shelves and in his larder. She needed to do something to occupy the time.

The rain had picked up, as had the wind. Not bothering to button her coat for such a short dash, Charlotte was nearly soaked through by the time she'd crossed the street and hurried into Michael's office. She pushed the door closed and let her eyes adjust to the dim light coming through the single window before crossing to the inner door.

The exam room was pitch dark. She felt along the wall for a switch.

The overhead light came on to reveal a high wooden table, the end leaves folded down. Gleaming counters and glass-front cabinets along the walls revealed the accoutrements of Michael's practice. It was a clean, neat space that showed her brother's attention to detail and dedication, and surely set patients at ease.

Another door on the left led to his living quarters. Charlotte went in and turned on the light. The bed near the door was neatly made. A woodstove in the far corner ticked and popped as it cooled from the dying fire. She kept her coat on against the damp chill settling into the room as she added more wood. The embers within the iron box quickly ignited the dry logs, and soon a merry fire was burning.

That would do for heat, but what about cooking? Across the room, a narrow coal stove and a small enamel sink were the entirety of Michael's kitchen. Along the walls, shelves held canned and jarred foods, tins of saltines, and something called Sailor Boy pilot bread. Cabinets above and below the sink held more food as well as cooking utensils, cups, and plates. A small square table and two straight-back chairs made up the dining area. It was a shabby room, but neat enough, and the braided rug on the wood floor looked clean.

Charlotte set a kettle of water on the woodstove and surveyed the shelves. Mostly home-canned salmon, by the looks of it, along with some jams and jellies, and commercial cans of vegetables and local clams. Not much variety, as he'd warned her. She took down a can of salmon and found a few spices in the cupboard. She pried open the tin of pilot bread.

"Huh. Hardtack." That would make a decent vehicle for a salmon salad concoction.

Michael's voice carried in from the front office. "Bring her in here, Eddington."

Charlotte froze. *Her*. They were bringing Darcy in for the autopsy. Lunch preparation forgotten, she quietly walked to the door leading into the examination room. It hadn't closed all the way when she'd entered, and through the gap, Charlotte saw Michael raising the leaves of the exam table.

Deputy Eddington carried in the tarp-wrapped body and laid her down with a gentleness that made Charlotte's throat close. He was a big man, and Darcy's body seemed so small by comparison, even under the heavy canvas.

"That's fine, Deputy," Michael said. "I'll make my report and deliver it soon. We'll want to have her interred as soon as possible."

Eddington straightened, about to respond, and caught Charlotte peeking at them. She held her breath. Was he going to say something to Michael? She wasn't doing anything wrong.

Then why are you spying on them and not announcing your presence?

He stared at her for a moment longer before answering Michael. "I'm sure Brigit and the girls'll want to arrange something. Don't think Darcy had any family in these parts."

"No," Michael said softly. He reached out to touch the tips of his fingers to the canvas. "They were all she had."

Eddington glanced down at Michael's hand, then his gaze flicked up to Charlotte again.

"We chatted some when I went to check on the girls." Michael lifted his head. He saw the deputy looking past him and turned. Seeing Charlotte at the door, his face flushed red. "What are you doing here?"

Charlotte stepped into the exam room. "I told you I'd come back to make us lunch." She nodded toward the table. "You're going to be busy this afternoon. I want to help."

Michael opened his mouth, but Eddington spoke over him. "You don't want to be here for this, Miss Brody."

"No, but I'm guessing neither do you, Deputy." Eddington's lips pressed together. "I can help my brother by taking notes, and you can continue your investigation."

He held her gaze, but addressed Michael. "Doc?"

Charlotte knew Michael would be harder to convince, but with Eddington on her side her brother might relent. "You'll need someone to help prepare her body for the undertaker. Better a woman for that, don't you think?"

It was a stretch of an argument. Would he bite?

Michael grimaced. He removed his mackinaw and suit jacket, draping them over the lone chair in the room, then unbuttoned his cuffs before answering. "This isn't going to be pretty, Charlotte. It was a brutal attack."

Charlotte's mouth dried, and her stomach tightened. "I was there at the 1913 Washington parade, where women were beaten for merely stating their desire for equality. I spoke to some of those imprisoned with Alice Paul at the Occoquan workhouse in Virginia, days after their release. I heard the stories of their abuse, saw the broken bones, bruises, and scars, Michael."

"This is different," he said.

"I know." She swallowed hard. "Someone hurt this girl, and I want to help find out who."

Her brother gave the deputy a beseeching look, hoping for support even though he could have easily told her no himself. Eddington shrugged and started for the outer office.

"Your call, Doc," he said. "I have a killer to find. Let me know what your exam shows."

The exterior door closed hard, shaking the cabin. Charlotte kept her expression sober, but inside she was pleased as punch.

Between not calling her out for spying from the other room and his neutrality on her providing help, Eddington seemed to be on her side. Though for the life of her, Charlotte couldn't figure out why.

"Fine," Michael said. "Let's get some lunch, and then we'll start."

The warm feeling of the deputy's support fizzled like a Fourth of July sparkler in the rain. Charlotte's stomach churned. "Lunch? Do you think eating beforehand is such a good idea?"

"If you're not up for it . . ."

His implication—no, challenge—put steel in her spine. "I have some salmon out. Let's eat, then get to work."

Charlotte found it hard to concentrate on creating conversation with Darcy's body waiting for them in the next room, and Michael was lost in thought much of the time. She picked at her food, eating little more than a pilot bread cracker. It was something bland to settle her already jittery stomach, and better than nothing.

They stepped into the exam room, and he continued to the outer office to secure the front door.

"I don't think we need anyone dropping by unannounced," he said upon returning. "My patients would probably rather not think about this aspect of my job."

He squatted down in front of a cabinet and opened the door. Out came several glass jars with metal screw-top lids, a tray of shiny metal instruments, and a folded piece of black cloth. Atop the cloth was a pair of black rubber gloves.

"How many autopsies have you done?" Charlotte asked.

"More than a few." The sour look on his face told her how he felt about doing them at all. "Most causes of death are obvious, and my findings merely confirm that someone died of natural causes, accidentally, or was shot or stabbed."

Michael secured his sleeves with garters, then pulled on the black gloves. Charlotte helped tie the rubberized apron over his clothing. He opened a drawer and passed her a fountain pen, a jar of ink, and a form with the Alaska Territory seal and CORONER'S REPORT at the top.

"Just write what I say. I'll have to stop now and again to draw diagrams or pictures." He caught her eye when he turned around. "Unless you want to do that too?"

Charlotte's mouth dried. "I can't draw."

His wry smile did nothing to alleviate the heaviness of the task ahead. "I know. Don't worry. You just keep your back to the table. But to be on the safe side . . ." He withdrew a tin of Vicks VapoRub from the drawer. Opening it, he dabbed some inside his nostrils. "I suggest you do the same. The aroma of internal organs can be overwhelming."

Suppressing her grimace, Charlotte dipped her finger into the camphor and mentholated ointment and spread some under her nose. Her eyes teared at the bite of the strong scent; she recalled having the gooey stuff spread across her chest as a child fighting a cold. After a minute or so, she became accustomed to it and nodded to Michael that she was ready.

She sat on the edge of the chair, the form on the counter that ran along the wall of the exam room. Positioned with her back to the table, head bent, she tapped excess ink into the jar and readied herself for Michael's narrative.

"The subject," he began, his tone solemn, "is Miss Darcy Dugan, approximately twenty-two years of age. Miss Dugan was employed by Miss Brigit O'Brien as a . . ." He coughed, but Charlotte couldn't say if it was real or out of a need to find the right word. "As a lady of the evening. She is—was—" His voice cracked, and he cleared his throat again. "She was known to me over the last year from biweekly health exams. I last saw Miss Dugan yesterday afternoon at three. She had complained of exhaustion and a general feeling of malaise. She refused a comprehensive examination. The abbreviated exam I performed revealed a slight pallor of her skin and somewhat elevated heart rate, but no other indications of disease. I prescribed rest, fluids, and iron pills."

Michael didn't speak too quickly for her to keep up, but Charlotte was glad for her shorthand classes in high school.

"Miss Dugan," he continued, "was found at eight this morning by Mr. Paul Avery while he was out with his dog in the copse of spruce where Dock Road and the railroad tracks meet just beyond Council Avenue. There doesn't appear to be any disturbance or damage to the body by dogs, bears, or other scavengers."

Charlotte lifted her head and half turned toward her brother. "Bears this close to town?"

Michael had his back to her, blocking Darcy's body. He looked over his shoulder at Charlotte. "Black bears wander through all the time. Mostly at dawn or dusk, but they're active at night as well, so be careful if you're out and about. Ready to continue?"

She nodded.

"Miss Dugan was partially covered in duff, as if the killer kicked the debris onto her. A short, thick branch, believed to be the principal weapon in the attack, was found nearby."

Charlotte paused in her writing and interrupted him again. "A weapon?"

Michael now stood near Darcy's head, hands resting lightly on Darcy's shoulders, ready to lift the canvas. The strain lines around his eyes and mouth seemed deeper. "Yes. We'll run tests later, but it's most certainly covered in blood."

He started to unwrap the tarp. The rustling of the heavy material made Charlotte's mouth dry with apprehension. As though of their own volition, her eyes jumped to the young woman's face, a perfect view of her left-side profile. No one could mistake Darcy for being asleep. Her eyes were half open, and thick blood was smeared under the nose and across the slack mouth. Tendrils of reddish blond hair draped over the edge of the table, but it was matted, wet and black, close to her skull. Dirt spattered onto the floor.

Michael sighed, his face pinched with purpose and something Charlotte couldn't quite determine. Whatever it was, she didn't envy her brother the terrible task ahead.

Charlotte's stomach clenched like a fist, forcing what little she'd eaten for lunch back up toward her throat. She swallowed and returned her attention to the form. Being in the same room was proving to be more difficult than she'd anticipated. She had no desire to see the injuries inflicted on Darcy, if she could help it, but the need to know what, exactly, had happened challenged her ability to keep her back to the table.

"Miss Dugan is wearing a blue dressing gown over a white chemise, undergarments, and black boots. Her boots are loosely tied and covered in mud, as are her clothes. The lower half of her gown and chemise are darker, perhaps due to the rains we've had," he said with cool formality that belied his earlier emotion. "There is severe bruising on the face. Swelling of the left eye, with a five-inch laceration along the orbital bone, suggests the assailant was right-handed. There's discoloration at the throat as well. The skull has been crushed in on both sides."

Charlotte heard Michael move around the table, but dared not lift her head. He picked up the sketchbook and pencil set out on the counter. Of course he had to provide pictorial records. There was a resident photographer, Michael had said at lunch, but he was out of town. The scratching of lead on the thick paper seemed loud in the small room. Charlotte breathed deeply, and a renewed burst of camphor burned in her nose.

After a few minutes of sketching, Michael set the book and pencil down. The tray of instruments near Charlotte rattled when he reached for a pair of blunt-nosed scissors. She glanced up, careful to keep her gaze on him.

"I'm going to remove her clothing." He spoke as if remarking on the color of paint, but she noted his unusual paleness. Michael might be going about the postmortem in an outwardly detached manner, but it bothered him, that much was certain. He'd said he'd performed autopsies before. Was he always so disturbed or was this one different somehow? Because Darcy had been a patient? Because of the manner of her death? "We'll cover her with some blankets or sheets I have here for the undertaker."

"Do you need my help?" Charlotte was relieved when he shook his head. She tried not to think about the further indignity Darcy had to face of being handled by yet another stranger. "When will the undertaker arrive?"

Michael shrugged. "Later today. He'll get things from Miss Brigit for the burial."

The sound of his moving Darcy's body about continued for several minutes.

"I'll be God damned," Michael said in a harsh whisper.

Charlotte rose, startled by his expletive. Darcy's folded dressing gown was under the table. Michael stood near her lower legs, staring down at her with wide eyes. Charlotte followed his gaze and immediately wished she hadn't. The bottom half of Darcy's chemise was dark with blood, not rain or mud.

"What happened?" Charlotte asked, her throat tight. "Was she stabbed?"

Michael shook his head. "We didn't see any cuts in her clothing when we rolled her onto the tarp. I think she hemorrhaged."

Charlotte glanced down again, curiosity momentarily overtaking repugnance. Darcy's bared arms were bruised. Several fingers were bent at odd angles. She'd attempted to defend herself against the blows, or perhaps fight back.

You poor girl.

Mud and water had seeped through her dressing gown to the cotton undergarments. Despite her revulsion, Charlotte peered closer at the muck on Darcy's clothing. "Look at this, Michael."

She pointed to the mud stain. “The edges here are too perfectly curved to be random.”

He bent closer, frowning. “I’d say it’s a shoe print. Or a boot. Difficult to tell. But there’s more than one, for certain.”

Charlotte straightened. “Most of the mud that came through to the chemise and knickers is concentrated on her lower body. The killer was aiming for her stomach.”

Michael’s already pale complexion turned ashen. “I think you’re right.” He reached for the scissors and began cutting the front of Darcy’s chemise. “Faster and easier this way.”

Folding back the thin material, Michael exposed her breasts and belly. The discoloration of her abdomen confirmed her attacker had focused his attention there. It took a bit more effort to cut through the blood-soaked lower half, and when Michael revealed the area of her hips and upper thighs, both he and Charlotte startled. Charlotte’s body went cold.

Darcy’s smallclothes were nearly black with blood.

“Go sit down, Charlotte.” Michael’s roughened voice seemed to come from far away. She remained standing. He came around the table and, using the insides of his forearms to avoid touching her with the exam gloves, gently urged her back to the counter. “I need you to record this. Please.”

Charlotte didn’t sit, instead positioning herself so she could watch him out of the corner of her eye while she wrote. Michael gave her a long look, though he himself appeared as shaky as she felt. Satisfied she was as removed from the proceedings as she would get, he stood between the table and Charlotte to block her view as he continued.

“Severe bruising of the lower abdomen and thighs. Hemorrhaging from the—” His voice caught, but he recovered quickly. “Hemorrhaging from the vaginal canal indicates ruptured organs. No other exterior injuries evident. I will commence the internal exam.”

Michael retrieved a galvanized bucket from the corner and arranged the tarp to funnel into it to catch fluids. He took up a shiny scalpel from the tray, gave Charlotte a quick check, then returned to the body. His brow furrowed with determination. "I've made a Y incision from under each armpit, meeting below the sternum, down around the umbilicus, then to the top of the pubis."

Charlotte tried to write without thinking about what the words meant, without connecting them to the procedure. She had to distance herself, as Michael had. Later, when she transcribed the coded marks of her shorthand, she hoped she could retain that distance.

"Heart and lungs appear normal," Michael said. "Stomach and intestines slightly enlarged. On the left, rib three is cracked and ribs four and five are broken. Ribs four and five on the right are cracked." There was a pause and the squelch of scissors on something thicker and wetter. "Stomach contents are not identifiable, so she'd eaten several hours before her death. I'll collect them to test for poisons, just to be sure."

He took a specimen jar and spoon from the counter. Charlotte looked over her handwriting until he was finished filling the jar and set it back on the counter.

"Spleen has been ruptured, and there is blood within the abdominal cavity, as expected. Pancreas and liver swollen. The reproductive organs appear discolored. One ovary is ruptured; the other appears bruised. The womb is dark and distended." More wet scissor sounds. "I'm dissecting the womb to determine its condition. Quite a bit of blood and—Oh, my God!"

Charlotte spun around and peered over his shoulder. Dark blood and pale pink and gray tissue were their own sort of horror, but what Michael held in his hand made her knees watery and her lower body cramp. A two-inch-long gray, curled form stood out against the palm of his black glove.

"She was pregnant."

Chapter 4

The room tilted and blurred. Charlotte felt herself sway and automatically reached out to steady herself on the nearest object: the exam table. The sudden realization she was about to touch Darcy made her jerk back, only increasing her disorientation.

"Are you all right?" Michael started to grab for her, but immediately withdrew his gore-slick hand.

Charlotte waved him off, not trusting herself to speak without vomiting. The image of what he'd held burned into her brain. She collapsed onto the chair, bent forward with arms crossed over her knees and forehead resting on them. Her skin felt clammy through her cotton blouse sleeve.

Swallowing to keep her stomach contents down, she heard Michael moving around with some urgency, muttering. The wet peeling sound was probably his gloves coming off. The squeal of an opening cabinet. The soft snap of cloth. His footsteps faded into his living quarters, and Charlotte heard the squeak of the pump handle and splashing water. He returned, his warm hand on her shoulder.

"Drink."

Charlotte straightened and drew in slow, even breaths. Michael stood beside her, blocking her view of the table, an enameled mug in hand. She wrapped her shaking hands around his and brought the cup to her lips. Michael's steady hold kept the water from splashing out. Something stronger would have been preferred, but the water helped. The roiling of her stomach subsided to a quiver after several sips.

"I'm sorry. I didn't realize I'd be so squeamish."

"You did better than I did my first time at an autopsy." His mouth quirked into a sympathetic grin beneath his moustache. "Barely got through the Y incision before I passed out cold."

The weak smile she managed faltered when Charlotte caught a glimpse of Darcy's now-shrouded body behind him. She looked down into the mug and swallowed hard. "I remember you becoming ill when I gashed my forehead falling off the swing in the yard. Always wondered how you'd manage being a doctor."

"I guess my desire to heal overcame my nausea after a while." He gently tugged a loose lock of her hair. "Maybe having you bang yourself up all the time helped too."

She chuckled and nodded. Charlotte had rarely been without some bump, bruise, or laceration, but the head wound had been positively gruesome, if not deep. Between her history of childhood injuries and the aftermath of her procedure, she thought she'd be used to blood by now.

But it wasn't the blood, she realized, so much as Darcy's situation. Surely the girl had known she was pregnant.

"You were her doctor. Didn't you know?"

Michael's lips pressed together, and he looked pained again as he shook his head. "I haven't conducted a full exam on her for a couple of months. Mostly just quick visits and a few swabs to test for syphilis and other diseases. She'd said everything was fine with her menses."

"So she lied to you."

"Probably." Michael let Charlotte hold the mug. "It's possible she didn't know for sure. But more likely she lied and tried to hide it from me. She might have been afraid of being let go from Brigit's. Babies aren't particularly good for that business."

Charlotte drank the last of the water, then set the mug on the counter. "What would she have done once the baby arrived? How would they have made do?"

"If she'd kept it and Brigit didn't want her around? Server at one of the cafés or clubs. Laundress. She could have found something." His gaze focused elsewhere as he became lost in thought. After a moment he shook off whatever he'd been considering and met her eyes. "I can finish up the rest of the examination and report. Go lie down for a bit."

She straightened in the chair and picked up the pen. "No, I'll be all right." He started to protest, but she held up a hand. "Honest. It was a bit of a shock, but I'm fine."

Liar.

She knew exactly what the dead girl on the table had gone through. Passing off morning sickness as a bit of a cold or a bout with bad food. Explaining away tiredness as having stayed up too late or working too hard. Secrets to be kept, hidden away from friends and family until a solution could be found.

Michael nodded, his expression one of sorrow. "All right, stay. But keep your back to the table and let me know if you need to stop."

Her stomach threatened to rebel again. Charlotte pasted as much of a smile onto her face as she could and held up three fingers. "I will. Scout's honor."

The remaining details of Darcy's autopsy were far less jarring, though it would have taken quite a revelation to top what Michael had already discovered. Charlotte concentrated on taking notes rather than on what the words meant. Still, the ache in her stomach migrated into her head. By the time the autopsy was finished, it felt as if someone were squeezing her temples inward, trying to get them to meet within her skull.

Michael touched her shoulder, making her jump. Gently, he

took the pen out of her hand. "Go into my room and rest. I'll fetch the undertaker."

Charlotte nodded. Deliberately ignoring the table, she entered his living area and pushed the door closed. It didn't latch, leaving a gap like the one she'd spied through earlier that morning. Not that it mattered. She had no intention of watching the undertaker removing the body.

She lay down on Michael's bed, wishing she'd asked him for some aspirin or bicarbonate of soda. With her hands and brain no longer occupied by concentrating on dictation, Charlotte couldn't force the thoughts and images out of her head.

Though she'd seen other murder and assault victims, she didn't recall being so affected by them. She was supposed to be a tough New York journalist, one who'd waded into the fray at more than a few protests.

But it wasn't the blood and bruises that had turned her stomach. It was the obvious rage of Darcy's murderer. The merciless blows meant to kill, meant to convey how the person felt. Pregnancy—particularly one that was unplanned or unwanted—stirred up strong emotions. Darcy's had clearly sent someone over the edge.

Sudden tears burned Charlotte's eyes and closed her throat. She curled into a ball, arms wrapped around her middle. Unexpected news like that could even change a lover into someone you hardly recognized.

Like Richard.

He'd been as shocked as she was after her doctor's visit confirmed what she'd suspected. Dreaded. They'd been using birth control, but even Margaret Sanger had stated that nothing was 100 percent guaranteed. Charlotte's immediate reaction upon learning her condition was that she didn't want a child. Not yet, anyway. But when she told Richard her plans to seek an abortion, he'd been furious.

Abortions were for poor, desperate women or prostitutes.

Not for women of their social standing. She would marry him, he'd said, and have the baby.

Charlotte had considered it for a few seconds, half a breath from accepting, until he continued. "After the baby's born, you'll stay home, of course."

She would become the wife and mother he'd need to maintain his family's standing in the business community. No outside pursuits like a career to distract her from her *real* duties.

Charlotte had been stunned into silence. He'd been a staunch supporter of her efforts to tell important stories about women's rights and equality until then. At least while they were attending lectures and dances, or as they fell into bed pulling at each other's clothes. Equality was fine for everyone except whomever he married.

The bastard. The lying, self-centered bastard. How had she not seen the truth of him?

But it was the truth within herself that caused her the most anguish.

The outer door squealed open, interrupting her thoughts. Heavy footsteps and the rattle of the door closing again followed.

"I've cleaned her up as best I could." Michael's voice carried in from the exam room.

A pang of guilt went through Charlotte, shaking her out of her bout of shame. She was supposed to have helped him, but she couldn't bear to see Darcy Dugan again.

Another man replied, his tone too low for her to catch the words. Wood clattered on the floor. A third man asked if Michael had an extra sheet or tarp.

Charlotte listened as the men prepared Darcy for the undertaker, her limbs locked. She'd withstood the chaos of marches and counterprotests. She'd pulled a man off a woman old enough to be his mother as he assaulted her because he didn't agree with her views. She'd recorded interviews with women who had bruises and broken bones, women who had seen friends hurt because they wanted equality with men.

Damn it, she should be tougher than this.

"Put 'er on the stretcher, Jimmy." Feet shuffled. "We'll get somethin' from Miss Brigit. The missus'll fix her up right pretty."

"Thank you, John," Michael said. "And no talking to Toliver or allowing pictures. This is still an open investigation. Eddington and Blaine will have your hide."

"Learnt my lesson last time, Doc. Okay, move 'er out, Jimmy."

Two sets of heavy footsteps retreated from the exam room. The front door slammed closed, rattling the log cabin. Charlotte heard Michael move about, cleaning up by the sound of the clattering instruments, cupboard doors closing, and sweeping.

Charlotte closed her eyes, pushing memories out of her head. Maybe she could help Darcy some other way. Her desire to help Michael and the deputy find who had killed a young prostitute was now a quest to seek justice for a kindred soul of sorts.

"Sis."

Charlotte startled and her eyes flew open. Her face felt hot. Michael crossed the room to sit on the edge of the bed.

"You all right?" He brushed a strand of damp hair off her forehead.

She pushed herself up into a sitting position. "I'm fine."

His brow furrowed.

Charlotte dropped her gaze and nudged him so she could swing her legs off the bed. "It's fine. Just a temporary shock."

More lies. There was nothing temporary about the guilt and sadness that dwelled within her; they were always there, waiting for an opportunity to reappear. It had been several months since she had woken up shaking, if not crying, after one terrible dream or another. Now those dreams would surely return for the next few weeks.

Charlotte and Michael both stood, and she busied herself

with straightening her clothes so she wouldn't have to look at him. She grabbed her coat from the chair where she'd left it earlier. Michael helped her slip it on.

"Maybe you shouldn't go to the party tonight," he said, sounding a lot like their father.

Charlotte cocked her head, confused. "Party?"

"The mayor's gala. You can stay here, if you'd like."

That party. He meant well, but there was no way she would stay in his room with the constant reminder of the day's trauma just beyond the door.

"No, I think a party is exactly what I need." He looked skeptical. Not a surprise. Charlotte pecked him on the cheek. "I'll go back to my room and freshen up."

He followed her through the exam room, where she avoided looking at the table, and to the front door. "Are you sure?"

"The distraction will do me good." She put as much of a smile on her face as she could muster. "Seven o'clock?"

"I'm supposed to escort Ruth from her house. Can you meet us at the Windsor?"

Charlotte's jaw muscles tightened, fixing the grin on her face. Of course he'd have to escort his fiancée. What else should she expect? "I'll do that."

Michael reached past her to open the door. Watery sunlight dappled the stone step and street beyond. "See you there, but if you don't feel like it later, don't worry. It's completely understandable."

Charlotte walked the three blocks to Sullivan's without speaking to anyone. Folks went about their business, allowing her to hurry past as if invisible. That suited her just fine. There was no way anyone in Cordova knew what she'd been through. Not today, not last year. But Charlotte couldn't help feeling that, if she made eye contact with any of the shopkeepers sweeping mud from the walkway or patrons carrying their purchases, they'd know everything, as if she wore a sandwich board outlining the grim details.

She pushed open the door to the rooming house, grateful for the next several hours during which she could write up the day's events and get ready for the gala. Her words might never see the pages of *Modern Woman*, but perhaps if she made them just words on paper, it would help reduce their visceral kick.

Charlotte unlocked the door to her room and got to work.

Mrs. Sullivan offered to press the burgundy gown while Charlotte bathed. One of the Sullivan boys—who was older than Charlotte by a good fifteen years and sported a fresh black eye—hauled in the heated buckets of water to fill the claw-foot tub in the bathroom. Though she'd just had a bath the day before, this one felt particularly cleansing.

After she donned the gown and slipped on her shoes, Charlotte stopped at Mrs. Sullivan's door for a final inspection.

The older woman smiled, her blue eyes damp from emotion. She grasped Charlotte's hands in hers. Strong hands that had been through so much. "You look lovely, dear."

Charlotte knew Mrs. Sullivan was seeing her daughter yet again. She smiled and squeezed the older woman's fingers. "Thank you. I promise not to disturb you when I return."

Mrs. Sullivan patted her arm. "If it's not too late, dear, stop in for a sherry and you can tell me all about it."

Adjusting the embroidered silk wrap around her bare shoulders, Charlotte waved good-bye as she stepped outside. The sleeveless gown with the deep neckline was more revealing than her typical garments. It had been a less than practical selection while she packed necessities, but now she was glad she'd thrown it into the trunk. As she walked toward the four-story hotel—the tallest building in Cordova—Charlotte wondered what her future sister-in-law might think of the dress. Ruth didn't strike her as the type to share Charlotte's fashion choices. Or many other choices, to be honest.

Whatever had drawn Michael to her?

The late afternoon sun had allowed the wood walkways and

road to dry, somewhat, assuring there would be little mud caked on her shoes as she arrived at the Windsor. The hotel's vertical sign, brilliantly painted with red letters trimmed in gold, dominated Second Street. The double doors had been propped open.

Charlotte followed the well-dressed couples into the lobby. A crystal chandelier sparkled overhead, giving a warm glow to the hardwood floor. A curving staircase carpeted in a deep green led to the upper floors. Behind the long registration desk, a middle-aged man stood with a tight smile on his face.

Fifty or so men and women chatted in small groups, while waiters in starched uniforms served what had to be mock-alcoholic cocktails in tall glasses, Alaska's dry law having gone into effect earlier that year. Folks managed to skirt the law, like Mrs. Sullivan with her after-dinner sherry, as long as they kept consumption limited to private settings. Public venues were a different story.

The tableau could have been set in New York or Philadelphia, except for the men wearing knee-high leather boots, canvas trousers, and the occasional gun. Not the sort of accessory one found displayed in polite society. The dichotomy of civilization and the Last Frontier, all in one room.

Most people had clearly already veered off toward the coat-check room, just beyond the front desk, but Charlotte opted to keep her wrap. After the chilly walk, she still felt gooseflesh on her shoulders and arms. She should have worn her coat. "Fashion be damned" seemed to be the local motto. She could certainly see herself getting behind that sentiment sooner rather than later.

The hum of conversation was punctuated by bursts of laughter. Charlotte smiled, feeling more of the day's earlier trauma retreat to a small knot in the pit of her stomach. That would have to do for now.

"May I escort you in, Miss Brody?"

She looked up into the freshly shaved face of James Eddington. His dark hair was slicked back. The tin star with DEPUTY U.S. MARSHAL in the middle and DISTRICT OF ALASKA etched in the surrounding circle stood out against his dark blue wool shirt.

"Thank you, but I'm waiting for Michael and Ruth."

Eddington nodded, then eyed the crowd. "I haven't seen either of them yet." He gestured toward the right. "But there's Reverend and Mrs. Bartlett talking to Mayor Kavanagh and his wife."

Charlotte followed Eddington's line of sight to where a thin man in clerical garb chatted with a tall, barrel-chested gentleman with a mole on his cheek, smoking a thick cigar. Their wives stood nearby, conversing, but occasionally glancing up to wave at someone. She assumed the woman with the thick, white hair in the neat bun and conservative dress was the reverend's wife. The younger, raven-haired woman in red had to be Mrs. Kavanagh.

"They seem quite friendly with one another," Charlotte said.

Eddington clasped his hands behind his back. He wore the same sort of canvas trousers and leather knee boots as some of the other men, and of course his revolver was at his hip. "All in the name of making Cordova the biggest little town in the territory."

The tone of his words implied the deputy might not be too keen on the idea.

"Oh? How do they plan on doing that?"

"Let's just say they each have their ways of approaching the public and making their case that civility leads to prosperity." Charlotte laughed, and Eddington's smile grew, showing off his dimpled cheek. But the amusement faded from the deputy's eyes. "I haven't heard from your brother yet. How'd it go earlier?"

The knot in her stomach tightened. "It was as horrid as you can imagine. I'll transcribe the notes I took, but you can talk to Michael about the details."

Eddington stared at her for a few seconds, frowning, his eyebrows nearly meeting over his crooked nose. "I'm sorry. I didn't mean to upset you."

She forced a smile back onto her face. "No, it's all right. You and Michael both warned me it would be difficult. It'll pass."

Some aspects of the day would fade eventually. The rest of her memories would be with her forever.

He watched her for another few moments, then nodded. "I'll talk to him soon. As much as I hate to leave a lady unescorted, I'm afraid I have to go back to work."

A small pang went through Charlotte. She hid it by giving him her best overdramatic pout. "You aren't staying? Who will I dance with?"

"I'm on security duty here." He leaned forward and winked. "Though perhaps we can steal a dance later."

The pang became an unexpected surge of warmth that flooded her cheeks. "I'd like that."

Eddington touched his forehead in his standard salute, then moved off to police the growing crowd. She watched him disappear in the sea of bodies and wondered what was wrong with her. The deputy was flirting, just as she was. Why was it affecting her so? The only answer she could manage was that the day's events had left her shaky.

"Sorry we're late," Michael said as he and Ruth approached from her left. "Waiting long?"

Relieved to have them to distract her, Charlotte smiled. "Not at all."

He wore a simple black suit and tie, the starched collar digging into his neck, and his mackinaw slung over his arm. Ruth unbuttoned her heather-gray coat to reveal a green silk gown. The long sleeves billowed, buttoned at the wrists. The collar dipped to the top of her sternum, revealing little more than the hollow of her throat.

Charlotte adjusted her wrap around her almost bare shoulders. "I've just arrived."

Ruth handed Michael her coat and leaned forward to press her cheek to Charlotte's in greeting. "I'm glad you decided to come. Michael told me you were positively traumatized this afternoon."

Charlotte shot her brother a glare.

"I said you were disturbed by the condition of the body," he said defensively. "Ruth embellished the rest on her own." He headed to the coat-check room.

"Well, of course you were disturbed, darling." Ruth slipped her arm under Charlotte's and held it to her, as if they were old friends. "A horrible thing to witness, I'm sure."

"I'd rather not dwell on it." Had Michael told his fiancée about Darcy's other condition?

Ruth patted her arm. "I understand. Let's put such dreadful things out of our minds for the evening. You look quite fetching, so urban and smart," she said, considering Charlotte's dress. "Especially compared to the rest of us bumpkins."

"Everyone looks wonderful," Charlotte replied. Her gown had been popular last year, and the other women in the room wore frocks no older than her own. "That color is absolutely gorgeous on you."

Ruth blushed a deep pink. "Thank you. Was that Deputy Eddington you were speaking to?"

Heat bloomed in Charlotte's chest. "It was. He's on duty this evening."

The blond woman leaned closer and lowered her voice to a conspiratorial whisper. "He's a bit of a rogue who tries to have his way with every pretty girl who comes to town." She pressed her lips together and nodded to make sure Charlotte understood the danger that was James Eddington.

"Is he?" Charlotte asked, feeling a tickle of mischief. "A rogue can be exciting at times, don't you think?" She winked and smiled wickedly.

The reverend's daughter stared at her, wide-eyed. After a

moment, she forced a laugh. "Oh, Charlotte, you are such a card. Michael, you never told me your sister was so hysterical."

Having returned from depositing their coats, Michael stood at Charlotte's other side. "Yes, she's a regular Fanny Brice."

He met Charlotte's gaze, an eyebrow quirked in his "What did you say now?" expression. She shrugged and shook her head. Surely he didn't expect her to be on her best behavior all the time.

"I can't wait for Mother and Father to meet you," Ruth said.

She guided Charlotte through the crowded lobby, greeting several people, but not stopping to chat. Michael briefly spoke to a few men and caught up to them by the time they made it to Ruth's father and another man, the mayor having disappeared in the crowd of guests.

"I absolutely agree, Reverend," the other man said, "but it takes more than godliness to stop some from drinking, law or no."

Charlotte's attention piqued. Along with several states, the territory of Alaska had enacted its dry law months ago, but the federal Volstead Act would be voted upon in October. The argument over its effectiveness raged in and out of Washington DC. "Perhaps the problem lies in forcing adults to curtail perfectly legal activities."

Beside her, Michael groaned. She felt Ruth stiffen. Both older men turned. The reverend nodded a greeting to Michael and Ruth before fixing his pale blue eyes on Charlotte. "Legal they may be, young woman, but that doesn't make them correct."

"Or virtuous?" she asked.

"Charlotte." Michael's tone held an unmistakable warning. "This is Reverend Samuel Bartlett. Ruth's father. And U.S. Marshal Thomas Blaine. Gentlemen, this is my sister."

She shook both men's hands. Bartlett's grasp was loose, cool, and moist. Blaine's was more firm, but he still held her fingers rather than her hand.

"So you're not keen on the Volstead Act, Miss Brody?" Blaine hooked his thumbs in the pockets of his black vest. The silver badge on his chest gleamed in the light of the chandelier.

"Not particularly, Marshal. Forcing extreme limits on personal behavior tends to make people react to the extreme, don't you think?"

Michael bowed his head. Her second day in town and she was creating havoc, the gesture said. Ruth and her father exchanged glances, perhaps wondering what sort of people her fiancé came from.

Ones who aren't afraid to speak their minds, Charlotte thought. The Bartletts might as well learn that now. Surely she wasn't the first to challenge their ideology, especially here.

"I tend to believe that as well," the marshal said. "Unfortunately, the burden of enforcement falls upon my office, no matter my personal views."

She inclined her head slightly. "I don't envy you your position, sir."

Blaine chuckled. Reverend Bartlett, however, pursed his lips. "Alcohol abuse is a terrible thing," he said. "It destroys families and ruins people. Something needs to be done. The only way to keep on the right path is to eliminate temptation."

"I'm sure Charlotte agrees, Father." Ruth released her to step up to him. She grasped his arm and smiled a brittle smile at Charlotte. "Don't you?"

Charlotte suppressed a flare of irritation at Ruth. She didn't need anyone speaking for her. "I agree abuse is something that needs to be addressed." Michael was going to kill her for making waves with his future father-in-law. "But I don't see how—"

"Ladies and gentlemen," a voice boomed from the front of the room before she could continue and deepen the color on Michael's and Ruth's cheeks any further. Conversation petered to relative quiet, and everyone focused on Mayor Kavanagh. "Thank you for coming out on this fine evening. I'm sure you'll repay my generosity with food and beverages at the polls." Laughter filled the lobby. Kavanagh smiled broadly, his expression a perfect balance of geniality and political awareness. He knew his audience. "But we won't worry about that for a few months. Let's have some fun."

Two uniformed waiters pulled open the double doors. Mrs. Kavanagh joined her husband, and they led the procession into the room. Charlotte couldn't see much past all the folks ahead of her other than the sparkling chandeliers and some silver bunting draped along the far wall, but the oohs and aahs of the guests in the front told her it was a spectacle for Cordova.

A piano, fiddle, and accordion struck up the opening bars of "Alexander's Ragtime Band."

"Oh, I love this song." Ruth tugged her father forward along with the crowd.

Michael tucked Charlotte's arm under his and hesitated to let his fiancée get ahead of them. "I'd nearly forgotten about your perverse pleasure in putting folks on the spot, Charlie." He tilted his head, his mouth near her ear. She braced herself for a lecture about propriety. "Just save a little for your third day in town, eh?"

He kissed her on the cheek and drew her into the ballroom. The thin smile on his face could have been amusement or resignation. Charlotte wasn't quite sure.

Chapter 5

Charlotte hadn't danced as much in the last year as she danced in the initial hour of the mayor's gala. The first dance with Michael reminded her of their younger years when their parents hosted parties, and the two of them would waltz in the upstairs hall, pretending they were among the adults in the parlor as Debussy played on the Victrola.

After the first song, she was swept from partner to partner for just about every tune. With the ratio of men to women in Cordova nearly three to one, most of the females at the Windsor were twirled, swirled, and swung about as long as the music played. Despite her nonstop activity with partners ranging in ability from accomplished to toe-crushers, and dances jumping from the fox-trot to the waltz and back again, Charlotte enjoyed herself. She'd forgotten how much she loved to dance.

She'd forgotten how it felt to be treated like the young woman she was, not judged by anything but her actions in the here and now. Back home, familiarity had bred a mix of kowtowing from her father's business associates and derision from those opposed to her articles. In Cordova, she could just be Charlotte, and it was heavenly.

The only dim spot of the evening, so far, had been the number of partners who wanted to share their grim conjecture about the murder. Violent deaths weren't unheard of here, she learned, but this one sparked conversations on topics from the evils of prostitution to the need for better police protection in the growing town.

Charlotte did her best to change the subject. Luckily, most of the men were polite enough to indulge her "feminine delicacies."

The music of a two-step rag reached its finale, and Charlotte's current partner, a Mr. Abner Doig, spun her toward a table of cigar-smoking gentlemen. Mr. Doig, half a head shorter than she, was panting, his face beaded with sweat and his wire-rimmed glasses steamed.

"Thank you, Miss Brody." He bowed slightly at the waist.

Charlotte nodded back. "My pleasure, Mr. Doig." Two of the men seated at the table started to rise as Doig moved off, reaching for her when the music began again. Did the band never take a break? She held up her hand. "I'm sorry, gentlemen, but I need to catch my breath."

Charlotte headed for the punch bowl. It wasn't that she didn't appreciate the attention; she did, but a girl needed to quench her thirst now and again. Several small glasses of pink punch were set out. She picked one up and moved out of the way of a young couple seeking refreshment. Moving off to a corner, Charlotte engaged in one of her favorite activities: people watching.

The Windsor ballroom easily held two hundred people, while still allowing for a good-sized dance floor, and for the dais where the three-man band played. Couples danced past her to a Cohan tune, most laughing or smiling. A few, however, appeared to be merely enduring until the song was over.

Charlotte drew a freshly pressed handkerchief from her clutch purse and daubed at her forehead and throat. She caught a glimpse of Michael and Ruth on the dance floor. They moved well together, a handsome couple with their lives set. A twinge of jealousy threatened Charlotte, and she pushed it out of her head and heart. She was happy for Michael. Her time would come.

Determined to maintain her buoyant mood, Charlotte shifted her gaze to another part of the ballroom. Deputy Eddington strode the periphery, his eyes missing nothing.

So serious, she mused. What sort of trouble did he expect to find at the party?

"Care for another, Miss Brody?" Marshal Blaine stood beside her, offering a glass of punch. "It doesn't quite pack the kick of a good shot of whiskey, but it'll do."

His crooked grin made her smile.

She downed the last mouthful of the fruity sweetness punctuated with seltzer bubbles, and set the empty crystal on the buffet table. Taking the proffered drink from Blaine, she touched glasses with him. Charlotte sipped hers while the marshal swallowed his in two quick gulps.

"Ah." He smacked his lips. "Frank sure knows how to throw a shindig. This is his first party without alcohol, and I hardly miss it. Much."

Charlotte laughed at the marshal's candor.

"How long have you been in Cordova?" She took another small sip. In a way, she was grateful for the dry law, or surely the gin and champagne would be flowing. Dancing wasn't the only thing she hadn't done much of in the last year.

"It'll be five years come spring. Came in on one of the first boats of the summer." He placed his cup beside her first one, then hooked his thumbs in his vest pockets. The move displayed the circled star pinned to his chest and the revolver at his hip. Though he spoke to Charlotte, he scanned the room much as his deputy had. Searching for something specific, or was that the nature of a lawman? "The missus and I were looking for something a little different after our youngest married and moved out."

Charlotte couldn't imagine her parents leaving their Yonkers home for the "wilds" of Seattle, let alone Alaska. "This sure is different," she said.

Blaine chuckled. "That it is. Some folks can't handle the cold and dark of winter, but a number of them go just as off-kilter with too much light in the summer. Don't sleep like they should."

Sleep deprivation might put someone on edge. Her own bouts of insomnia resulted in days of muddled thought and short temper. During those times, she'd entertained the idea of throttling people for minor irritations.

Could Darcy's murderer have been similarly affected?

"Marshal, what are your thoughts on the Dugan case?"

Blaine pressed his lips together under his moustache. He didn't meet her gaze as he spoke, but continued watching the crowd. "Could be a tough one. No witnesses so far, no threats to her that we know of, but her profession wasn't the safest." He gave Charlotte a sidelong glance. "You helped your brother at the autopsy, I hear."

Was that a hint of accusation in his voice? Worry about breaking some law or, worse, getting Michael into trouble, kept the images from that morning at bay. "I took notes, yes. Did we do something wrong?"

He shrugged. "Not so far as I'm concerned. I'm sure Dr. Brody kept things official. As long as you don't compromise the case, it's all good."

Tension eased from her shoulders. "I wouldn't dream of it." Sweat still trickled down her back and dampened her cleavage. "If you'll excuse me, Marshal, I think I'll get a bit of fresh air."

Blaine bowed. "It's been nice chatting with you, Miss Brody. May I call upon you for a dance later?"

"I'd be delighted."

Charlotte made her way along the perimeter of the room, sidestepping couples and groups. A dozen or so men smoked cigars and chatted in the lobby, squat glasses of colorful liquid in hand. She crossed the polished floor to the main doors and stepped out onto the walkway. A salt-tinged breeze from the bay ruffled the edges of her shawl. The sun was just sinking below the horizon, yet there was sufficient daylight where shadows didn't lurk.

Not one to lean and loiter, Charlotte strolled to the corner. Music filtered from the Windsor. She hummed along with the tune, turned around, and walked back past the alley between the hotel and the bathhouse next door.

Charlotte caught a flicker of light and movement from the alley. Someone had opened the hotel's side entrance thirty or so feet down.

Probably one of the staff dumping garbage in a bin or perhaps popping out for a smoke break.

"I told you not to come here." The sharp-toned words, meant to be whispered, echoed off the walls. A second person responded, but their comment was too low to hear.

Charlotte was about to continue back inside when the first speaker's next words stopped her cold in her tracks.

"That bitch got what she deserved." A woman by the pitch, but anger and the attempt to keep her volume down gave her voice a gruff quality. "The filthy whore should have kept her legs and her mouth closed."

With bins and pallets between them, Charlotte couldn't see who was in the alley, and she didn't dare risk trying to see them. They had to be talking about Darcy Dugan. Charlotte stood still, hardly daring to breathe so she wouldn't miss a word.

"I don't care," the woman said. "Just get those papers. They have to be in her room somewhere. I can't—won't—go to that horrible place, so it has to be you."

The other replied, then footsteps retreated toward the opposite end of the alley. A man? Light flashed onto the bathhouse wall, then went out when the hotel door thudded closed.

Charlotte's heart pounded. It wasn't surprising to hear people discussing that morning's shocking discovery, but the woman had sounded positively incensed. Not by the murder, but by Darcy herself.

What had instigated such hatred? The mere existence of prostitution, or something more significant?

Charlotte dashed back inside to see if she could catch the person returning to the mayor's party. She nearly bowled over a man and his companion on their way out.

"Pardon me," she called, pushing past them.

Others in the lobby looked after her, curious, as she hurried by. Charlotte stopped at the doorway into the ballroom. Of course, none of the other attendees appeared agitated or rushed. Where would the woman have accessed the alley? Through the kitchen? Off to the right was a hallway. She might have gone into the powder room to freshen up before returning to the ballroom.

Charlotte made her way to the corridor where she found doors marked LADIES, GENTLEMEN, and KITCHEN. At the end of the hall was an unmarked door. She turned the knob of that one, peered into the dark alley, and pulled it closed again. That explained how the pair got in and out of the hotel, but where were they now? The man had gone off . . . somewhere. What about the woman?

Charlotte took a deep breath and opened the door to the ladies' room. A dark-haired woman in a red gown sat at one of the two vanity tables, kohl pencil in hand. The mayor's wife, Charlotte realized. Mrs. Kavanagh glanced at her and smiled, but went back to fixing her makeup. A black compact and a small jar of blush sat on the table next to her purse.

A blue velvet upholstered divan and two matching armchairs shared the room. Another door led to, Charlotte assumed, the lavatory.

"Looking for someone?" Mrs. Kavanagh asked.

"Did you see—" Charlotte couldn't very well ask if the woman had heard anyone come in from the alley. She could *be* the woman from the alley, for all Charlotte knew. "Did you see a tortoise shell compact in here?" Charlotte made a show of searching the vanity, then crossed to one of the chairs.

"Sorry, no. Care to borrow mine?" Mrs. Kavanagh held up the black lacquered case.

Charlotte took the offered compact and sat at the other vanity. "Thank you."

"You're the doctor's sister, aren't you?"

Charlotte tilted her head. She shouldn't be surprised that people knew her before she knew them. "I am, and you're the mayor's wife."

She offered her hand to Charlotte. "I am."

Charlotte had only seen her briefly when Deputy Eddington pointed her out earlier in the evening. She seemed younger up close.

"Mrs. Kavanagh. It's a pleasure."

"Welcome to Cordova." She released Charlotte's hand and continued primping.

"Thank you. You have an interesting town here."

Mrs. Kavanagh gave a short laugh. "We certainly do." She set her pencil down and swirled her finger in the pot of blush to brighten her cheeks. "How are things in the States?"

Charlotte had seen the *Cordova Daily Times* for sale at the drugstore and the café, so the question was more polite than from a true need for news. "It's getting back to a semblance of normal. The flu pandemic and the war certainly took their toll."

"It was rough here too," Mrs. Kavanagh said. "Entire villages were wiped out. We had our own losses, of course. Your brother and Dr. Hastings were practically run into the ground, especially after Dr. Garrett succumbed. But overall, we managed to pull through."

"I'm glad to hear that." Michael had written about the long hours of tending patients and of a few losses that seemed to hit him particularly hard; he and Miles Garrett had been friends.

Mrs. Kavanagh packed her purse and snapped it shut. "But let's not speak of such things tonight. This is a party, after all." She smiled as she stood. "Shall we return to the festivities, Miss Brody? I'm sure there are a good number of gentlemen awaiting their chance to dance with you."

Mrs. Kavanagh introduced Charlotte to her husband, the Honorable Francis "Call me Frank" Kavanagh, who was standing with the Reverend Bartlett, another gentleman, and their wives. The mayor stuck his thick cigar into his mouth and took both Charlotte's hands in his to shake them. The burnt-orange-scented cloud of smoke was more pleasant than most, but it still made Charlotte's eyes water.

Kavanagh was almost immediately drawn into an argument with Reverend Bartlett and the other man, a city council member, over land-sale laws. The mayor had left the council meeting early the night before, missing that point of contention. Kavanagh was attentive and good-natured, though the set of his jaw told her he was no pushover.

Mrs. Kavanagh and Mrs. Bartlett made a grand effort to include Charlotte in their side conversation, but it was difficult to focus while surreptitiously searching for Deputy Eddington in the crowd. She needed to tell him what she'd heard in the alley.

She saw Marshal Blaine dancing with a woman who might have been his wife. Despite the older man's friendliness, she didn't feel comfortable seeking him out. Granted, Eddington wasn't particularly approachable, but he was leading the investigation into Darcy's murder.

The exchange in the alley played through Charlotte's head again. Whatever she could add—if there was any significance to what she'd heard, and there was no assurance there was—would have to be relayed to him anyway. Better to speak directly to the deputy than to be brushed off by the marshal.

"Don't you agree, Miss Brody?" Mrs. Bartlett said.

Charlotte jerked her head around to face the women she was supposed to be conversing with. Damn it all. What had they been talking about? She had no idea. "Um."

Mrs. Bartlett pressed her lips together, her brow wrinkled with agitation at Charlotte's obvious slight.

"Are you all right?" Tess Kavanagh asked with more concern than annoyance. "You seem a bit flushed."

Charlotte pulled her handkerchief from her purse and daubed at her throat. Maybe she could pass off the embarrassment as a dizzy spell or some other feminine malady. Her inner feminist cringed, but better that than insulting the women any more than she had. "I am feeling a little lightheaded. Will you excuse me, please?"

Without waiting for a response, she walked away from the others. Instead of heading to the powder room, or to the main doors, Charlotte skirted the outer edge of the crowd. Surely she'd run into Deputy Eddington.

There he was, speaking to a middle-aged couple. Now she just needed to get him alone.

Just as she reached them, the music changed to a slower tune. Perfect. She loosely knotted her wrap around her shoulders so it wouldn't slip off. "Pardon me, Deputy. I'd be honored to take you up on your offer of a dance."

Eddington's dark eyebrows rose. At her boldness, perhaps? But then he grinned. "It would be my honor and pleasure, Miss Brody."

He excused himself from the couple, then held his left hand out, palm up. Charlotte took it. His fingers gently closed around hers, and he led her to the dance floor. When they found an open spot, Eddington lifted their hands and twirled her into position, facing him. The move surprised Charlotte. Who would have thought the gruff deputy could be so suave? His right hand rested on her waist, and he stared into her eyes. She moistened her lips. "I hope I didn't take you away from any important business, Deputy."

"Nothing of the sort. And please, call me James."

The musicians were at the opposite end of the floor, making conversation possible. Other couples spoke to one another without her hearing them, and Charlotte hoped she could discuss the pair in the alley in some semblance of privacy. She moved in closer, inhaling a combination of tobacco and wool. His hand at her waist slid to the small of her back.

"I need to tell you what I heard," she said, her mouth near his ear.

"Gossip about the Bartletts' cook?" he whispered. "I know she keeps a bottle of rye in the root cellar."

Charlotte squeezed his hand in rebuke, but she laughed. "No. Something serious."

Eddington drew his head back to look at her, but kept their bodies close. There was a glint of amusement in his eyes. "Violation of the Alaska dry law is serious, Miss Brody."

"But probably not heeded as the government wishes. No, this is about Darcy Dugan."

His amusement fled. "What about her?"

She gave him a brief description of what she'd heard and the circumstances. Though he continued to lead her through the dance steps without faltering, his gaze darted throughout the room. She knew he was listening, but he seemed to be searching for suspects as well.

"And you have no idea who it could have been?" he asked as he spun her around an older couple.

Charlotte surveyed the attendees. "No. They could have been anyone. I'm sorry."

Eddington immediately brought his attention to her. "Nothing to be sorry about. You've given us more to go on. At least two people know more about the murder than they're willing to admit."

"Do you think they were working together?" The possibility startled Charlotte. "Planned it?"

He shrugged and went through the motion of giving her a

polite bow as the music ended. "Or one told the other. I'd wager a man delivered the fatal blows, though some women are certainly strong enough. I've questioned Brigit and the girls, but either they saw nothing or are lying for some reason. Hard to say."

"Why would they lie? I'd think they'd want to find out who killed one of their own." It made no sense, but human nature was often a mystery. It also led to some of the best stories.

"The houses here and the marshal's office have an understanding," he said. "They operate more or less freely as long as they aren't blatantly advertising, but that doesn't translate to trust."

Perhaps an unbiased third party like herself could get more out of Brigit and her girls. Charlotte already had a rapport with Marie. That would be a good place to start.

Deputy Eddington tucked Charlotte's arm under his and escorted her to the table where Michael and Ruth sat with another couple. Michael glanced between her and his fiancée, his expression a familiar one of exasperation. What had she done now?

"Are you all right, Charlotte?" Ruth asked coolly. "Mother said you were feeling poorly."

"I'm—" Oh. Right. She'd been "unwell" while in conversation with Mrs. Kavanagh and Ruth's mother. Charlotte's malaise being miraculously alleviated by dancing with Deputy Eddington didn't go over well with Ruth. "I am feeling better now, thank you."

"I couldn't let Miss Brody leave without dancing with me," Eddington said. He turned to Charlotte and inclined his head. "I hope I didn't exacerbate any symptoms of nausea."

It took considerable effort for Charlotte to control the laughter that threatened to bubble out of her. He was a rogue, just as Ruth had said. She gave him a wan smile. "I'm sure I'll recover, Deputy."

Their shared pretense shone in his eyes as he bowed to her,

then the others at the table. "I'm afraid I have to return to my duties."

The deputy bid them good evening and, with his hands clasped behind his back, resumed his patrol of the perimeter of the room.

"If you're feeling ill, Charlotte, perhaps I should bring you back to your room." Michael stood and straightened his coat.

Charlotte started to protest, then thought better of it. "I'd appreciate that. I promise to send him back here right away," she said to Ruth.

Ruth's pinched expression, so like her mother's, softened slightly. She offered a tight smile. "Of course he should take you home. I think that's for the best."

I'm sure you do, Charlotte thought.

She bade good-bye to the others. Michael came around the table and gently grasped her upper arm. He guided her toward the coatroom to pick up his mackinaw. On the way, he shook his head. "I don't even want to know."

"No," she said, "you probably don't."

Chapter 6

A light rain fell throughout much of the morning, lending a cold dampness to the room. Charlotte snuggled under the down comforter, loathe to move lest she touch the cooler portions of the sheets. The patter against the window and the warmth of her bed lulled her into an in-between state of consciousness. She had no reason to be up with the sun, such as it was on a gray Sunday. She certainly had no plans to attend morning services. Let Cordovans see her as a godless heathen, for all she cared. She'd behave herself in other public forums. Mostly.

Would Michael be joining Ruth and the Bartletts at the Lutheran church? Charlotte and Michael had gone to services now and again with their parents, but it was more for show than due to any sort of piety. What had possessed him to become engaged to a preacher's daughter?

Must be love, she thought with a surprising lack of envy.

Eventually, her bladder determined it was time to get up. The rest of the house was quiet as Charlotte made her way to the lavatory. She returned to her room, dressed, and read through the first installment of her series she'd be sending to Kit. It couldn't be posted until the next day, and it would take at least a couple of weeks to reach New York, but Kit and Mr. Malone should be pleased.

At ten thirty, her stomach rumbling, Charlotte decided to see if the café was open. It should be late enough afterward that Miss Brigit's house would be stirring. Hopefully Marie would be willing to talk to her. Charlotte donned her mackinaw and wide-brimmed hat and headed out into the rain.

Henry was just setting up the coffeepot in anticipation of the after-church crowd. "Morning, Miss Brody."

"Good morning, Henry." Charlotte shook off rain from her coat. "Goodness, what a day."

"At least it isn't snowing yet. We usually don't get this sort of weather until late in September. Might be a bad winter this year if it keeps up."

Charlotte hung her hat and mackinaw on the provided coatrack. "That's something to look forward to." Henry cocked his head, not getting her sarcasm. "Never mind. Can I have some coffee and toast, please?"

They chatted about the weather—the possibility of thirty feet of snow by the end of February boggled her mind—then Charlotte steered the conversation to the mayor's party the night before. Henry had been washing dishes in the kitchen the entire night, but had enjoyed the music.

"Did you see or hear anything unusual?" she asked. No one else was in the café yet, assuring privacy with her inquiry.

He continued stacking cups and saucers. "Nope. Just the chef yelling about limp lettuce and soggy toast points." He gave her a sidelong glance. "Why?"

Chances were slim that Henry knew anything about Darcy Dugan, but he might have overheard something at some point.

"Just wondering. A lot of folks were talking about Darcy last night." From what she'd heard, the attendees had been horrified, but certain the young harlot had tried to cheat a customer, thus instigating a drunken rage.

"I bet," he said. "There hasn't been an outright murder here for a good bit, and that one was more of an accident than anything."

She recalled Michael mentioning something of the sort. "What about other problems with Miss Brigit's girls? Does the marshal get many calls about them?"

Henry refilled her coffee cup, a pensive look on his smooth face. "Not that I've heard. Miss Brigit is a bit of a stickler. Doesn't let the girls get too wild. They're kinda nice, really." Charlotte caught his eye, and the boy's cheeks flamed. "I mean, when they come in for lunch or something, they're always nice to me and tip well. Like you do." His dark eyes widened, and the color on his face deepened. "Not that you're a—I didn't mean—"

"I understand what you mean, Henry." Charlotte smiled, suppressing a laugh, and deposited a dime and a nickel on the counter. "Let me know if you hear anything, will you?"

With his eyes downcast, he nodded, swept the money into his palm, and concentrated on sorting coins in the till.

"Speaking of Miss Brigit," she said. Henry met her gaze, his cheeks still flaming. "Can you direct me to her house?"

Other than his eyes widening with shock and curiosity, he gave no other outward reaction. Henry described the house that was located just below Michael's office, closer to the railroad tracks.

Back outside, a gust flung cold rain into Charlotte's face. She ducked her head, one hand holding her hat to keep it from blowing off, and made quick time to the two-story clapboard. This unassuming residence housed Brigit and her girls? She knocked on the green door and waited.

No one responded, so she knocked again, louder. Was she too early? It was after eleven. Did the girls get Sundays off? The railroad tracks were less than fifty yards away, and she wondered how anyone living there got any sort of rest.

"Get locked out, girlie?" called a deep voice from the road.

Charlotte turned around. Three men sauntered past the house, heading toward the canneries closer to the water along the railroad tracks. All were bearded, wearing rough clothing and rubber knee boots. One passed a brown bottle to another. They didn't seem interested in approaching her, thank goodness, but her heart pounded at the possibility of having to deal with the men. Would someone in the house hear if she called out?

"Is she a new girl?" one asked.

The man with the bottle shrugged. "Who the hell looks at their faces?"

All three guffawed and, thankfully, kept walking.

Heat rose on Charlotte's face. She'd received her share of rude remarks, especially when she confronted a man who didn't think women should be journalists. There were more of those than she cared to count, but this was the first time she'd felt so vulnerable.

The one man's words echoed in her head. *Who the hell looks at their faces?*

Was that how they saw, or didn't see, these women? As anonymous playthings? Did a man like that kill Darcy because she'd been nothing to him? Easy to get rid of?

They were no better—or worse—than Richard.

The thought turned her stomach. Something had to be done about antiquated attitudes of people who viewed a woman, any woman, as less than a man.

Charlotte stepped down from the low wood porch and walked around the side of the house. There wasn't much of a yard, mostly scrubby grass and overgrown patches of fireweed. Wood stacked against the wall beside the back door. A couple of old folding chairs.

And a narrow, beaten path leading up the slope to the walkway that paralleled Main Street.

Charlotte mentally followed the trail that ran behind the buildings. A small cabin, Michael's office, a clothing store, the tailor. There was a gap between buildings where the wooden walk was supported by pilings that had been sunk down into the water twenty feet below the main part of town. The trail continued all the way to Sullivan's rooming house, then down the slope on the opposite end. This was the path Darcy took the other night while trying to escape her killer.

But why did she leave the house if she was ill? What could have been such powerful motivation? And why hadn't she yelled for help?

"Can I help you?"

Charlotte spun toward the voice coming from the back of the house. A petite, dark-haired woman of thirty or so stood in the open doorway, hands on her hips. She wore a pale green, Oriental-inspired dressing gown, and her feet were bare, the toenails painted bright red.

"Good morning," Charlotte said. She made her way toward the door. The aroma of bacon frying made her stomach gurgle. Perhaps she should have eaten more than toast at the café. "I was hoping to talk to Marie. Is she available?"

The woman gave Charlotte a slow perusal, taking in her drooping hat and wet mackinaw. "Who are you?"

"Charlotte Brody. Marie knows me."

"Marie's not up yet." The woman smiled wickedly. "She had a busy night."

Apparently the death of one of Brigit's girls hadn't stemmed the flow of customers. Did business take precedence over grief, or was it an attempt to keep things as normal as possible?

If the comment was meant to scandalize, this woman was wasting her efforts on Charlotte. She returned the mocking grin with one of sweet innocence. "I'm sure Marie made a lot of clients happy. Does she get some sort of bonus for a job well done?"

The woman's smile dropped into a tight-lipped frown. "I'll let her know you're looking for her, Miss Brody."

She started to retreat into the kitchen. Charlotte took a quick step forward, her hand out in a placating gesture. "Wait. Are you Brigit?"

The woman stopped. "What of it?" she said curtly.

Charlotte had to make amends or she'd never get anywhere with Brigit, and likely not get a chance to question Marie. "I apologize for the flippant remark. I'd like to talk to you about Darcy."

Brigit drew in a sharp breath, obviously surprised by Charlotte's request. "Why? What do you care about her?"

How could Charlotte explain to this woman that Darcy's death—and the reason it might have occurred—had affected her in the short time Charlotte had been in Cordova? That the young woman's condition had churned up Charlotte's own painful past? Did Brigit know Darcy had been pregnant?

"I helped my brother during her autopsy yesterday," Charlotte said. Brigit's dark eyebrows rose, but she didn't respond. "I want to help find out who killed her."

Brigit reached back into the kitchen and picked up something from the windowsill. She stuck a cigarette between her lips and concentrated on flicking the wheel of her silver lighter as she spoke. "Some drunk, I'd reckon. It happens."

The flame caught, and the pungent aroma of burning tobacco cut through the rain.

"You have no idea who it could have been? Who she was . . . with that evening?" Charlotte found that hard to believe.

Brigit blew a stream of smoke from the corner of her mouth. "She was supposed to be taking the evening off. Doctor's orders." The emphasis on that last bit told Charlotte exactly what the madam thought of Michael's directive. "No one went up to her room, and no one saw her come down. Eddington was already here asking."

He'd mentioned that while they danced last night, but Charlotte hoped she could talk to Marie in a more relaxed and friendly manner than would likely have been used in an interrogation by the local law.

"She hadn't been having trouble with anyone lately?"

"No."

Charlotte tried to read the truth behind the woman's simple denial. Brigit held her gaze, challenging Charlotte to come right out and refute her too-pat answer. But why wouldn't Brigit let James know if there had been trouble?

Unless there hadn't been, and Darcy's death was a spontaneous reaction by an angry customer. That didn't sit right with Charlotte. The beating Darcy took was too specific, too personal to be a random act.

What would it take to get Brigit to talk?

"Look, Miss O'Brien—"

"Brigit will do," she said. She drew deeply on the cigarette, then flicked the butt into the damp bushes. The cloud of blue smoke she released obscured her scowl for a moment.

It took considerable effort for Charlotte not to huff in frustration. "Miss Brigit, I only want to help."

"You've been here for, what, two days, Miss Brody? You have no reason to stick your nose in my business." She stepped back into the kitchen, hand gripping the edge of the door. "I'll tell Marie you want to talk to her, but unless you're willing to pay the five-dollar minimum or looking for work, I'll kindly ask you to otherwise leave me and my girls alone. If you'll excuse me, I have a funeral to arrange."

Slam.

Charlotte stood in the overgrown yard, staring at the scuffed door while rain soaked the lower half of her skirt and blew into her face with each gust of wind.

Damn it.

Chapter 7

Charlotte trudged back up to the main road, berating herself with every step as a raven in a nearby spruce seemed to chuckle at her. Even he thought she should have handled the encounter with Brigit better. With the madam on the defensive, there was no guarantee she'd relay Charlotte's message. Charlotte might not get to talk to Marie without catching the girl outside of the house. Maybe she could wait a few days and try again. But the more time that passed, the more difficult it would be to find the killer.

"Charlotte, is that you?"

Charlotte lifted her head and squinted into the rain. Ruth stood in front of Michael's office, a black umbrella dripping over her head. "Good morning. Is Michael in?"

"He's had an emergency call." Ruth glanced at the door to the office and shrugged. "Such is the life of a small-town doctor."

"He is dedicated."

"He is, but it does impede at times. We were supposed to have an early Sunday dinner with my parents." Ruth brightened. "Why don't you join us? I'm sure Mother and Father wouldn't mind."

Had Ruth forgiven her for leaving Mrs. Bartlett's company? She'd seemed rather perturbed last night. Maybe it wasn't as big an indiscretion as Charlotte imagined. Still, she wouldn't want to risk insulting them again by arriving at their door in anything but her Sunday best.

She scrunched her toes in her boots. "I'm not exactly dressed for socializing."

"Oh, pish-posh," Ruth said. "We won't worry about that. Come on."

She hooked her arm through Charlotte's and tugged her toward the next street up the hill. They passed Second Street and the Windsor, continuing on to a more residential section of town. The umbrella covered them both, so Charlotte removed her hat to avoid hitting Ruth with the brim.

"Were you out for a walk?" Ruth asked.

"Just getting a little fresh air, yes." There was no polite way to tell her she'd been at Miss Brigit's, or why. Charlotte wasn't supposed to be interfering. If word got back to Eddington, Charlotte would have to suffer his ire.

Ruth's nose wrinkled. "There are better places to stroll than by the railroad tracks or along that particular row." Was she referring to the aroma of the clam cannery or Miss Brigit's? "Did you enjoy the party last night?"

"Very much. I haven't danced like that in a long time."

"You seemed to be very popular."

Charlotte looked up from watching her step. Ruth smiled prettily at her, then set her gaze ahead. Was she criticizing Charlotte for dancing so much? "There were fewer women than men. I think it was more of a matter of numbers than popularity, but I had fun."

"I guess that's all that matters." Ruth patted Charlotte's arm, then unhooked her own from Charlotte's. "Here we are."

They'd come up to a two-story home. Its white clapboard siding, green door, and green shutters made it look remarkably like Miss Brigit's. There was even a small covered porch. Charlotte decided it was best not to point out the similarities.

"What a beautiful home," she said.

Ruth closed the umbrella and shook off the rain before opening the front door. "Let's get you out of those boots and into something a bit more comfortable."

She slid the umbrella into a wooden stand to the left of the door. The tiled entry was as large as Charlotte's room at Sullivan's. Cabbage-rose paper adorned the walls. Straight ahead, stairs led up to the next floor, and doorways to the left and right stood open. A telephone table to the right of the front door held a candlestick phone and a vase of flowers. Two straight-backed chairs in the entry provided comfortable places for visitors to deal with their footwear.

Through the arched doorway on the left, the parlor was brightly lit by lamps to enhance watery sunlight coming in the front bay window. The overstuffed furnishings, Persian rugs, and delicate knickknacks gave visitors a dignified, yet homey welcome. Clattering dishes and the murmur of voices carried in from the right. The dining room, Charlotte guessed. The tantalizing aroma of roasted chicken and fresh-baked bread from that direction confirmed it.

Ruth opened a panel under the stairs and withdrew two wooden hangers. She waited for Charlotte to shed her coat, then hung both it and her hat in the closet. She then handed Charlotte a pair of soft, black slippers. Charlotte removed her boots, set them to the side along with others already there, and donned the slippers.

"Thank you," she said, smoothing her hair and skirt.

Ruth hung up her own coat. She replaced her boots with a pair of dark green slippers and brushed at her skirt. "There," she said, smiling at Charlotte.

"Is that you, Ruth?" Mrs. Bartlett called.

"I think everyone's already seated." Ruth took Charlotte's

arm again and escorted her into the dining room. The Bartletts weren't alone, making Charlotte even more aware of her disheveled appearance.

Wonderful.

Reverend Bartlett presided at the head of the table, Mrs. Bartlett at the foot. The mayor sat at the reverend's right, Tess Kavanagh to Mrs. Bartlett's right. An older couple sat across from each other, and a young blond man in his late teens sat to Mrs. Bartlett's left. The men rose, the younger one reluctantly, with his head down.

"Hello, dear," Mrs. Bartlett said, smiling at Ruth. The skin around her mouth tightened when she looked at Charlotte. "How lovely to see you again, Miss Brody."

It seemed her dashing off to find James Eddington hadn't quite been forgiven. Charlotte inclined her head and vowed to be as polite as possible throughout the meal. "It's a pleasure to see you too, Mrs. Bartlett."

"Michael had to see a patient," Ruth said, guiding Charlotte to an empty seat near the older woman sitting to Reverend Bartlett's left. "But I ran into Charlotte." She introduced the other couple as Mr. and Mrs. Robert Landry. Charlotte sat between Mrs. Landry and Ruth. "That's my brother, Sam." Ruth gestured toward the young man beside their mother. "Sam, say hello to Charlotte. She's Michael's sister."

Sam glanced up, barely making eye contact with Charlotte through the fall of hair that curtained his face. He mumbled what might have been "hello."

"Hello, Sam. It's nice to meet you."

He dropped his gaze to his lap, shoulders hunched.

Ruth straightened her silverware and water glass. "He's a bit shy."

A woman wheeled a cart in from the swinging doors that led to the kitchen. A perfectly browned bird, surrounded by potatoes and onions, steamed upon a silver tray. The server went directly to Reverend Bartlett. He bowed his head and clasped his hands together at the edge of the table. Conversation stopped, and everyone followed his example.

"Thank you, Lord, for these bountiful gifts we are about to receive. Bless our friends and family and the people of Cordova. And please, Lord, look after the lost souls, particularly that of Miss Darcy Dugan. Amen."

Charlotte's head came up at the mention of the girl.

Mrs. Bartlett made a dismissive sound. "Honestly, Samuel, to mention that harlot's name at this table."

Reverend Bartlett began carving the meat as the server set bowls of side dishes on the table. "It's my job to concern myself with all the souls in Cordova, Mother, not just the godly."

"She certainly wasn't that." Ruth reached for the water pitcher and filled glasses for everyone.

"I've known a few ladies of the evening who attended church," Charlotte said. Though she had no reason to believe Darcy had been particularly religious, she felt the need to defend the girl. "Some seemed more dedicated to God than regular parishioners."

Everyone at the table froze and stared at her. Reverend Bartlett held a slice of breast between the carving knife and serving fork. The spoonful of potatoes Mrs. Bartlett had scooped plopped onto her plate. The Landrys stared at her, wide-eyed, as did Ruth. Only the Kavanaghs appeared more amused than stricken.

Well done, Charlotte. The sarcastic words in her head sounded like Michael. So much for polite conversation.

Ruth let out a short bark of nervous laughter. "Charlotte, you're such a card. I said as much last night. Didn't I, Mother?"

"So you did." Mrs. Bartlett's blue eyes burned into Charlotte. She flicked another spoon of potatoes onto the plate and set it before Sam with a thunk.

"What I meant—" Charlotte sipped her water. "What I meant was that the decision to become a pros—a sporting woman doesn't necessarily exclude or eliminate her faith."

"That may be true," Reverend Bartlett said, "but the act itself is unacceptable in the Christian faith."

Charlotte couldn't argue that point, but she didn't think the preacher would mind a little friendly ideological challenge. "Yet even Christ befriended prostitutes."

Grinning, Mayor Kavanagh set an unlit cigar on a saucer beside his plate. "She has you there, Samuel."

"Hate the sin, love the sinner," the reverend replied.

"It seems that someone hated her quite a bit," Charlotte said.

"Such a terrible thing." Ruth shook her head.

Was she talking about Darcy's being a prostitute or her murder? The others made sympathetic noises around the table, except for young Sam, who kept his head down and continued to eat.

"Does the marshal's office have any idea who did it?" Mrs. Kavanagh asked.

"Blaine says they're following every lead they have," the mayor said, flicking the colorful paper band of the resting cigar. "Unfortunately, it's not much." He turned to Charlotte. "Deputy Eddington questioned you and a few of the other residents at Sullivan's, didn't he, Miss Brody?"

"My room is at the back of the house," she said. "I told him what I heard that night, but I doubt it was of any help."

Ruth's head whipped around. "You heard something? I didn't know that. Did you see anything?"

Charlotte shook her head. "Deputy Eddington believes Darcy and her killer made their way from Brigit's along the path behind the house and down to the tracks. They bumped into my wall, but I didn't see who was outside."

"We certainly can't have a madman running about," Mrs. Landry said. "What if he harms someone else? Someone from a good family?"

Charlotte's mouth dropped open in shock. She almost began to rail about what difference it made who was assaulted, but hesitated when she saw Reverend Bartlett's expression. Surely he wasn't warning her away from addressing this ignorant woman? Charlotte pressed her lips together and took a deep breath.

"I saw the condition of Darcy Dugan's body," she said quietly. "It was horrible. Bruised and bloody. The killer took special care to make her hurt as much as he could before dealing the fatal blows. That's something no one, no matter her station or lifestyle or faith, should have endured."

Mrs. Landry stared at her, rheumy eyes still wide.

"But there are no witnesses, no suspects," Ruth said. "It could have been anyone. Cordova can be a dangerous place for someone out and about so late."

"The attack was very personal." Charlotte had to be careful about revealing too much. She'd promised Marshal Blaine she wouldn't compromise the case. "Once we get a little more information about Darcy and what she'd been up to lately, I think Deputy Eddington and Michael will be able to figure it out."

"What do you mean, 'we'?" Ruth asked. "Charlotte, you can't possibly be involved in this terrible affair."

She had already become involved, and more concerned than anyone realized. Not because she was working with Michael, or even because she'd gone over to Brigit's to speak to Marie. She was involved because she had to be. Because someone with a better idea of what Darcy might have been experiencing with her pregnancy needed to seek justice for her. Not that Deputy Eddington wouldn't do his best, but how could he understand a woman's place in the world, particularly one of Darcy's condition and station? And even he had said Brigit and the girls weren't opening up to him. Charlotte could very well have the advantage there.

"Everyone should do what they can to find out who murdered Darcy, don't you think?"

Ruth's gaze darted around the table. Seeking support? What was there to dispute in bringing a murderer to justice?

"Of course," she said, looking at Charlotte again. "But some things are better left to professionals."

Charlotte gave her a tight grin. "I am a professional. I've been involved in several investigative stories that required work with the local police."

"Including murder?" Mrs. Kavanagh interjected. "That's a rather different kettle of fish, Miss Brody."

"It is," Charlotte admitted, "but I'm ready and willing to do whatever it takes."

Mayor Kavanagh cleared his throat with a deep rumble that garnered everyone's attention. "I'm sure your statement to Deputy Eddington is a great help. We want to get the case wrapped up as soon as possible. Cordova isn't perfect, but it's not a town that allows any of its citizens to be harmed without repercussion. The bigger we get, the more likely ruffians will attempt to set up shop and take advantage. I won't have it in my town."

That sounded like a reelection speech if Charlotte ever heard one. Raised glasses and exclamations of "hear, hear" went around the table.

The rest of the meal was filled with speculation on who would head the annual Quilt Show committee, ideas for marketing Cordova's growing clam fisheries, and other less controversial subjects. When Mrs. Bartlett suggested they gather in the parlor for coffee, young Sam mumbled something, then dashed up the stairs. After another hour of keeping to safe, mundane topics, Charlotte thanked her hosts and took her leave.

"I'll see you to the door," Ruth said, accompanying Charlotte. "I'm glad you were able to visit."

Charlotte peeled off the slippers and donned her boots. She wouldn't call her future sister-in-law on the polite fib. Charlotte knew she probably should apologize for the discussion at the table, but in all honesty, she wasn't sorry. "I appreciate the chance to get to know you all. Michael isn't one for giving much detail."

Like the fact that he was seeing a girl, let alone engaged.

"He's a good man and a good doctor. Once Doctor Hastings retires, Michael's hours will be more regular and his client list much more suitable."

Charlotte hesitated shrugging into her coat. "Will there be another doctor brought in?"

"Of course. We're too big a town to have just one, or even only two. The junior doctors will pick up the less profitable patients."

Like the cannery workers and the prostitutes, Charlotte assumed. "I can't imagine Michael forsaking his regular patients in the name of status. He wants to help people. All kinds of people."

Ruth tilted her head as if bemused by Charlotte's words. "Being a doctor is about status as well as helping people. He can do both, but most of his patients will actually be able to pay him in something other than canned goods or wood for his stove."

This was the sort of woman Michael wanted to marry? One who saw his life's work as a way to better his standing—and presumably hers? "That's not why he became a doctor, Ruth."

"Oh, I didn't mean to suggest he doesn't want to help those in need." She laid her hand on Charlotte's arm. "Goodness, no. Charity will absolutely be part of his schedule. But you have to agree that after all his hard work in school, and dealing with the most difficult of circumstances, he deserves to have a practice that's a bit more comfortable."

Michael had indeed worked hard and had seen some of the worst of human conditions. He'd admitted that his recent letters home hadn't included the reality of his practice here, but there'd been no indication that it was getting to him. On the contrary, he seemed much more content than when he'd been in the States.

"Good intentions and humble beginnings are fine," Ruth continued, "but no one truly wishes to stay in that position for their entire life. Michael can serve Cordova and still achieve his proper due. Everyone should have grand aspirations, don't you think?"

Even Charlotte had had dreams of working for bigger periodicals like the *Washington Post*, the *New York Times*, or the *Herald*. Ambition wasn't a bad thing. "I guess you're right."

Ruth grinned, but her blue eyes were hard. "Of course I am. I know he'd be very worried if you were to get involved with this vile business, so please, Charlotte, for Michael's sake . . ."

Ruth didn't finish the sentence, but the implication was clear: Don't jeopardize Michael's comfort or his standing in local society.

"We wouldn't want to upset him, no." Charlotte couldn't get to the door fast enough, not even caring to see if Ruth had picked up on her derisive tone. "Thank you again for inviting me. I'm sure we'll see each other soon."

She was on the small porch and headed to the street with her coat unbuttoned, Ruth calling farewell behind her. What made Ruth think she knew Michael—knew what he wanted—more than his own sister?

Because she's been closer to him than you have in the past year. You don't know all that he's been through. Just like he doesn't know what you've been through, does he?

Charlotte quelled the voice in her head. It wasn't the same.

Was it?

She hurried down the street, the front of her coat clutched in one hand.

Chapter 8

Charlotte spent the rest of the day writing and reading. Mrs. Sullivan had invited her in for a light evening meal, but Charlotte left before the after-dinner sherry, claiming a headache. The dreariness of the day had continued into evening, prompting her to turn in earlier than usual.

The next morning she woke to still more rain—thankfully it wasn't snow as Henry had mentioned—feeling no better than when she'd fallen asleep. The conversations from the previous afternoon at the Bartletts' still rang in her ears. Between the dismissal of Darcy as a victim worthy of their sympathies and Ruth's expectations that Michael would fob his patients off on a new colleague for the sake of status, Charlotte found the ache in her head renewed rather than relieved.

Deciding a walk in the rain was not only necessary for her errands, but might help get rid of her headache, Charlotte washed up and dressed. She wrapped the first installment of her serial in cardboard and waxed brown paper given to her by Mrs. Sullivan. She'd stop at the post office to send it to New York, then have a heart-to-heart talk with Michael. That definitely would require some mental preparation. Her stomach rumbled. And food.

She locked the door to her room and headed out, the packet tucked inside her coat to protect it from the rain. Charlotte waited for the lone vehicle on the road to pass by, avoiding the splash of a puddle, then crossed. The post office was housed in the federal building, upstairs from the U.S. marshal's office. She entered the main doors, then hurried up without too much thought of James Eddington's proximity.

A bell tinkled over the door as she entered. A woman behind the waist-high counter chatted with a female customer. To the right of the counter, rows of numbered brass boxes filled the wall. The postal clerk glanced at Charlotte and nodded a greeting to her.

Charlotte set her packet on a table near the door and waited for the clerk to finish. A list of postal regulations and another of unclaimed letters were tacked to the wall. Beside them were several "Wanted" posters from the U.S. marshal's office, including one that was two years old for an Edward Krause, with the words ***Captured, Convicted, Executed*** scrawled across it. After reading the walls, Charlotte double-checked the address Kit had given her and the knots in the string.

"Can I help you, miss?"

The bell over the door tinkled as Charlotte turned. The female customer had departed, and the clerk looked at Charlotte expectantly.

"Yes, thank you. I need to send a package to New York." She carried her parcel to the counter.

"Sure thing." The clerk brought a ledger up from beneath the counter and took the address information. "The steamer leaves tomorrow night. It'll go out on that."

"Perfect," Charlotte said. "Do you know if I can pick up paper and carbon at McGruder's?"

"Probably have better luck at the drugstore, I'd imagine. They have stationery and such." The woman hefted the package and gave the New York address of *Modern Woman* a closer look. "You a writer?"

"A journalist. I'm chronicling my travels to Alaska and my time in Cordova."

The clerk laughed. "Ain't gonna have much to write about from here except clams and copper. Hardly nothing happens now that the dry law's in effect. It's settled into downright tedium."

"Oh, I don't know," Charlotte said. "The mayor's party the other night was fun. And of course, that poor girl."

The woman's expression clouded. "Yeah, a terrible thing. Darcy was a decent sort."

"You knew her?"

She shrugged. "Seen her around. She'd come in with Marie or other gals who were sending letters, or if they were picking up mail for Brigit."

"Didn't Darcy send letters out?" Charlotte asked.

The clerk tilted her head, a thoughtful expression wrinkling her brow. "Not that I recall. Isn't that funny? Most everyone here has some sort of correspondence with the outside world. But not Darcy, not to my recollection."

Charlotte thanked the clerk for her help, held the door open for a woman holding two youngsters by their hands, then descended the stairs and walked toward the café. Half a block ahead, young Sam Bartlett stared into the café window. He wasn't directly in front of the glass, but stood off to the side, as if he didn't want to be seen by anyone inside.

"Good morning," Charlotte said when she drew closer. "Would you care to have a cup of coffee with me?"

Sam's head snapped up, his eyes wide. His pale face blossomed to deep pink, emphasizing a long scratch on the left cheek. He ducked his head and hurried past without a word. His boots clattered on the wooden walk until he came to the first alley. There, he dropped down onto the muddy path and disappeared behind the building.

Ruth had said he was shy, but that bit of behavior had Charlotte wondering if his was some sort of phobia.

She entered the bustling café and found a seat. Henry greeted her with a smile, a cup of coffee, and a menu. After enjoying the chef's special omelet and a side of toast, Charlotte set off for Michael's office. She'd promised to make meals for him in return for his purchasing food for them both, and wanted to inventory his shelves before a trip to the grocer.

"Miss Brody. I mean, Charlotte," a female voice called from behind her.

Charlotte turned. "Oh, Marie. I'm glad to see you."

The girl was wearing a conservative day outfit beneath her waterproof coat and sturdy boots. Her black umbrella rippled under the assault of wind and rain. "Brigit said you'd stopped by to see me."

Charlotte hid her surprise that Brigit had passed along the message.

"Yes, I need to talk to you." She glanced back into the café, but there were too many people in too small a space. She didn't want to have a private, potentially sensitive conversation there. "Is there someplace we can go to chat?"

Marie scanned the street in both directions with red-rimmed eyes, then nodded up a side road. "The pool hall? It's just opened for the day and shouldn't be terribly crowded." Her brow furrowed. "Unless you think that's not an appropriate place."

Charlotte laid her hand on the girl's arm. "I've spoken to folks in prisons and opium dens. I think I can handle a pool hall."

Marie led the way up the road. The Edgewater Pool and Billiards Hall was a long, low building with a large front window. Inside, a pair of men in shirtsleeves sat at one of six dining tables drinking coffee. Eight pool tables filled the rest of the room, most unoccupied so early in the day. A man leaned over to line up a shot at one while another chalked his cue. A large man with glossy black hair and a dark complexion, suspenders straining over his belly, stacked glasses behind the counter.

"Hey, Marie." A gap-toothed grin appeared on his face. "Good to see you."

Charlotte had never heard a Native Alaskan speak before, and this man's soft voice didn't match his formidable size.

Marie shook out her umbrella before closing it and smiled, but Charlotte noted it was an effort for her. "Just looking for a quiet place to talk to my friend. Charlotte, this is Albert." They exchanged greetings. "Can we get a couple of coffees and use your card room?"

Albert set cups and saucers on the bar. "McKinney's back there with his crew. They've been at it all night. How about a table in the corner?"

"That's fine. Thanks."

They carried their coffees to a dim corner. The small round table and two wobbly chairs seemed to have been shoved into the shadows to be kept out of the way of the larger settings. But the distance from the men and the crack of ivory balls guaranteed a bit of privacy.

Charlotte draped her damp coat on the back of the chair and set her hat on the far side of the table. Once Marie settled into her seat, Charlotte covered the girl's hand with her own. "I'm so sorry about Darcy."

Marie only nodded, blinking rapidly, but Charlotte saw the tears. "I couldn't believe it when the deputy told us. Who would do such a thing?"

"They'll catch whoever did it," Charlotte assured her, but she honestly wasn't sure. Yet it wasn't like the murderer could have gotten far, unless he'd hared off into the wilderness.

"I hope so." Marie raised her cup, hands shaking with emotion.

Charlotte sipped at her coffee to give Marie a chance to collect herself. The brew was on the strong side, and Albert hadn't offered cream or sugar. *I guess men who play pool drink their coffee black.* Though Charlotte wondered if there was a little something extra in the men's cups, dry laws be damned.

Marie daubed at her eyes, then cleared her throat. "I wanted to thank you again for having your brother come see Darcy the day before . . . the day before. She seemed better after he'd left."

All Michael had prescribed for Darcy was rest and fluids, but perhaps that was all the girl needed at the time. And maybe a bit of sympathy, if Brigit was after her to get back to work.

"I'm glad," Charlotte said. She didn't want to upset Marie, but questions needed to be asked. "About that night. Did Darcy seem worried about anything?"

Marie thought for a few moments. "Not that I can recall. She was in her room when business started to pick up. Kevin Hartney was celebrating his birthday with some friends. We were all busy, what with being down a girl and all."

"And no one asked for Darcy? Made any sort of fuss?" The idea that a disgruntled regular might have been so irritated by rejection seemed far-fetched, but sometimes the oddest things set a person off.

Marie shook her head. "There were a few requests for her, but most of the guys are willing to see whoever's available."

"So no one went to her room. And no one saw her leave."

"No. Even Brigit was working."

Which meant Darcy could have come downstairs without any of the others knowing. But why? And how did the killer get her out of the house?

"I know Deputy Eddington already questioned you, but is there anything about Darcy's behavior that seemed off lately? Was there anything bothering her?" Charlotte didn't want to mention the pregnancy unless Marie did. As close as they seemed to have been, it was possible Darcy hadn't shared her condition with her friend.

"Other than her feeling poorly? Not really. Brigit had her staying at the house more than usual." Charlotte cocked her head in silent query. Marie leaned closer and lowered her voice, though there was little chance of the men overhearing her. "We visit the clubs or here at the pool hall to bring in business, though legally we're not supposed to. Brigit schedules who goes. It can be fun, but sometimes it's real work to drum up a customer or two on slow nights. Darcy didn't particularly like it, and Brigit didn't force her."

"Does she force you?" Choosing to become a working girl meant a certain amount of exploitation, but requiring the girls to solicit customers off-site strained even Charlotte's feminist limits.

Marie shrugged, a guarded look in her eyes. "She reminds us that we're as responsible for the house succeeding as she is, more so maybe, and going out helps."

"But Darcy didn't have to."

"She went for a little while, but stopped a few months ago. The other girls were jealous. It's sort of a luxury to stay back and wait for customers to come to you."

Could one of the other girls have been angry enough to attack Darcy? When would she have had the opportunity if everyone was working that night?

"How long had Darcy been working for Brigit?"

"Just about a year," Marie said. "She came down from Fairbanks with some folks looking to work in the canneries. Found out that was *real* work, and stinky to boot. She and I met here at Albert's. She asked about becoming a working girl, so I introduced her to Brigit."

Charlotte studied Marie a little closer. She was no more than twenty, if that. "How long have *you* been with Brigit?"

Even in the shadowy corner, Charlotte saw Marie's blush. "Two years."

"How old are you now, Marie?" Charlotte was afraid of the answer, but felt compelled to ask.

Marie ducked her head and said softly, "Eighteen." Her head jerked up again. "Please don't tell. Brigit and everyone think I'm twenty-two or thereabouts."

Charlotte patted Marie's hand, all the while her heart breaking a little for this girl—this child—who had likely started in the life before she truly understood what it meant. "I won't, but is this what you want to do?"

Marie shrugged again. "No, but the money's good, and it's less backbreaking than working the laundry or the canneries. My mama worked herself near to death for years. Got old before her time. I swore I'd never do that."

It wasn't the first time Charlotte had heard that very argument from a sporting woman. Being in control of their own destiny, their own financial situation, had lured many a girl into prostitution, if they weren't desperate to begin with. Most were taken advantage of by pimps and madams, though some went on to create legitimate business opportunities for themselves. She hoped Marie would end up in the latter group.

"Funny thing is," Marie continued, "most of us girls talk about getting out, maybe going south back to the States to start a business or marry. But not Darcy. She seemed content, even when she wasn't working and making money."

Charlotte wasn't surprised to hear a young woman enjoyed having sex, even with strange or numerous men. It wasn't her idea of a fulfilling relationship, but she wasn't qualified to judge another woman's proclivities. Far from it. Still, the majority of prostitutes she'd met considered the job marginally better than working in another menial position.

"Was Brigit angry that Darcy wasn't working like the rest of you?" Charlotte couldn't imagine the madam murdering a girl who wasn't bringing in money. Fire her, perhaps, though a threat to the madam's livelihood could be motivation.

Marie rolled her eyes. "Brigit's always angry about something. Not in front of the customers, of course, but we'll get a tongue-lashing if something goes wrong."

"Does she ever get physically violent?" From what Charlotte had seen, Brigit had a temper, and despite her smaller stature she might be able to inflict serious injury. Especially if she had a weapon like a sturdy tree branch.

"No." Marie blinked at Charlotte, and her mouth dropped open. "You don't think Brigit hurt Darcy, do you?"

"Do you?"

Marie thought about it for a moment, slowly shaking her head in denial, but then stopped, uncertainty in her eyes. "I don't know. I don't think so, but you never truly know people, do you?"

"No, you don't." For some reason, Michael's face popped into Charlotte's mind's eye. And Richard's. Charlotte pushed aside the issues she had with both her brother and her former lover. Those issues were nothing compared to solving a girl's murder. "You were Darcy's best friend, Marie. Did she share anything with you—anything at all—that made you think she was in trouble or having a problem with anyone?"

"No, I told the deputy that. She'd been fine, except for being sick. Got quiet just before, but I figured it was her coming down with whatever illness she'd picked up. Do you think it wasn't?" The girl's face crumpled. "Why wouldn't she tell me if something were bothering her? We were friends."

Marie buried her face in her hands and sobbed. Charlotte wrapped her arms around Marie's shoulders, offering what little comfort she could. The billiards players and Albert glanced their way, but probably preferred to stay out of "women's business."

The door of the Edgewater opened, allowing a swath of gray light into the room. A dark-haired boy, eight or nine years old, in knee-pants with suspenders and a long-sleeved shirt, stopped at the entrance and looked around. Albert, leaning on the counter reading a newspaper, nodded in Charlotte and Marie's direction. The boy came toward them.

"Marie, Brigit needs you back at the house."

Marie looked up, sniffed back tears, and wiped her eyes with a handkerchief from her coat pocket. "What for?" The boy pressed his lips together and glanced between Marie and Charlotte. "It's okay. She's a friend."

"I'm Charlotte," she said, holding her right hand out.

He shook it quickly and shoved his hands in his pockets when he let go. "Charlie."

Charlotte smiled. "My brother calls me Charlie sometimes."

She was hoping the similarities of their names would set the boy at ease, but it didn't. He remained vaguely suspicious of Charlotte's presence and spoke to Marie. "Brigit needs you to help with Darcy's service and all."

Marie stiffened under Charlotte's arm. "Tell her I'll be right there."

"She said to find you and send you home," Charlie said. "I'm going to pick some flowers for her."

He ran back through the doorway, waving to Albert as he went.

"Does Charlie run errands for Brigit?" Charlotte asked. If the boy was regularly at the house, maybe he knew something.

"Sometimes. He's Brigit's son."

"Really?" Charlotte couldn't help her startled response. In her few years talking to women from every walk of life, she'd never met the child of a prostitute or madam living with his mother.

Marie sighed, and the two of them rose together. "I heard you helped Doc with his report," she said as she put on her coat. "Are you looking at helping Deputy Eddington too?"

"If I can," Charlotte replied. *If he'll let me.*

Marie nodded and suddenly pulled Charlotte into a hug. "Thank you."

She hurried out after Charlie, the door slamming behind her.

Charlotte clamped her hat onto her head with one hand and held the collar of her coat closed with the other as wind and rain whipped between buildings. By the time she arrived at Michael's office, both her hands were numb and dripping wet. The thought of wearing gloves in August seemed ridiculous, yet not. How long before she could take the weather in stride, like most here?

She pulled open the door and hurried inside.

Michael and the three people with him in the office all looked at her. An older Native woman, a teenage girl, and a boy of six or seven with a plaster cast on his left arm all stared at her with curiosity in their dark eyes. The three wore heavy trousers and boots. The two women had long tunics, almost but not quite dress-length, of deep red with black trim. The boy wore a too-large plaid shirt tucked into his pants.

"Excuse me," Charlotte said, stepping aside.

"Charlotte," Michael said, "this is Mary Ivanoff and her grandchildren Rose and George." He looked at the Ivanoffs in turn. "This is my sister, here from the States."

Charlotte carefully removed her hat to avoid flicking rain on them all. "It's nice to meet you."

The girl spoke softly to the woman, the language a mix of glottal consonants and flowing vowels unlike anything Charlotte had ever heard. The woman responded in quiet tones.

"Grandma says welcome to Alaska," Rose said, offering a shy smile.

"Thank you," Charlotte replied. "Sorry to interrupt your appointment."

"We're just finishing here." Michael ruffled the boy's shiny black hair. "George is healing just fine." He spoke to the girl and her grandmother. "I want the cast to stay on for another couple of weeks. Either come back in and I'll take it off, or you can do it on your own if you're not able to make it to town. Just be careful when you cut the plaster. And be sure to stop in when you can, so I can look him over."

Rose translated once again. The older woman nodded and spoke a few short sentences. She reached into the woven bag slung over her shoulder and pulled out a bundle of newspaper. The smoky fish aroma was strong; it made Charlotte's stomach rumble.

"Grandma says thank you for your help. We'll return when we can."

Michael took the offered packet, smiling at his patient and the family. "Thank you. Safe travels back home."

The trio put on foul-weather gear that had been hanging on the hooks behind the door and left the office.

"How far do they have to go?" Charlotte asked as she hung up her wet mackinaw and hat. She knew little about the Native settlement along the lake shore several miles away, and made a mental note to include women from that culture as well in her articles.

"They live in Alice Cove, about ten miles northwest by boat." Michael headed back toward his room. Charlotte followed. "Mary makes the best salmon jerky this side of the sound."

"Ten miles by boat?" Charlotte looked out the window at the rain and wind slashing through the trees near the cabin. What was it like on open water in this weather? "And they come all this way to see you?"

He set the bundle on the shelf near the sink. "No, not specifically. They came to town for some goods and to visit family and friends. George broke his arm pretty badly a few weeks ago when they were here last, so I set it. I expect I won't see him before they remove the cast themselves."

Rural living wasn't so unusual to her, but that sort of travel seemed on the extreme end of things. What if there was an emergency? How did such isolated people cope when foul weather set in?

"I was going to call down to Sullivan's for you in a bit," Michael said, turning around and going back through the exam room.

"Oh? What for?" Charlotte followed him into the office area.

Michael sat at his desk. He pulled open a drawer and removed patient files and the gold fountain pen he'd received upon graduation from medical school.

"A copy of the autopsy report needs to be sent to the territorial governor's office." He held up several sheets of paper, one covered in familiar symbols.

"I'm sorry, Michael. I completely forgot." She took the pages and sat opposite him. "If you have some blank forms and another pen, I'll transcribe my shorthand right now."

He provided both. Charlotte took up the outside corner of his desk while he continued to make notes on living patients' files.

She tried not to attach images to the words she spelled out, but it wasn't easy. The memories were too fresh. After twenty minutes of writing, only stopping to wipe her hands on her skirt, she handed the pages back to Michael.

"Make sure I have things as you recall them," she said. She didn't want to have to rewrite anything, or add a gruesome detail that might have been missed.

He read through the pages quickly, his lips pressed tight. Had she made a mistake or was it the content of the report? Michael signed the bottom and had her countersign as his secretary. "We want to make sure the official paperwork has you on it as a witness."

"Since I'm officially your secretary," she said with a grin, "do you want me to take them to the post office?"

He smiled back, but he looked weary. "I still have to write up a cover letter and ask Eddington for a copy of his report. It'll be another day or so."

"Let me know if I can help with anything. You don't need to do it all on your own, you know."

"Well," he said, drawing out the word, "I'm a bit hungry. Saw patients all morning then got caught up with paperwork."

Charlotte rolled her eyes. "Very subtle. I apologize for not keeping up my end of our deal with cooking chores. I promise to be better."

"Just a sandwich and a cup of coffee will suffice."

She swatted at him, then headed into his living quarters to make him lunch.

While they ate bowls of soup and salmon salad sandwiches at his desk, Charlotte considered the best way to approach the subject of Ruth and her plans. Charlotte started to speak a couple of times, but stopped herself before she could get the proper words out. How was it she could speak her mind with the Bartletts and the Kavanaghs, but she couldn't with her own brother?

"What?" Michael asked around a mouthful of bread and fish.

Charlotte heaved a mental sigh and sat up straight, girding herself for what was sure to be a knock-down, drag-out confrontation. "I was at the Bartletts' yesterday for lunch."

"I know. Ruth told me. Sorry I missed it." He took another bite of his sandwich and looked at her expectantly.

Ruth had told him Charlotte had been there, yet Michael hadn't stormed over to lecture her on proper behavior? Odd. Either Ruth hadn't told him everything for some reason, or he was getting used to Charlotte's way of doing things. She would bet on the former.

"I'm glad you weren't there."

He cocked an eyebrow at her. "Oh?"

Charlotte cleared her throat. "We got on to the topic of ladies of the evening and some who decide to pursue the profession."

"Oh, my God, Charlotte. What did you say now?"

"Probably everything you think I did, and worse. But that's not the point."

Michael squeezed his eyes closed, a pained expression on his face. After a moment, he opened them. Pain had turned to suppressed anger. "They are to be my in-laws. *That* is the point."

"We had a lively discussion. It's not like I insulted them or their beliefs." Well, maybe a little, she thought, but that's not what she wanted to discuss with him now, if ever. "Honestly, Michael, I wouldn't have said anything, but the reverend brought up Darcy during grace. I just expanded the conversation."

Michael wiped his mouth, glaring at her over the linen napkin. "I'll bet. Why must you irritate people?"

She couldn't deny that her approach could be annoying. Her job was to get people to talk to her, and sometimes that required stirring things up. "My irritating your fiancée's family isn't as big a concern as the conversation I had with Ruth afterward."

"What did you say to her?"

"Why do you assume I was the one to say anything?" Charlotte held up both hands, palms out, to ward off his growing anger. "Never mind. I didn't say a thing. It's what she told me that has me worried." Charlotte lowered her hands and leaned forward. "Have you spoken to Ruth about her plans for your future?"

"Of course we've discussed our future. It's natural when two people get engaged."

She shook her head. "No, not the future she sees for the two of you, together, but your professional future as a doctor."

Michael frowned, more in confusion than anger. "What did she tell you?"

"That once you become the senior doctor here in town, you'll be dropping your less prestigious clients to maintain your income and image."

He didn't say anything for a few moments, and Charlotte couldn't read what he was feeling. Was he angry at her? Upset that Ruth was making critical decisions for him?

Finally, he sat back in his chair and tossed the napkin on top of his plate. "She's not completely wrong."

Charlotte stared at him, mouth agape. Surely she had heard him wrong. Their parents had instilled in both of them the duty to serve the less fortunate. Michael had gone into medicine to heal physical ills, while she had opted—to her parents' dismay at times—to shine a journalistic light on unfair conditions and injustices. How could Michael turn his back on the very people he'd sworn to help?

"I don't understand," she said, finding her voice.

"It's the way of the profession, Charlotte. Here, Yonkers, DC, wherever I choose to practice, that's the way it works. If there's more than one physician, the older, more experienced one will have the most affluent patients." He stood, gathering his plate, bowl, and spoon. "I've worked damn hard under some deplorable conditions. Don't I deserve a break from that?"

"But what about the people you see now? What about families like the Ivanoffs?"

Michael brought his dishes into his living quarters. Charlotte followed. "I'll still be seeing patients of all sorts for some time, don't worry. Another doctor might arrive soon, and Doctor Hastings won't retire for years." He set the dishes in the sink. "I'd never leave people in the lurch, but I have to think about my reputation and standing in the community as well. I'll have a family to consider."

Something darkened his expression, but he turned to pump water into the sink before she could tell what it might mean. "You can maintain an honorable reputation while still seeing to poorer people, you know. When did a patient's income become more significant than his or her health?"

Michael slammed his coffee cup into the sink, splashing water onto the floor. He snatched a towel off the counter to mop it up. "It's not, but maybe I don't feel like being a doctor to anyone for the rest of my life. We're looking at statehood, and Alaska will need some significant bolstering in Washington. It would be a boon to everyone if we could get in."

"Politics?" The idea of Michael chatting up politicians boggled her. "You can't be serious."

"A lot of professionals use their standing in the community to get things done on a higher level for a greater good." The outer door of the cabin opened, then shut with a significant bang. Michael checked his pocket watch. "That's my two o'clock with Mr. Perkins. You'll have to go."

He ushered Charlotte through the exam room to the office. A gray-bearded man of about fifty in a worn wool shirt and patched canvas trousers looked up from the newspaper he was reading.

"Hey, Doc." Mr. Perkins scrambled to his feet and swept his fedora off his balding head. "Ma'am."

Charlotte smiled at him, but went directly to where her coat and hat hung. "I'll see you later, Michael."

She shoved her hat on her head and was still slipping the mackinaw on as she left. Standing on the walkway out front, she sucked in a couple of deep breaths of cool, rain-washed air.

Politics. How could he give up his medical practice for politics?

Charlotte strode down the walk toward Sullivan's, her heels hard on the wooden slats.

This was all Ruth's idea, she'd bet. Michael had been perfectly content to be a doctor until he'd met Ruth, happy to tend to the unfortunate and needy.

Hadn't he?

Her step faltered in front of the tailor's shop. She stopped and looked back toward her brother's office. Maybe he'd become overwhelmed by it all, or tired of barely making a living. Michael was right; he deserved to have a decent life, especially now that he was getting married and, presumably, going to start a family.

A man's reputation was everything, wasn't it? Richard had taught her that.

Charlotte resumed walking to the rooming house, feeling the weight of . . . disappointment? Loss? Whatever it was, it slowed her steps and made the walk seem much farther than a few blocks.

She opened the door to Sullivan's as a burly man lumbered

down the stairs. He gave her a nod, then sat in one of the armchairs near the telephone table. He picked up the set and flicked the hook to get the operator. Charlotte continued down the hall to her room, giving the man what little privacy was to be had in the public space.

Unlocking the door, she pushed it open, and a piece of paper fluttered across the floor. Had something fallen off her table? After compiling the copies of her story that morning, Charlotte had filed notes and stashed them in her trunk. There was a page in the typewriter, but clean paper was boxed to stay neat.

She picked up the folded page and flicked it open.

DARCY IS NONE OF YOUR BUSINESS.

A threat? She almost laughed. Someone was threatening her because of the questions she was asking? She'd learned nothing at all that would help the case.

But who would have sent it? Charlotte stared at the paper, rereading the line several times, though it gave no clue to the author. Only a handful of people were aware of her interest. Which one would want her to steer clear of the investigation? Miss Brigit had told her just yesterday to stay out of her business.

You need to talk to Eddington, her more cautious inner voice insisted.

She slipped the paper into her coat pocket and retreated from the room, locking her door behind her. The gentleman in the parlor was on the telephone, cooing to some loved one on the other end of the line. Charlotte hurried past him and out the door.

The rain and wind had picked up in the few minutes she had been inside. Twice she had to clamp her hand atop her head to keep her hat from blowing off. Did it ever stop? The few others on the street scurried by, as intent on their destinations as she was on hers.

She crossed to the federal building, knocking as much mud from her boots as she could before entering the marshal's office. James Eddington looked up from the desk where he smoked a pipe while reading papers. The sweet, earthy tang of tobacco and leather hung in the air. The room held the deputy's desk, a chair for visitors, a long bench along the far wall, and a filing cabinet. One door led to Marshal Blaine's office; another was simply marked JAIL.

"Miss Brody," James said, rising. He set his pipe down. "What can I do for you?"

Charlotte removed her hat and tried to smooth down her hair as best she could. She probably looked a fright, dripping wet and windblown, rushing in like her tail was on fire. She withdrew the somewhat crumpled and damp paper from her pocket. "I found this in my room."

James glowered as he came around the desk and took the note from her. The aroma of pipe tobacco clung to him, not in an unpleasant way.

"I was out most of the morning and just got back from talking to Michael."

The frown deepened when James read the six words. Then his body stiffened, and his hand clenched. "What have you been doing that's related to the case?"

Charlotte swallowed hard. She'd expected the question, and knew he'd be displeased with her answer. "I spoke to Brigit and Marie. Mostly Marie. I asked her if there had been anything bothering Darcy in the last few days or weeks." His expression darkened into a scowl, as she'd also expected. "You admitted you hadn't gotten everything you thought you could from her. I just wanted to help."

"You must have learned something that someone didn't cotton to." His frustration and anger were coming out in the increasing thickness of his Southern accent. "What did Marie say?"

Charlotte told him what Marie had said about Darcy's not

being as concerned with making money as the others. "That was about it."

"So Brigit knew you were looking into Darcy's death, and at least five men at the Edgewater saw you chatting with Marie." James narrowed his gaze, gauging her for truthfulness. No, she wasn't telling him everything Marie had said—she'd promised she wouldn't—but Charlotte wasn't lying either. "Anything else? Anyone else know?"

"I had lunch at the Bartletts' yesterday, with the Kavanaghs and the Landrys."

Three of Cordova's upstanding families. Surely there was no harm in their knowing.

But James's face darkened. "The mayor knows you're asking questions while I'm investigating an open murder case?"

"No, of course not. But he knows I spoke to you about that night, and that I helped Michael. I told them I'm interested in seeing the case solved."

He shook his head and stomped back to the desk. "Damn it, Charlotte." He slapped the note down onto the open file. "Someone in this town beat a girl to death and knows you're poking about. How the hell am I supposed to keep you safe?"

"I'm trying to help." He was concerned for her safety? She hadn't learned anything worth threatening bodily harm over.

He sighed, then rubbed his hands over his face. "I know, but obviously someone feels you shouldn't, or you're getting too close to something. Even if you aren't in danger, they're skittish now, and that makes my job all the more difficult."

"Oh." Guilt flushed her cheeks. She approached the desk, stopping on the opposite side. "I'm sorry, James. I had no intention of doing anything like that. I didn't think word would get out so fast."

"Small town," he said, "with nothing as exciting as this happening in a long while. Ears are everywhere."

While that could be advantageous for gaining information, it worked against the lawman as well.

"I guess you want me to stop nosing around."

James crossed his arms and leaned a hip against the desk. "That would be ideal, yes."

She crossed her arms as well. "I don't think I can do that."

"Why not?" he growled.

"If information is out there that will help you catch the man responsible, I'm going to make sure it's revealed."

"Revealed, not sought. Revealed. To *me,* Charlotte, or to Marshal Blaine."

Charlotte's jaw tightened, and she pressed her lips together. "I have the right to investigate a story."

"But not the right to jeopardize an open case."

Her righteous indignation faltered. "No, of course not." She gestured toward the desk. "I brought the note, didn't I?"

He nodded. "You did, which only proves my point. You need to step back, for your own good. The person who wrote this likely killed a girl. I don't want you anywhere near that animal."

Charlotte glanced at the note. Images of Darcy, bloody and bruised, flicked through her mind like a picture show. The note with its single line of six simple words took on a more ominous tone. Would the killer come after her? James believed so. She'd never backed down from dangerous assignments, had even waded into riots. Rocks through the window were one thing. A threatening note left in her room made it all too personal.

"I'll be careful," she said.

"Somehow I doubt that." He snatched his coat and hat off the rack behind his desk. "I'll walk you home."

"I don't think a police escort is necessary, Deputy."

Ignoring her, James held the front door open and stood aside, waiting for her. Charlotte rolled her eyes, making sure he knew exactly how she felt about his overprotective gesture, and led the way out.

They walked back to Sullivan's with nary a word passing between them. She had to admit, she felt safer walking beside him, but who wouldn't feel safe with a six-foot-tall man carrying a large pistol escorting them home?

He held the front door open for her, then closed it gently behind them. "Did you ask Mrs. Sullivan if she heard or saw anything?"

"No."

James strode to the landlady's door and knocked respectfully, not pounding on it as he had to rouse Charlotte two days in a row. Mrs. Sullivan answered, and he swept the hat off his head.

"Afternoon, ma'am."

"Deputy." She glanced between him and Charlotte, worry on her face. "Is something wrong?"

"No, not at all," he said. Charlotte admired the way he was trying to keep Mrs. Sullivan at ease. No sense in frightening the woman. "I was just wondering if you'd seen or heard anyone down by Miss Brody's room earlier today."

Mrs. Sullivan peered down the hall, as if she'd find someone lurking there now. "No, I haven't, but I was feeling a bit under the weather until late this morning and stayed in bed." She gave Charlotte a beseeching look. "Was there trouble, dear? Did someone try to get into your room?"

"Nothing like that, Mrs. Sullivan." She smiled to reassure the woman. "I think there was someone looking for me, that's all."

True enough.

"Make sure any visitors check in, Charlotte," the landlady said. She gestured toward the parlor. "Rules are clear as day in the parlor."

"I'll let them know."

Mrs. Sullivan nodded curtly. "Anything else, Deputy?"

"No, ma'am. I'll just escort Miss Brody to her room, then be on my way."

She gave them a look that said there'd better not be any hanky-panky, then shut her door. James followed Charlotte, standing behind her as she unlocked and opened the door to her room. She turned around to see him in the doorway, scanning the room as if he expected someone to be inside.

"You didn't have to bring me to my door," she said. Charlotte placed her hat on the table and unbuttoned her coat.

James clutched his hat in both hands. "I don't mind. Besides, I needed to ask you something."

"I can't imagine what else there is to know."

"I need to know if you'll have dinner with me tonight." She stared at him, blinking. Was he teasing her? There was no glint of amusement in his blue eyes. In fact, he appeared all too serious. Uncomfortable, even, as he gripped the brim of his hat. He cleared his throat. "I guess that wasn't really a question. Miss Brody, would you do me the honor of having dinner with me tonight?"

"I—" She should say no. They hardly knew each other.

But wasn't this how people got to know each other? Over dinner? Was she even ready to get involved with a man again?

It's just dinner.

"I'd be delighted, Deputy Eddington." She hesitated, suddenly unsure of his motive. "Unless this is your ham-handed way of making sure I stay out of trouble."

His brow furrowed for a second, then smoothed out when he smiled. "It's not. Not entirely."

He winked, and she laughed, the awkwardness of the last few minutes fading.

"I'll come collect you at seven thirty," he said, putting his hat back on.

"What should I wear?" Charlotte hadn't experienced much of the town's culinary offerings and was unsure of the dress code.

A different kind of glint lit his eyes. "That burgundy gown you wore at the mayor's party the other night. You were—" He blushed, yet didn't seem embarrassed in the least. "Something like that would be a fine dress for tonight. See you at seven thirty, in the parlor." He tugged the brim of his hat and strode back down the hall.

Charlotte borrowed an iron from Mrs. Sullivan and pressed the worst of the wrinkles out of a dark blue dress. The sheer long sleeves made the dress more modest than the arm-baring burgundy gown, but it was appropriate for a friendly dinner. Besides, the burgundy gown had to be laundered after all the dancing she'd done in it. She'd rather disappoint James by wearing a different dress than offend his senses with a soiled gown.

She slipped the silk over her head and smoothed it down. The slightly flared skirt fell to just above her ankles, showing the leather shoes she hoped wouldn't be ruined in the mud. The rain had eased late in the afternoon, though Mrs. Sullivan predicted the lull wouldn't last long.

A few essentials in her clutch purse, and Charlotte was ready. Well, as ready as she could be for a date, if that was what this was. But what about outerwear? Her mackinaw and hat were fine for daytime traipsing through town, but not for an evening out. Back home, she'd risk wearing a less protective garment and her cloche, knowing a taxi would be nearby. There was no such luxury here.

"Mackinaw it is," she said, draping the practical coat over her arm. Giving in to vanity and fashion, she left her heavier hat on the hook and donned her cloche before locking the door behind her.

Mrs. Sullivan waited in the parlor. She smiled at Charlotte. "You look beautiful, dear."

Charlotte smiled back and rested her hand over her thudding heart. Why was she so nervous? It was just dinner. "Thank you. I wish I knew what sort of restaurant we were going to."

The landlady giggled like a schoolgirl. "You don't have much choice here, I'm afraid. Either the Windsor Hotel or The Wild Rose. The cafés and other restaurants close by six."

Charlotte hadn't heard of The Wild Rose. Before she could ask about it, the door rattled open, and James stepped inside. He swept his hat off and smoothed his dark hair back as he shut the door. Gone was the seemingly permanent shadow of a beard. Clean-shaven cheeks emphasized his square jaw. His blue eyes assessed Charlotte, and a slow smile curved his lips.

She felt her heart flutter.

When their eyes met, he was flat-out grinning. "Hello." He laid his hat on one of the chairs and took her coat to help her don it. "I hope you don't mind walking a little."

Mrs. Sullivan leaned close. "The Wild Rose," she whispered, nodding with approval.

"I don't mind," Charlotte said, buttoning her coat.

James glanced down at her feet. "We'll avoid as much mud as we can. I'd hate to see your shoes or that fine, fine dress ruined."

"So would I."

They didn't say anything for several moments, just stared at each other. Heat blossomed in Charlotte's chest and up her neck to her cheeks. Why was he looking at her like that? Why was she looking at him like that?

Mrs. Sullivan cleared her throat. "No visitors after nine. The door will be locked, and I'll hear you come in."

The gentle reminder broke their temporary paralysis.

"Of course," Charlotte said. James picked up his hat and opened the door. "Good night, Mrs. Sullivan."

"Good night," she called after them. "Have a lovely time."

On the walkway, James offered Charlotte his arm. "It's a couple of blocks up the hill from here."

They strolled up the street, greeting others taking advantage of the break in the weather to get out and about or run last-minute errands. Light spilled out of the large front window of The Wild Rose. When James opened the door for her, delectable aromas wafted out into the cool night.

Five of the seven tables in the front room were occupied by

smartly dressed men and women. A man of about forty in a black suit met them at the door.

"Good evening, Deputy. Glad to see you've finally made it."

"How could I resist after all your boasting? Will, this is Miss Charlotte Brody."

The maître d' bowed slightly at the waist. "Nice to meet you, Miss Brody. Let me take your hats and coats."

James helped her off with her coat, then handed both their garments to the man, giving Charlotte the opportunity to see his attire. He'd changed out of his heavy wool shirt in favor of a fitted white cotton one with a high collar and even wore a necktie. From his slicked-back hair to his black suit, waistcoat, and trousers, and down to his polished leather shoes, James Eddington appeared more the dandy than the deputy.

He faced Charlotte and caught her eying him. "I do clean up once in a while," he said with a crooked smile. "For special occasions."

She pinched the side of her skirt and dipped a curtsy. "I'm honored, sir."

He folded one arm across his stomach, the other behind his back, and bowed, his blue eyes never leaving hers. "My pleasure, Miss Brody."

There was less of a jesting air about their exchange. Or perhaps Charlotte was reading too much into his intense gaze. Deciding she was, she laughed it off and took his offered arm when Will returned to show them to their table.

Gilded pendant fixtures with crystal globes hung over each table, yet the illumination was soft enough to make the diners feel as if they were in their own little sea of light. Gold-edged china and goblets atop brilliant white table linens rivaled any settings Charlotte had seen back home. Even the dark wood of the chairs and the burgundy velvet upholstery on the seats belied The Wild Rose's location.

"This is amazing," Charlotte said as Will held out her chair.

"Thank you," he replied. "My wife and I have owned it for

a couple of years now. We're trying to bring a little civilization to the wild frontier." He winked at her and handed them each a menu after James sat down.

"With poached salmon and finger sandwiches?" James quipped.

Will laughed. "Whatever it takes. The special of the house tonight is braised pork with potatoes and garlic green beans. The razor clam soup is especially fine. I'll have Joseph take your order in a few moments."

Will strolled back toward the front of the restaurant, stopping along the way to chat with other customers.

"Will's originally from your neck of the woods," James said, perusing the menu as he spoke. "He was a chef in some fancy restaurant in Baltimore, but likes to talk too much to stay in the kitchen for long."

"What brought him out here?"

"The same thing that brings most everyone to Alaska," he said. "A chance to start over."

That certainly applied to both Michael and herself. A clean slate. No one who knew anything about her past. There was no harm in trying again, was there?

"Is that what brought you up here?"

James raised his eyes from the printed sheet with its curling script. "I was born in Georgia. Came up here with my parents back in ninety-eight during the gold rush. At ten years old, I wasn't exactly looking to start over, but I guess they were."

Charlotte set the menu aside and clasped her hands together at the edge of the table. "That's quite a change, especially for a young boy."

"Not that I had a choice or a chance to state my opinion. My brothers and I did as we were told, went where we were told to go."

Joseph arrived and took their orders, the special for both. After he departed, Charlotte and James exchanged bits and pieces about their younger years. Having grown up in a more urban setting, she was equal parts delighted and amazed at the antics James and his brothers had engaged in. She, in turn, explained that there were certain expectations for girls in her parents' social circle, even if the Brodys were more liberal in their attitudes.

"So you were a good girl, were you?" he asked.

"Well . . ." A few of her more daring actions came to mind. Like the time she and Kit snuck out while Charlotte was spending the night at the Camerons' and the two of them went for a late-night swim in the river half a mile away. James smiled and shook his head.

Joseph returned with their meals, saving Charlotte from relaying the part in which they had ducked behind a hedgerow to avoid the constable patrolling the neighborhood. The waiter asked if there was anything else they needed, then departed to attend to other diners.

Charlotte laid her napkin on her lap and waited for James to do the same so they could begin eating. The aroma of the pork and roasted potatoes was too tantalizing to resist for long. But James didn't touch the white linen cloth.

"Not going to tell me more about your midnight swim?"

"I'm sure my silly, girlish endeavors won't hold your interest, Deputy."

He narrowed his gaze, studying her, then snapped his napkin open before laying it on his lap. "I'm sure there was never anything silly about you, Miss Brody."

She felt a flush rise to her face. What was he doing? Flirting?

They ate in silence for several minutes, then James looked up from his plate. There was an intensity in his gaze that set her stomach a-flutter. "What?"

"Why are you here, Charlotte?" His curiosity seemed genuine, not just a way to make conversation.

She couldn't tell him the real reason, could she? So she made a joke of it instead. "Because you asked me to dinner."

His wry grin told her he recognized what she was doing, but

it didn't deter him in the least. "You've come to visit your brother, but that's not everything, is it?"

She took a sip of water, then carefully set the glass down. Delay tactics wouldn't work for long. "I'm writing a series of articles about life up here on the new frontier, particularly from the point of view of women."

"You'll be talking to some of the gals who've been here a while then."

Charlotte nodded. "I've had lovely conversations with Mrs. Sullivan."

"As well as more recent arrivals, like Brigit and Marie." There was no hint of his earlier unhappiness with her involvement. That was something. "But perhaps their activities here are a bit too delicate a topic for your readership."

"On the contrary," she said, indignation forming a knot of heat at the back of her neck. "I plan on writing about every aspect of living in Cordova: the good, the bad, and the delicate."

"Think they can handle that sort of thing?"

"Women are made of sterner stuff than you think, Deputy." Was he intentionally baiting her or just making conversation?

"If I didn't know you, even for as short a time as I have," he said, "I would not have thought you were made of sterner stuff." Charlotte prepared to admonish him for assuming that, as an Eastern-raised female, she was too fragile to live in any but the most controlled environments. But his next words rendered her speechless. "There's steel in you, to be sure, but also a sadness that makes me wonder who or what hurt you enough to bring you way the hell out here."

She stared at him for several seconds. His observation cut too close. How had he known? Was her shame evident on her face? Charlotte dropped her gaze to her plate. "It's nothing like that."

Liar. She was lying to a man whose job it was to discern the truth.

James reached toward her arm where it rested on the white-clad table, but before he could make contact, he closed his hand into a fist and moved it away. "I'm sorry. I didn't mean to make you uncomfortable. I shouldn't pry."

Her head came up. "You're not prying. You're making conversation. I asked you the same thing. It's only fair."

Fair, but that didn't mean she'd tell him.

Leaving it at that, they continued their meals. Despite the unnerving accuracy of James's question, Charlotte found herself relaxing as their conversation flowed into more neutral topics. James was an avid reader and had enjoyed many of the same books as Charlotte.

After the dishes were cleared and coffee was loitered over, James paid the bill, leaving a generous tip, and rose. He held her chair out as she stood, allowing her to precede him to the front of the restaurant. There was only one other party left in the restaurant. Charlotte hadn't noticed the others departing, or whether new diners had entered. Will asked if they had enjoyed their food—they assured him they had—then retrieved their coats and hats.

James helped her don her coat and hat before putting on his own. Will held the door open and bade them both good night. The rain had picked up again, and Charlotte lifted her collar against it. Her cloche wouldn't be much protection against the rain.

As if reading her mind, James plucked the flimsy hat off her head and set his wide-brimmed hat on it, startling her as the crown dropped over her eyes. She lifted the front and blinked up at him. He smiled, his face mottled in light and shadow.

"Don't want you getting soaked through or ruining your nice hat on the way home," he said, handing her the cloche. He threaded her arm up under his.

"What about you?" Charlotte had to keep the hat tilted up a little so it wouldn't cover her eyes again.

James shrugged. "I won't melt."

"Neither will I," she said.

But when she moved to take his hat from her head, James caught her hand. "Indulge my archaic notions, won't you, Miss Brody? Just this once?"

Charlotte lowered her hand. "I guess a sincere act of chivalry won't offend my feminist senses much."

James grinned and made a sweeping gesture for them to be off.

The short, muddy walk back to Sullivan's required constant vigil against puddles and slick walks. Her poor shoes would be ruined if she didn't remember to clean them off as soon as she got to her room. There was hardly a soul on the street when they stopped at the door.

Charlotte dug her keys out of her purse and unlocked the door. She faced James. The awning overhead kept the rain off them, but he was soaked. His dark hair was plastered to his head, and water dripped off his nose.

"Thank you for the wonderful dinner and fine conversation. And for the use of your hat. You didn't have to."

"But I wanted to."

Charlotte grasped the brim of the hat to return it to him. James covered her hand with his, the calluses on his palm gently scratching the back of her hand. He leaned in, ducking under the brim, and kissed her.

His sweet tobacco and leather scent, and the tangy bite of his aftershave surrounded her. She closed her eyes and pressed forward. Not parting her lips beneath his, but definitely telling him . . . something. Could it be called stealing a kiss if she allowed it? She felt James's other hand at her shoulder steadying her, not pulling her to him.

This was more than the "friendly" dinner she had expected. Part of her enjoyed the attention, the sturdiness of him, but another part warned her that this was similar to the way things had started with Richard. Charming, witty Richard, whom she'd met at a suffrage meeting, then later at fund-raisers, dancing like Vernon Castle. He'd made her think he was one of those rare men who supported the cause. The prospect had fooled her completely, right into his bed.

James wasn't like that bastard, was he? Charming in his way, yes. Witty, yes. But would letting him get closer prove to be just as painful?

All too soon—or not soon enough, she wasn't quite sure—he straightened, breaking the kiss. He wasn't smiling, exactly, more like gauging her reaction. Did he expect an invitation of some kind? Another kiss?

Charlotte didn't move.

James took the hat from her head, placed it on his own, and stepped back. He gave her shoulder a gentle squeeze before lowering his hand. "Good night, Charlotte. I'll see you tomorrow. Be sure to lock the door behind you."

"I will. Good night."

Such normal conversation while her brain whirled.

He touched the brim of his hat, waited for her to go in and secure the door, then walked down the dark street. Charlotte watched him through the parlor window, her forehead pressed against the glass and butterflies dancing in her belly. When he was lost to shadow and distance, she closed her eyes and tried to figure out what to do next. What it meant. *Just act normal and see what tomorrow brings.*

Charlotte turned from the window and headed to bed, realizing as she walked down the hall that she was smiling.

Chapter 9

It was the perfect day for a funeral. Low, heavy clouds obscured the surrounding mountains, and a steady drizzle added to the current state of saturation. A flock of crows mobbed a bald eagle, chasing it across the gray sky, as Charlotte made her way to the Red Dragon social club.

A murder, Charlotte remembered. *A flock of crows is called a murder.*

The plain pine casket sat on a long table at one end of the room. Brigit read a short eulogy for Darcy. She hadn't felt right about having the gathering at the house, Marie had told Charlotte as they entered. They couldn't afford such gloom to impact business.

Brigit, Charlie, and the three women of the house attended, and Mr. Manning of the Baptist church read scripture. Charlotte sat in the back of the overly perfumed room, along with a couple of men who hadn't realized there'd be a service rather than a card game that afternoon. In the front row of folding chairs, one of the other girls kept her arm around Marie's shaking shoulders.

After the short service, the attendees followed the black

horse and carriage carrying the casket over the quarter mile of road beside the stream connecting Eyak Lake to Odiak Slough. People stopped to watch, and some of the men even doffed their hats despite the rain, as did a couple of women wearing trousers and oiled mackinaws. Others looked on with pinched expressions, as if their day had been disturbed not by the death of a young woman, but by the inconvenience of her funeral procession on a public street.

The cemetery at the southeast corner of town was atop a low hill overlooking the slough and the railroad yard. The procession gathered around the open grave under black umbrellas. Mr. Manning read more passages from the Bible.

Charlotte wrapped her arms around herself, shoulders hunched, to ward off the chill in the air. If this was August in Cordova, she could only imagine what January would be like.

"Sorry I'm late," Michael said in a low voice beside her.

His sudden appearance startled her. No one else seemed to notice him, their heads down while Manning droned.

She gave him a sidelong glance, noting his dripping hat and damp coat. His face was pale and haggard. "What are you doing here?" she asked in equally low tones.

"I was her doctor," he said, eyes on the proceedings. "I feel responsible. If I had gone to see her sooner, maybe she would have been well enough to get away from her attacker."

"You did nothing wrong."

"Legally, no. Not even ethically, as far as that goes." He shrugged his slumped shoulders and shook his head slowly. "Still."

Charlotte looped her arm under his in a gesture of understanding his feelings of guilt and sadness. "Some doctors see their patients as just patients." She felt his arm and body stiffen. "I mean, you cared about her as a person, like a good doctor should." How did Ruth think he'd be able to shove his patients off onto a new doctor? Michael cared too much about people to do that. Speaking of Ruth . . . "Does your fiancée know you're here?"

Lines deepened along his mouth, and his jaw tightened. "Of course she does."

"But she's not happy about it." Not a surprise.

Michael nodded toward the preacher, indicating they should be more attentive. His diversion tactic worked, and Charlotte silently listened to the final words of Darcy's interment. When Mr. Manning finished his sermon, the ladies and Miss Brigit each dropped a stalk of purple-pink flowers into Darcy's grave. They slowly filed out of the cemetery.

Brigit held Charlie's hand and glanced at Charlotte. When the madam looked at Michael, her gaze hardened, and she stopped in front of him. "She'd asked for you, you know."

Was Brigit blaming Michael? How dare she? Darcy's death had nothing to do with him. Charlotte was about to say as much, but Michael seemed to sense her anger and stilled her with a hand on her arm.

"I know," he said. "She deserved better."

"Even though she was a whore?" Brigit asked with such vehemence that Michael winced.

"I should have been more attentive to her psychological needs, even if her physical illness was only minor."

The madam raised an eyebrow. "Are you admitting to malpractice, Doctor?"

Michael shook his head. "Not at all. Just regret."

"I'm sure." Brigit turned to Charlotte, who braced herself for her own dressing-down, but Brigit's gaze softened. "Thank you for coming, Miss Brody. I'm sure it meant a lot to Marie to see you here."

She strode out of the small cemetery with Charlie in tow.

"How could she blame you?" Charlotte asked Michael. "Darcy's presumed illness had nothing to do with her murder."

"No, but if I'd tended her sooner, maybe she would have

been working and would not have gone out of the house." He guided Charlotte through the opening in the low, iron fence surrounding the cemetery. "Brigit's upset, that's all."

"Understandable, but—"

"Leave it alone, Charlotte." Michael's harsh tone surprised her. He cast a sidelong glance her way, the softening of his gaze saying he realized his reaction had been stronger than necessary. "Sorry. It'll blow over soon enough. Between Brigit and Ruth, I'm about at my wit's end with women today."

She bumped his hip with her own. "Hey! *I'm* a woman."

"You're not a woman; you're my sister."

A burst of laughter was inappropriate after a funeral, and Charlotte managed to stifle the sound. But it felt good to have Michael talking to her like this again.

The tap-tap-tapping of the black Royal typewriter filled her small room. It was just before nine at night, and the sun had gone down, prompting Charlotte to use her desk lamp. The next installment of her serial for *Modern Woman* would touch on Darcy's murder and law enforcement in the territory. She would interview Michael and James to get their professional input for the article.

Typing James's name on the page, however, brought to mind the very unprofessional kiss from the night before. Charlotte shook her head, knocking the memory aside before she lapsed into a fantasy that had no right to exist. She wasn't here for that. She was here to show readers back in the States what Alaska was like from a woman's point of view.

And reinvent yourself a little, like everyone else?

She'd denied it to James during dinner the other night, but couldn't lie to herself that easily. Of course her travels to Alaska were a way to put her past behind her. But she didn't have to admit that to anyone else.

The potential for dredging up more pain and memories was

a good reason to leave the investigation of Darcy's murder to James. Yet she couldn't. Her journalistic and justice-seeking instincts overrode the desire to hide her feelings and her past. If she could help find the killer, wasn't it worth reliving some of her own anguish?

A soft knock on the door barely broke through the sound of the keys hitting the paper-covered platen. Who could be calling on her at this hour? There were no visitors permitted after nine. Could Mrs. Sullivan be asking her to share a sherry or two now? As much as Charlotte liked the landlady, she wasn't in the mood to be sociable.

Charlotte smoothed a stray hair back behind her ear. She'd tell Mrs. Sullivan she was about to go to bed. But when she opened the door, it wasn't the older woman.

"Marie." Charlotte couldn't hide her surprise. She leaned into the hall. No one else was about. "What are you doing here?"

Marie slipped past her, carrying a large floral carpet bag. "I'm sorry to bother you so late," she said in a breathy whisper. "But I needed to see you."

"How did you get in?" Charlotte closed the door quietly and also spoke in low tones. She didn't think Mrs. Sullivan would be as upset with Charlotte's having a female visitor after hours, but she wasn't sure.

"I came in with someone I knew. Promised him a little something special next time he came over to the house, though I won't be able to make good." Her cheeks pinked with the admission. She put the bag on the chair and opened the buckles. "I don't have much time. The ship leaves at ten."

"Ship? Where are you going?"

Marie rifled through the bag, then faced her, an old, black fur coat in hand. "Got a cable. My sister's real sick down in Seattle. I needed to give you this before I left." She held the bedraggled garment out to Charlotte.

"I'm sorry to hear about your sister, but you don't have to—"

Marie stepped closer, shoving the coat into Charlotte's hands. "Please, it's important. Darcy—" Her eyes filled. "Darcy told me to take it for myself if anything happened to her, but I can't make heads or tails of it, and I can't take—" She stopped herself, flustered, and shook her head. "You'll know what to do with it. I have to go. Ralph's waiting in his motorcar to take me to the dock."

"No, wait—"

Marie whirled around, snatched up her bag, and was out the door before Charlotte could ask her any more questions.

"Make heads or tails of what?" she asked the empty hall.

Charlotte held the old coat at the shoulders, her fingers sinking into the warm fur. It was heavy enough to be a decent coat for the environment, though not her style or her size. The girls at Miss Brigit's had probably divided up Darcy's belongings, since she didn't have family. But if Darcy and Marie were so close, why hadn't Marie kept the coat herself?

Charlotte draped the coat over the back of the chair and heard a faint rustling. She lifted it again, feeling along the arms and panels. At the back panel, something crackled between the fur and the satin lining. But closer to the bottom, the coat felt thicker. Charlotte inspected the seam. Though the stitches were neat and even, there was a section that had been sewn with different thread.

She sorted through her belongings and found a small pair of scissors in her travel sewing kit. Carefully, she snipped the odd threads. Before she was half done with the row, a stack of five-dollar Federal Reserve notes slid out of the gap. Charlotte stared at the ribbon-tied bundle. There were perhaps twenty notes in the stack. One hundred dollars wasn't a fortune, but it was a nice little nest egg. How had Darcy gotten the money? Had she saved it? Had Marie known it was sewn into the seam? She must have.

Charlotte gently pulled the money all the way through and set it aside. She felt along the inside panel of the coat. Her hand stilled. There were at least four more bundles and some other papers. Quick work of the rest of the thread proved her right. She retrieved another four hundred dollars or so and some yellowing newspaper pages folded in half.

Five hundred dollars cash. No wonder Darcy wasn't as anxious to work the clubs as the other girls. Where did she get so much money? It was doubtful Brigit paid the girls that well. Tips from her patrons? Possibly. Why hide it? Why not open a bank account if she was afraid the money would be stolen? Perhaps the local bank wasn't keen on doing business with ladies of the evening.

Charlotte laid the folded newspaper in front of her. The partial article facing her was something about the dwindling gold strikes in Nome. She glanced at the top of the page. The *Fairbanks Daily News-Miner,* dated October 16, 1909. The front page, with its bold masthead, was creased from several folds. Charlotte smoothed it out. The picture centered on the page showed several people coming down the steps of a large building. Three men and two women, all wearing heavy dark coats. The headline at the top read, in large letters, **CASE DISMISSED!**

She read the caption at the bottom of the picture. "John Kincaid, Mary Jensen, Elizabeth Jensen, and their lawyers Herbert Grimes and Richard Barlow leaving the Fairbanks Courthouse."

Why would Darcy keep the article? Did she know any of the people involved?

Charlotte read the article through. Kincaid, owner of a gambling den, and the two women, prostitutes on the Line in downtown Fairbanks, had been accused of theft and fraud by a patron, Cecil Patterson. Patterson claimed the Jensen sisters had lured him to their small cabin on the Line, convinced him to attend a gathering at Kincaid's club, then proceeded to cheat him out of his gold. Unfortunately for the territorial prosecutor, Patterson had disappeared shortly before he was scheduled to testify, and the case was dismissed.

A second page, dated May of 1910, showed nothing of interest as far as Charlotte could see. Advertisements for men's clothing, the announcement of a wedding, and the continuation of a story from the previous page regarding the hassles Judge Wickersham faced in civilizing interior Alaska. But at the corner of the page, a small piece, almost an afterthought, noted that a body found during the breakup of the Chena River had yet to be identified. No one had come forward to claim the poor soul, who was barely recognizable as male due to injury by weather, ice, and scavengers. The suspected cause of death was exposure as a result of excessive alcohol. How else could his lack of clothing be explained?

Charlotte reread the two paragraphs. She went back to the front-page article about the fraud case. Nothing else in the two pages seemed remotely connected. Was the body found in the icy waters of the Chena River Cecil Patterson?

She peered more closely at the picture of the people at the courthouse. There was something vaguely familiar about the man, Kincaid, but she couldn't be sure. Not that Charlotte expected to know anyone from Fairbanks. Perhaps Michael or James might, though how likely was that?

She found her magnifying glass in the top drawer of her wardrobe trunk and focused it on the picture. The two women wore fashionable hats of the day, lovely, but half their faces were hidden. The lawyers appeared to be appropriately smug after having gotten their clients off on the fact that there was no witness.

Charlotte studied Kincaid. His tall, robust figure dwarfed the women. She focused on his face, and her breath caught. There was a mark on his cheek, just above the line of his mutton chops. The smile beneath his whiskers said this whole situation had been a mistake from the get-go. She'd seen both the birthmark and the smile before, on Mayor Kavanagh.

She set the magnifying glass on the table. Had John Kincaid fled Fairbanks for Cordova, clean-shaven and with a name change to help hide his identity?

Improbable, especially if someone who knew him well in Fairbanks happened to be in Cordova, but not impossible. Alaska was a land of starting over, a place to reinvent yourself. Maybe Kincaid/Kavanagh didn't feel the need to travel too far for that, despite having been accused of terrible acts, and perhaps linked to the disappearance of a witness.

How did Darcy figure into this?

Charlotte considered the paper then the stacks of notes. A lot of money for a young sporting woman to be hiding. Unless she was involved in something as illicit as theft or fraud. Something like blackmail.

Suppose Darcy had known Kavanagh was really Kincaid. Suppose she had pressed him for money to keep quiet and maintain his upstanding reputation. Suppose the Honorable Mayor had gotten tired of paying.

"Was that what got you killed you, Darcy?"

Was that *who* killed her, was the bigger question.

Charlotte would need more information before going any further than speculation. There was no proof of anything, and no one to ask with Darcy dead and Marie having left town. Had Kavanagh been at Miss Brigit's that night? He would have been a hard man to miss. Would he have hired someone to do his dirty work?

A shiver ran down Charlotte's spine, closely followed by a cold dose of reality. This was getting ridiculous. It was an outrageous scenario, one for dime novels and pulp-fiction magazines. She couldn't even be sure the man in the picture was Kavanagh. It could be someone who looked similar to the mayor, and maybe her own brain had jumped to a very wrong conclusion.

That had to be it.

Though it didn't explain why Darcy had stashed money and the articles in the coat. She might have been afraid of being robbed, but why hold onto the newspaper clippings?

Damn it! Marie had brought Charlotte the coat for a reason. Had Marie been in on Darcy's secret or had she found the money and the pages the same way Charlotte had, by accident? Why hadn't Marie taken the money?

Nothing made sense.

Except that Charlotte was now in possession of a large amount of cash and items that could be connected to a woman's death. And someone in Cordova had warned her away from looking into that death. What if that person found out what was in the coat and that she had it?

Charlotte shoved the money and the papers back into the gap between the fur and the lining. She threaded a needle and hastily sewed the seam. It was nowhere near as neat as the one she'd torn out, but it would do. She'd bring the evidence, such as it was, to James. But it was so late, after ten. He wouldn't be at the office now, and Charlotte had no idea where he lived. She'd have to ask Michael. There was no way she'd be able to wait until morning to do so.

She dumped her notebook out of her tapestry bag, shoved the coat inside, then donned her outerwear. The rubber boots squeaked softly as she forced herself to walk down the hall rather than run. No one was in the parlor at that hour. Charlotte quietly unlocked the front door and slipped outside. She was careful to lock it behind her.

The night was cold and damp. There was no one else on the street, and her heels thudded with unusual loudness along the walk. The glow of the streetlamps provided pools of safety, though she couldn't put a name to what she was afraid of. There was no indication that anyone was nearby. Not a sound, not another soul.

You're being ridiculous.

Be that as it may, Charlotte hurried along the walk to Michael's.

The curtains were drawn over dark windows. Taking care on the slick stone in front of his door, she knocked and waited. Rain pinged on the metal roof. The scents of the sea and of coal smoke were stronger than that of the rain. She pounded the side of her fist on the door.

Where the hell could he be?

Charlotte scanned the dark street. The businesses were all closed, of course. Lights shined in homes farther up the road, standing out against the otherwise dark slope of the residential area above Main Street. Was Michael visiting his fiancée and her family? There was only one way to find out.

Clutching the tapestry bag to her chest, she headed toward the reverend's home. Once past Main Street, there were few streetlights. Charlotte's pace slowed. The dim glow of the watery pools of light was barely enough for her to navigate the muddy street. She should have brought a flashlight.

You should have stayed home, her more practical inner voice admonished.

Probably, but there was no changing that now.

Halfway between the third and fourth streets paralleling Main, the back of her neck prickled, and Charlotte stopped. The sound of squelching feet abruptly halted somewhere behind her. She whirled around, peering into the darkness and listening. Michael's warning of bears roaming town set her heart racing.

But would a bear stop when she did?

Of course not. And no one else was fool enough to be out in the rain at this hour. It was her own footsteps echoing back at her. She was letting her imagination get the better of her. Chiding herself for foolishness, Charlotte resumed her trek to the Bartletts', plodding through muck.

There it was again. The sucking sound of feet pulling from mud, as if someone were treading not on the relatively packed road, but along the side. Following her. Trying to not be seen.

Charlotte's heart hammered. She broke into an awkward run, her boots slipping and sliding. The windows of the Bartlett home spilled light into the front yard, promising safety if she could just reach them.

Her feet went out from under her, and Charlotte fell. She landed on her right side. A sharp pain shot from her hip up along her spine. "Damnation!"

The wet footfalls came closer, the fall of boot soles on earth, not paws.

Without waiting to see if her follower was friend or foe, Charlotte scrambled to her feet, the bag tight to her chest, and bolted the last fifty feet to the front door. Under the harsh porch light, she slapped her palm on the pristine surface, leaving muddy handprints.

"Hello! Please, is anyone there?"

Heavy footsteps behind her sent Charlotte's heart into her throat. She spun, back against the door. A dark figure lurched up the walkway.

"Who are—" The door jerked open, and Charlotte tumbled into the house.

Chapter 10

Charlotte hit the foyer floor with a jolt that rattled her from tailbone to teeth. She caught herself with one hand behind to keep her head from cracking. The fur coat spilled out of the bag, into her lap.

"Good God, Charlotte, what are you doing?"

She tilted her head up to peer into Michael's astonished face. Movement from outside flickered at the edge of her vision. She faced the shadowed figure and scooted back against Michael's legs. "There's someone—"

The words died on her lips as Ruth's brother Sam stepped into the circle of light. He swiped his wet hair away from his forehead, staring at her, hands clenched at his sides. His coat gaped open to the wind and the rain, the second oblong toggle button missing.

Muttering, "Sorry," he dashed over her splayed legs and ran up the stairs.

"Sam!" Ruth called after him from behind Michael, but the boy didn't slow down. His feet pounded overhead. A door slammed.

Charlotte stuffed the fur coat back into her bag, hands shaking. Her wrist twinged from the fall, but she didn't think it was sprained or broken.

"Goodness." Ruth helped Charlotte to her feet. "Come up off the floor. What on earth is going on?" She brushed her palms together, knocking off bits of mud collected from grasping Charlotte's arm.

Michael shut the door, his features now set in agitation. He was wearing his mackinaw, likely having been on his way out when Charlotte burst in. "I'd like to know the same thing."

She held the bag containing the coat against her chest, the damp fur emitting a slight odor of wet dog, and opened her mouth to explain. But something stopped her. Ruth's pursed lips of disappointment? Michael's exasperation?

"Why don't you come in and sit down, Miss Brody? Tell us what the fuss is all about."

She hadn't noticed Mr. and Mrs. Bartlett standing near the doorway leading into the parlor. Reverend Bartlett looked concerned, but Mrs. Bartlett wore the same sort of disapproving expression as her daughter.

"I'm sorry to bother you so late," Charlotte said. "I was hoping to find Michael here, and on my way up I thought—"

Telling them all she thought someone had been following her seemed ludicrous now. Of course someone had been following her. Young Sam had been on his way home, traveling in the same direction she was going.

Charlotte's cheeks warmed; she felt like a silly girl.

"Is there some sort of emergency?" Michael asked. Ruth passed him his hat. Her hand lingered on his arm.

"No, not really." Charlotte stammered the words and realized she was shivering. Cold mud had seeped through her dress, and caked on her hip and leg when she fell. "I just needed to see you."

Michael narrowed his gaze at her, his lips pressed tight. Before he could say anything, Ruth gestured to the bag. "What is it you have there?"

Charlotte stifled the impulse to hide the bag behind her back, like a child caught stealing cookies. "Nothing." A terrible lie that, by Ruth's frown, was easily detected. "Nothing important. It's just—I need to speak to you, Michael." To hell with dodging the other woman's curiosity, though to be fair Charlotte had fallen into her house. The Bartletts deserved some sort of explanation. "It's about the case."

Michael cast guilty glances toward Ruth and his future in-laws. "Not here. I'll walk you home." He gave Ruth a peck on the cheek. "Good night, darling." Then he shook hands with the elder Bartletts. "Sorry about the disturbance."

"Nothing to worry about, son," the reverend said, waving them off as if young women stumbled into his home on a regular basis. "I hope everything works out all right. Good evening to you, Miss Brody."

"Good evening, Reverend. Mrs. Bartlett." Charlotte nodded to him and his wife. "Again, please accept my apologies. Good night, Ruth."

"Good night, Charlotte," she said tightly. She opened the front door, glaring.

Another wedge between them, Charlotte realized. At this rate Christmas dinner was going to be hell.

Michael took her arm and escorted her out, his pace down the walk a bit too fast for the wet conditions. The door shut firmly behind them.

"Are you out of your ever-loving mind, coming here like this?" His fierce whisper carried down the dark street. "You've already managed to upset Ruth's mother and her closest friends. Are you trying to add Reverend Bartlett and Ruth to that list?"

Charlotte was pretty sure Ruth was already on that list, but now wasn't the time to be flippant. "I needed to talk to you or James about some things I have in my possession."

"You mean that ratty coat? Where'd you get it?"

"Marie. It was Darcy's."

His step faltered, but he pressed on. "Darcy's? Why did Marie give it to you?"

Charlotte glanced around, seeing nothing out of the ordinary and hearing nothing but their own footsteps. *It was only Sam*, she reminded herself. "I'd rather not go into details here. Can we go see James?"

"At this hour?" Michael's voice rose with incredulity. "Tell me what you have, and we'll see if it merits waking the man."

Which meant he'd decide if it was worth all the fuss. Charlotte shook her head. When had he become such a pompous ass? "If you don't want to help me figure out who killed Darcy, then fine. Just tell me where James lives, and I'll go alone. You won't be embarrassed or damage your precious reputation by waking an officer of the law with possible information on a murder."

At the edge of one of the pools of streetlamp light, Michael stopped, bringing her to a halt as well. "What the hell are you talking about? Of course I care about solving Darcy's murder. What's gotten into you?"

Charlotte jerked her arm out of his hold. "What's gotten into me? What's gotten into you? You're a totally different person from a year ago, Michael. I hardly recognize you anymore. You're more concerned with your standing in the community, not serving it." A ball of sorrow and anger swirled deep in her belly, then pressed into her chest, nearly choking her. "You're different, and I want my brother back."

Tears stung her eyes. She blinked hard, hoping any that fell would just mix with the rain.

"I'm different? What about you?" He stared at her hard enough to almost make her break. "While I was in med school and at the hospital, I'd get volumes of letters about what you were up to, who you were seeing. Then as of a year ago, barely a couple of pages' worth every few weeks with vague references to gatherings and facts that changed from one letter to the next."

Charlotte trembled. He knew something had been going on with her.

His expression softened, and he laid his hands on her shoulders. "People go through things," he said quietly. "Things that they can't share. And it changes them."

"I know," she said in the same low tones. "But this is us, Michael. We shared everything growing up."

Only two years apart in age, they'd been as close as siblings could be in their younger years. Whenever one of them got into trouble with Mother or Father, the other offered understanding and comfort. When Charlotte tried sneaking back into the house after breaking curfew, Michael had distracted Father long enough for her to scurry upstairs. She took the brunt of the punishment when playing baseball in the parlor resulted in a broken lamp.

But the most precious times Charlotte recalled were when they had stayed up late, talking about what they wanted to do with their lives, where their travels might take them, their latest crushes. Graduation and career choices meant less time together, but it shouldn't have driven them apart.

What had happened?

He gave her a sad smile. "We're not kids anymore."

"Which is why we should be able to talk rather than keep things bottled up inside." Charlotte realized what she'd asked for a split second too late to stop herself. What if he agreed? What if he asked her to tell him *her* concerns and struggles?

He stared down at her, his eyes intense under the watery lamplight. "I can't, Charlie," he said, his voice cracking. He swallowed hard. "Not yet."

Disappointment warred with relief, making her lightheaded. She wasn't ready either, but at least they each knew they'd be there for each other when the time came. "All right. We'll leave it alone for now. But I still need to get this to James."

Michael rubbed his palms over his face then down his cheeks. He looked tired, and not just from the lateness of the hour.

"Fine. I'll take you to his place. Hopefully he won't arrest us for disturbing the peace."

Charlotte took Michael's arm, and he led the way down to a muddy lane between Second and Third Streets. "I doubt that will happen. James is gruff, but he'll understand."

Michael grunted disagreement. He turned up a narrow path to a small cabin between two other buildings. A light glowed through the window. Good, James was up.

Michael knocked on the door. "When did you start calling him James?"

"At dinner last night."

Before her brother could comment, the door swung open. James filled the low doorway, bending to get a good look at his late-night visitors. His hair was mussed, and he wore a long-sleeved undershirt, the suspenders of his trousers dangling at his hips. One toe peeked out of a worn sock. "Doc. Char—Miss Brody. Is something wrong?"

Charlotte's gaze went back to his whisker-shadowed face. "Sorry to bother you so late, Deputy."

He cocked an eyebrow at her. "Not a bother. Please, come in."

He stood aside, allowing them to pass. Charlotte entered first and immediately noted the aroma of leather, tobacco, and smoke. While James hung their coats and hats on wooden pegs affixed to the log wall, she perused his tidy cabin. A book lay on the straight-back chair near the woodstove. On the floor beside the chair were an enameled mug and an open tin can. A black pipe rested on the can. Coats hung on wooden pegs; boots, snowshoes, and various trunks and boxes were stacked beneath a loft. An orange tabby sat above the ladder leading up to the loft. It scrutinized her and Michael, then sauntered into the shadows.

"Have a seat, Miss Brody." Charlotte handed the book—Dante's *Inferno*—to James, which he set on a shelf among other tomes. She sat with the tapestry bag at her feet. James retrieved a small wooden crate and a second chair from against the wall for himself and Michael. "Can I, um, get you anything?"

She smiled, getting the inkling social niceties were not his forte. "Thank you, no. We're here on official business."

James glanced at each of them. "Is this about the note?"

Michael startled. "What note?"

Damnation, she'd forgotten to tell him about it. "It's nothing to worry about, Michael."

James gave her a reproachful look. "Someone left a note in your sister's room, warning her away from investigating Darcy's murder."

Michael's eyes widened, his eyebrows shooting toward his hairline. "What? Why didn't you tell me?"

"I forgot."

He slumped on the wooden chair, shaking his head, and pinched the bridge of his nose. "You are unbelievable."

She and James exchanged glances. He grinned. A warm fluttering in her chest made Charlotte look away, but she smiled nonetheless.

James told Michael the circumstances of the note. "I warned her to stay out of it for her own safety," he said.

"Apparently that isn't working so well." Michael gestured to the bag at her feet. "What is it you've found now, Charlotte?"

She withdrew the fur coat and laid it on her lap. "Marie stopped by my room earlier this evening and gave me this. It had been Darcy's." The men appeared unimpressed by the garment. Charlotte suspected that was why Darcy had used it. No one would give the worn fur a second glance. "Deputy, do you have a pair of scissors or a penknife?"

James gave her a questioning look, but leaned back and dug a small folding knife from his front pocket. "Will this do?"

"That'll be fine, thank you," she said, taking it. It's not like she needed to be delicate about the operation now.

The men watched as she cut and tugged at her own poor stitching. When the gap was large enough, she reached in and withdrew one of the stacks of Federal Reserve notes. Their eyes widened. She handed the first stack to James, then retrieved the others.

"What in the hell is this?" the deputy asked.

"About five hundred dollars cash," she said, "along with these." Charlotte carefully removed the newspaper clippings from the lining. "Where did she get the money, and why was she hanging onto newspapers that feature a story that came out when she was a child?"

She handed the pages to James and pointed out the smaller write-up on the unidentified body. Michael read through them as well.

"Do either of you recognize anyone in the photograph or mentioned in the article?" she asked.

James tilted the paper toward the light. "Maybe. What about you, Doc?"

Michael reached into his inner jacket pocket for a pair of spectacles. He fit the wire earpieces over his ears and studied the page. "Is that Frank Kavanagh?"

Charlotte's heart raced. Michael saw the resemblance too. "Do you think so? I wasn't sure."

"Let me look at that again," James said. Michael handed the page over, and the deputy squinted at the figures.

"I used a magnifying glass," she said.

James gave her a look she couldn't quite interpret. Was he upset? Amused? It was difficult to read him sometimes. He went to a drawer near the sink. After rifling through it for a moment, he withdrew a small magnifier. Surprise widened his eyes as he studied the picture. "I'll be damned."

Charlotte rose, too excited to keep still any longer. She stepped beside James and peered over his arm. "You both think it's him. What about the women?"

James pointed to one of the women. "That might be Brigit, but I can't say for sure. Damned hat is in the way."

Charlotte grinned. "I thought the same thing. About the hats."

He smiled back, but it faded quickly. "The money is more than your typical lady of the evening can pull, even in this town."

"Combined with the pages from the paper," Charlotte added, "it makes me think Darcy wasn't just working for Miss Brigit."

"Darcy knew Mayor Kavanagh was really John Kincaid, the saloon owner. At the very least, she might have threatened to reveal that bit to his more conservative supporters." James scanned the article again. "But I'm willing to bet she connected him to the disappearance and probable murder of Cecil Patterson."

"How long has Kavanagh been in Cordova?" she asked.

"It was before I got here, maybe six years? He owns one of the clam canneries with a couple other gentlemen. Made a big deal of providing jobs and fair wages. He was elected to office in '16."

"How about Miss Brigit?"

James narrowed his eyes. "She came to town not long after him, I hear. You think they were in Fairbanks together. Involved in this theft case."

"And maybe the disappearance of Patterson, yes." If James was coming to the same conclusion, her earlier supposition didn't seem so far-fetched. Unless James was playing along with her silly ideas and was about to shoot them down. No, he wouldn't do that. That was a little game Richard had enjoyed, feeding her viewpoint in the guise of agreement just to turn around and take the other side. She didn't get the feeling James played such games. "So you think that's what happened?"

"Just a minute," Michael said. Charlotte had almost forgotten he was in the room. "You're jumping to some serious conclusions here. Even if the man in the picture is Mayor Kavanagh, or if the death of Patterson is connected to the Fairbanks trial, there's nothing to prove Kavanagh had anything to do with Darcy's murder. There's no physical proof leading to anyone specific, is there, Eddington?"

"No," James replied, "but it would certainly be motive."

"Who else would be angry enough to kill her?" Charlotte asked.

"The father of her baby, if he was a prominent man," James said.

She drew in a sharp breath, remembering Richard's face when she'd told him she was pregnant. She'd been feeling poorly for several weeks, and after missing her cycle she had suspected the cause even before her doctor confirmed it. Her first thought had been that she wasn't ready to be a mother, and that Richard deserved to know what she planned.

His predictable shock had turned to unexpected anger. "Don't be stupid, Charlotte," he'd said. "Prostitutes and sluts have abortions. Or women too poor to take care of yet another brat. I can't have you doing something like this. Think about how it would look if word got out."

How it would reflect on *him*. Would he have hurt her to preserve his own reputation?

"I can't think of a single man in this town who'd do such a thing." Michael's tone was pitched upward with his disbelief. "Not a one."

"No?" James raised a sardonic eyebrow. "I can."

"Who?" Charlotte didn't expect him to name anyone, and he didn't. He shook his head, indicating it wasn't his place to accuse.

"I'll talk to Brigit again about Darcy's regulars," he said. "Maybe that'll give us more of a lead as to who might've been concerned with her condition."

"Brigit won't talk, will she?" Michael asked. "I mean, if men aren't bragging about visiting her girls, they surely don't want to be named. Some probably go to certain lengths to make sure Brigit and the girls keep mum."

James gathered the stacks of Federal notes, wrapped the newspaper pages around them, and set them on the shelf above his sink. "Likely, but if I press her hard enough, maybe suggest not talking will get her into trouble, that might help loosen her tongue."

"Or it might shut her up, and we'll get nowhere," Charlotte said. She met James's glare with a calm expression that didn't quite match how she felt. She didn't want to risk being cut out of the investigation by irritating him, but she knew he would be wrong to push Brigit. "She's as stubborn as they come and already on the defensive. Let me talk to her. I think she trusts me."

"Because of your chats with Marie." He didn't sound convinced, but it didn't sound like he was dismissing the idea either.

Charlotte laid a hand on his arm. "Let me try, James. I think I can get answers you can't."

"You shouldn't be involved in this," Michael said. "Leave it to the marshal's office. Right, Eddington?"

"Your sister may have a point," James said, holding her gaze. "Brigit doesn't trust me or Blaine. With Marie's leaving town, we have no one who really knew Darcy coming forward to help." He covered Charlotte's hand with his. "But when I say it's time to quit, it's time to quit. Got me?"

Charlotte grinned and gave his arm a slight squeeze. "Thank you."

She stuffed the fur coat back into her bag while Michael continued to appeal to James.

"I forbid her to do it," Michael said with finality.

Charlotte spun around, mouth agape. Did he actually say what she thought he did? "I beg your pardon?"

James crossed his arms and watched the two of them. It was smart of him not to get in the middle.

"I told you before, Charlotte, this is none of your concern," her brother said. "You're insinuating yourself into this case and have already been threatened once." He crossed his arms as well, anger darkening his fair features. "I'm responsible for your well-being, and I forbid you to do anything more."

She stared at him, unable to believe he had said the words. James might have muttered something like, "Oh, Doc. Bad idea," but with the blood pounding in her head she wasn't sure.

"You forbid me? *Forbid* me?" Charlotte stepped forward until she was within a hand's breadth of Michael, controlling her breathing to keep from screaming. "I assure you, Michael, I've done plenty of things more dangerous than this. You're my brother, not my keeper."

"Maybe you need one now and again. Someone to keep you in line."

Surely he didn't mean that. Surely he was just concerned for her. He seldom tried to impose his will on her or demand she follow his direction. More often it was Charlotte trying to get him to yield to her, but that never worked either. His behavior now had become more akin to something neither of them had appreciated while growing up.

When had Michael morphed into Father? Or Richard? Why did the men in her life insist she wasn't capable of being who she wanted—no, needed—to be? She'd proven herself time and again. Had she made the effort to escape those men just to have her own brother take up the role of oppressor?

Charlotte drew in a deep breath through her nose, then let it out slowly.

"Maybe I do need someone, but it won't be you." She faced James and inclined her head. "Sorry for such a late night, Deputy. I'll speak to Brigit when I can and let you know what she says."

"Not to worry, Miss Brody," he said. "If you're ever uncomfortable or feel in any sort of danger, you be sure to come to me. Hear?"

Charlotte knew she should express her gratitude for his support and concern in a more friendly manner, but anger kept her words tight.

"I will. Thank you." Glaring at Michael as she passed him to get her coat, she said, "I'll walk myself home. I need some time alone."

"It's late. You shouldn't be out by yourself," Michael said, his overbearing attitude unwavering.

Charlotte gave him another scowl, opened her mouth to offer a string of epithets, then snapped it shut. It would be impolite to rant like a sailor in front of James.

The deputy laid a hand on Michael's shoulder. "I'd be more concerned for anyone crossing her, Doc. Let her go."

She donned her coat, set her hat on her head, and, nodding to James, left the cabin with only the slightest slam of the door.

Chapter 11

Charlotte spent the next morning at the *Cordova Daily Times* poring over page after page in search of information on Frank Kavanagh and Brigit O'Brien. A 1912 article about the clam cannery built by Kavanagh and his two partners, Jacob Feeney and Max Kruth, was the first mention she found, but the Kavanaghs hadn't arrived in town yet. The paper had run the piece to let Cordovans know there would be more opportunities for employment now that the railroad was finished and men were looking for work again.

Another article in early 1913 introduced the Kavanaghs to the populace, noting that the couple hailed from Virginia. A portrait of Frank and Tess Kavanagh accompanied the story, showing the couple as Charlotte knew them. Throughout the next several years, the Kavanaghs were mentioned in a number of social notations or in support of various local causes. Their standing in the community rose, culminating in Frank's campaign and election into the mayor's office. All the while, Tess Kavanagh quietly supported her husband and did everything right in the eyes of Cordovans, as far as Charlotte could tell.

There was nothing on Brigit at all. Not a mention, not a line. Not even a hint of the activities that went on in the house. There were a few incidents of women being arrested for solicitation on the police roundup, but none mentioned Brigit. Not surprising for a more conservative local newspaper, the criminal element in Cordova was confined to the back pages unless a particularly heinous act occurred. Those weren't common, but the town was less genteel than the postings on the social pages suggested. There was a seamier side of Cordova, that was for certain, though perhaps the citizens of the town didn't wish to be reminded of the fact.

"Finding everything you need, Miss Brody?"

Charlotte folded the last newspaper in the stack and rose from the long table in the back of the *Times* office. She smiled at Andrew Toliver, the *Times*'s editor, chief reporter, and printer. His shirtsleeves were rolled to the forearm, held by garters, so they wouldn't become inky when he set the press.

"I did, thank you. Let me help you return these to the archive shelves." She followed the rotund man to the storage room, the tang of ink and paper dust tickling her nose. "I appreciate your letting me look at these. I hope I didn't interrupt your work."

"Not at all. Always happy to help a fellow journalist," he said, hanging the more recent editions on the six-foot-tall, triangular newspaper rack set against the wall. The dozen wooden poles that crossed the lengths of the frame supported the structure and allowed the papers to be hung without creasing. Toliver grinned at her, then cocked his head to the side. "You looking for something specific?"

When she'd entered the newspaper office three hours before, he'd been in a bit of a frazzle while setting the linotype. He'd accepted her explanation of needing information for her articles in *Modern Woman* with barely a word, then ushered her to the archive room. "Just getting a feel for the area," she said. "Have you lived here long, Mr. Toliver?"

He scratched the back of his neck, mindless of the smudges of ink on his hands. "Ten years next spring. Moved here straight up from Seattle."

Charlotte's hope that Toliver had been in Fairbanks at the same time as Kincaid and the women were on trial died with a quiet sigh. "So you didn't know the mayor or his wife before they came here."

"No. The Kavanaghs didn't arrive until after the railroad had been finished for a couple of years. Lots of folks came into town about then, looking to make some money, to find a place in the world." Toliver shrugged and grinned. "Cordova's not a bad place to settle down."

"Michael seems to like it." She suppressed the flare of residual anger in her gut. She and Michael would have to have a serious talk about boundaries if she decided to stay.

"He's a good man, your brother." The newspaper man gave her a significant look. "Heard you helped him with the Dugan autopsy."

Charlotte recognized his technique. He was fishing for information, but she wouldn't keep James's confidence if she shared what she knew. "I did, but I'm not at liberty to discuss the case, according to Deputy Eddington. I don't want to jeopardize the investigation."

Toliver looked perturbed at first, then nodded curtly. "Understandable. Tell me, Miss Brody, do you need a job while you're here?"

Charlotte blinked at him. "You mean at the *Times*?"

"Sure, why not? I have a couple of boys who gather local tidbits and write copy, but we're growing by leaps and bounds. The *Cordova Times* could use a lady's touch. And I'm not getting any younger. I need someone who knows what they're doing when it gets busy."

Her heart gave a small leap. With a regular job in town she could stay even longer if she chose. "I'd have to complete my commitment to *Modern Woman*."

Toliver nodded. "Oh, sure, sure. We can talk later. I wouldn't refuse an insider piece on the Dugan murder, if you had a mind to write up a little something. Are you finished here, then?"

"I am." She gathered her coat and hat from where she'd been sitting. "Thank you again, Mr. Toliver. I'll be in touch."

She skirted the desk, glancing at the framed pages of the *Times* hanging on the walls that she'd read earlier, and hurried out the door. Her heart beat hard as she considered Toliver's offer. To be part of a newspaper, even in a town like this? It wasn't the *New York Times*, but it was something.

Charlotte bent her head against the wind and rain and made her way down the hill to Brigit's house. She passed Michael's office, but didn't feel ready to talk to him yet. Why was he being so overprotective? Even as kids, he'd been the one to encourage her to stand her ground and do for herself. Sure, he'd be there to back her up if things got out of hand, but otherwise he was more likely to push her into a fray to defend herself, rather than pull her away. What had changed?

Years of sorrow and secrets, she supposed with a sigh. All their closeness as kids couldn't overcome the distance of their personal lives as adults. Even when Michael had gone off to university, they'd kept in touch with weekly letters. She'd quit journalism school to start working at the *Yonkers Weekly*, and they'd still written regularly. The letters had become less frequent when he went to the army hospital and she became more involved in the suffrage movement. Their lives had become busy, as lives do. Then, of course, she'd met Richard and never seemed to have time for anything. She and Michael had lost their connection somewhere. She wanted to fix that, but not if Michael was going to be an ass about it.

Her rubber boots squished in the mud. She knocked as much muck off the soles as she could walking the stone path to Brigit's front door. Curtains were drawn on all the windows. Not a surprise, considering the hours the ladies kept. But it was noon, and Charlotte figured someone would be stirring.

Charlotte huddled beneath the overhang of the porch and knocked. The brass peep box set in the door remained closed. She knocked again. After a few moments, she heard noises. The inside peep-box door opened, but Charlotte couldn't see who was on the other side due to the grill and lighting. The small inner brass door slammed shut. More noise, like wood scraping on wood, she thought, and the door swung open.

Charlotte looked down at Charlie, Brigit's son.

"Yeah?" He eyed her with hostile suspicion, but his small stature, dark, unruly hair, and dusting of freckles made him less intimidating than intended.

"Is your mo—Is Miss Brigit available, please?" Charlotte had an inkling that asking for Brigit by name and playing along with his role of gatekeeper for the house would get her further than asking for his mother.

His brown eyes glinted with a sense of importance, telling Charlotte she'd managed to get that one right, and he opened the door to admit her. A straight-backed wooden chair scraped across the floor, pushed aside by the door. That explained the noises she had heard and how Charlie used the peephole.

Charlotte stepped inside the tastefully decorated entry hall. Somewhere in her brain she'd expected gaudy, gilded hardware, or paintings and statues of nude women. Instead, she found a polished cherry-wood side table with a sleek black telephone and a small area rug covering the tiled floor. There was a damp wool and tobacco odor in the air. A door to the right was marked PRIVATE, but beyond an archway to the left was an equally demure parlor with several couches and a couple of gaming tables set for faro or poker.

"Wait here," Charlie said. "I'll get her."

He shoved the chair against the wall, then knocked on the PRIVATE door. A muffled response prompted him to enter. He closed the door behind himself, leaving Charlotte alone in the hall.

Upon closer inspection, the rug was a bit worn, and the striped paper above the wainscoting curled near the ceiling molding. Charlotte stood in the archway leading into the parlor. The carpet and furnishings were clean, the crystal chandelier polished. The scent of floral perfume was heavier here. To the right of the arch, a black upright piano sat against the half wall where a stairway led to the upper floor.

"Miss Brody," Brigit said from behind her.

The madam wore her dark hair in a neatly pinned pile on her head. Her crisp white blouse, straight black skirt, and polished black boots were more in line with what a school teacher might wear, not the proprietress of a brothel. "Miss Brigit. I'm sorry to arrive uninvited."

Brigit gave her a slight grin. "Our door is always open. I was just on my way to the bank, however, so if you could tell me what you need . . ."

Charlotte glanced at Charlie, who stood beside his mother with a similar expectant look upon his face. "Is there somewhere we can speak privately?"

The grin faltered into a sigh of resignation. She knew Charlotte was there to discuss Darcy. "Charlie, go wake up Lizzie and Della. Tell them it's their turn to do the cooking. Mrs. Palmer won't be in until this afternoon." Brigit focused her bright brown eyes on Charlotte. "Come with me."

She spun on her heel and strode to the room across the entryway. Charlotte followed, trying to not let the woman's abrupt manner get the better of her. She knew Brigit would be difficult. The best way to counter that was to be equally calm and understanding.

A large walnut desk dominated Brigit's office. Behind it was a black leather chair, the only seat in the room other than a low divan in a corner. Artwork covered three walls; the fourth had tall windows dressed with lacy blue and white curtains.

Brigit gestured for her to have a seat on the divan. Charlotte unbuttoned her coat and removed her hat before sitting. Brigit's not offering to take them meant one thing: You aren't going to be here long.

"What can I do for you, Miss Brody?" Brigit crossed her arms beneath her breasts and sat on the edge of the massive desk.

"I'm looking for answers, Miss Brigit, much as you are, I assume."

She cocked an eyebrow. "I'm waiting for someone to do his damn job and figure out who killed Darcy."

"Yet you and your girls aren't fully cooperating with the marshal's office," Charlotte said. She wanted to question the madam about the arguments with Darcy that Marie had mentioned, but that would put Brigit on the defensive. Better to avoid it for now. Charlotte was here for a different purpose. "If you could tell me who Darcy had been seeing most of lately, it would help."

Brigit glared at her. "She was a whore. She saw a lot of men."

Charlotte leaned forward. "I mean someone who, perhaps, has some standing in the community and whose reputation might be damaged by coming in here."

Brigit stared at her for a moment, then started laughing. Not a mere chuckle, but a hearty laugh that shook her body. Charlotte felt an uncomfortable warmth rise on her cheeks. What was so funny? She just wanted to know about the men coming—

Ah.

When she realized what she'd said, the heat on her cheeks intensified with embarrassment, but she also couldn't help smiling a little. Making Brigit laugh probably wasn't a bad thing. "That's not exactly what I meant."

"I know." Brigit wiped the corners of her eyes with the sides of her hands, attempting to control herself. "Which is why it was so funny. In my line of work, you deal with a lot of references to such things."

"I can imagine," Charlotte said. She let the madam regain her composure. "What I meant was, could someone who didn't want his visits here made public be responsible for Darcy's death? Was anyone like that one of her regulars?"

Brigit's demeanor changed in the blink of an eye from amused to wary. "There are a number of men who fall into that category, Miss Brody. Proper gentlemen who don't want their friends or wives knowing they frequent my establishment."

"Please, call me Charlotte." Anything to create a rapport with the woman would help.

"This isn't the only house in Cordova, but we have a reputation for good women, fair gaming, and discretion. A man walking through that door," she said, nodding in the direction of the front of the house, "knows he'll get all three, no matter who he is. I wouldn't tell you the names of the poorest of cannery men or miners or the richest city councilmen who trust me and my girls."

"Even if he killed one of your girls?"

Brigit pressed her lips into a thin line and frowned. Charlotte read the conflict in her eyes. Brigit wanted to know who killed Darcy, wanted to help, but she couldn't betray the trust of her customers either.

"I know your business is important to you, Brigit, but more important than putting away the person responsible? What if he tries again?"

"I'm as determined to have justice for Darcy as you are," she assured Charlotte. "I just can't hand over a list of names. I'd be ruined, and there's no guarantee it would help."

"Just a few names that might come to mind." Charlotte got up and stepped in front of her. She grasped Brigit's forearm and gently squeezed. "Please. Deputy Eddington has little to go on. He needs your help. Darcy needs your help."

Brigit's expression became pained. "If there was someone about whom I could say, 'Yes, him,' I'd tell you, Charlotte. In a heartbeat. But there was no one from that night who'd fit the bill. Sure, Darcy had regulars, well-off and well-married regulars who'd have my head if I revealed their activities. But none were here that night. It's a delicate balance, running a house these days. Half the town shows up on my doorstep, while the other half wants to run me off."

The dichotomy of a growing frontier town, Charlotte thought. Ignore or even secretly participate in seamier behavior as long as it didn't interfere with public efforts to become "civilized."

She moved her hand away from Brigit's arm. Charlotte believed the madam, but that didn't help the case. Just as she was about to thank Brigit for her time, a thought struck her.

"None of those men came here," she said, "but did any of them get word to Darcy? A call or a note, maybe, to meet them? Something or someone drew Darcy outside when she should have been resting."

Brigit shook her head. "We were all very busy. No one had much time to answer the phone or run secret messages. Except—" Her eyes widened; her entire body stilled. She pushed herself away from the desk and went to the door. Opening it, she called out, "Charlie!"

Charlotte heard the boy's feet pound down the stairs then across the hall. "Yes, ma'am?"

She knelt down in front of him and grasped his shoulders. "Did you take any sort of message to Darcy that night?" He opened his mouth, then snapped it shut again, his eyes darting to Charlotte. Brigit shook him gently to regain his attention. "Look at me. Tell me what happened."

"I-I went outside to play night tag with Nick and Davey." His sheepish expression told Charlotte he wasn't supposed to be out at that hour.

"And?" Brigit didn't chastise the boy for his misbehavior. There were more important things to worry about than breaking curfew.

"A man called me over as I was coming home," he said. "Gave me a couple of tokens for the drugstore to take the note in." Charlie glanced up at Charlotte again.

Wooden or metal tokens were a popular form of currency in areas where government-issued coins were scarce. Inscribed with a specific store's name, they were as good as cash at that establishment. What kid wouldn't do something as simple as deliver a note if it meant a piece of candy or a soda?

"Who was the man?" Charlotte asked, keeping her tone soft despite the growing anticipation that the boy had critical information he hadn't shared.

"I dunno," he said. "He was kinda tall, wore a dark coat and hat."

Charlotte considered Charlie's age and height. Anyone over sixteen or eighteen was probably a grown man to him. "How about his build, Charlie? Was he fat? Skinny?"

"Not fat, like Mr. Toliver. More like Doc Brody, sorta skinny."

Charlie's associating her brother with Brigit's house threw Charlotte for a moment. Then she remembered he was here frequently to tend to the girls, and likely tended Charlie as well.

"Charlie, you know just about everyone in this town." His mother dug her fingers into his shoulders. "Who was he?"

"I dunno, Mama, I swear." Tears brimmed, but didn't fall. "It was dark and rainy, and I was in a hurry. He gave me the note and the tokens and nudged me toward the house. Didn't say anything but my name, and his hat was pulled way down." Charlie dug into his trouser pocket and withdrew two wooden tokens. He held them out. "Here. I didn't think it would hurt no one." His voice cracked. "I didn't think Darcy would get killed for it."

"Why didn't you tell anyone?" Brigit asked.

"I didn't see him good and didn't want to get into trouble for being out." Charlie's lower lip quivered. "I'm sorry, Mama."

Charlotte's chest tightened. "It's not your fault, Charlie."

"No, of course it isn't, honey." Brigit loosened her grip and caressed his narrow shoulders. She smoothed a lock of hair from his forehead. "You keep the tokens. It's all right. Go on now and help the girls."

Charlie spun around and ran out of the office. Brigit rose slowly. She faced Charlotte, looking weary and sad. Her obvious emotion combined with the boy's statement didn't completely exonerate her, but it was less likely, in Charlotte's mind, that Brigit had killed the girl.

"At least we know how he got Darcy out of the house," Brigit said.

"It's more than we had before." Charlotte set her hat on her head. She approached Brigit and gathered the woman's hands in hers. "I'm sorry your boy had to go through that, but please make sure he understands he's helped the case."

Brigit nodded and squeezed Charlotte's fingers. "I will. I think he was more at ease telling it while you were here than when Eddington came around. I didn't want Charlie in the room that morning. It was no place for a boy his age, talking about what happened. And we're kind of skittish around lawmen."

Charlotte grinned before releasing her hands. "James can be a bit intimidating."

Brigit quirked an eyebrow. "James, is it?" Charlotte felt a flush rise. "He is a handsome one, for sure. Here, I have to make my appointment with the banker. I'll walk with you, if you're headed back up."

Brigit retrieved her coat and umbrella from the hall closet. She and Charlotte walked the path behind the house and up toward town. At the top of the rise, not far from the back of Michael's office, Charlotte had a good view of the walkway behind the buildings that paralleled Main Street. The wooden footbridge spanning the sixty-foot gap in the ridge upon which

Cordova was built appeared solid, with safety rails to prevent anyone from falling onto the rocky beach below. The elevated railroad tracks, farther out over the water, serviced the canneries to the northwest.

Darcy and her killer had come this way. Did she cry out? Had the wind muffled her calls for help? A wave of guilt rippled through Charlotte. *I should have looked out the window sooner.*

"You all right?" Brigit asked.

Charlotte shook herself out of futile thoughts and offered an apologetic smile. "Just thinking. Sorry, I didn't mean to delay you getting to your meeting."

Rather than travel along the footbridge, the two of them walked to Main Street. The bank was near McGruder's store, a couple of blocks past the federal building, where Charlotte was headed, and just far enough to require more than companionable silence. It wouldn't hurt to gather some information on Brigit while they walked.

"Where were you before Cordova?" Charlotte asked as casually as she could.

A sidelong glance accompanied an enigmatic smile. "What makes you think I was anywhere but here?"

"I've learned that few people here are actually from Alaska," Charlotte said.

Brigit laughed. "True. I'm from Ohio originally, a tiny town west of Cleveland. Not much going for it. Moved to Virginia, then Dawson at the tail end of the gold rush there, and ended up heading west with the miners."

Charlotte tried to watch Brigit's expression without seeming too obvious. "Nome?" Brigit nodded. "Fairbanks?" A hesitation before affirmation. Was it Brigit in the picture?

As they drew closer to the bank, the door opened, and Tess Kavanagh stepped onto the walk. She smiled at Charlotte, but when she saw Brigit the smile fell. It wasn't the startled response of nearly colliding; there was too much distance between them for that fear. But they were all close enough for Charlotte to see Mrs. Kavanagh's eyes meet Brigit's. Recognition flared in each of their expressions, as did something else. Not anger, precisely. Surprise? Wariness?

Mrs. Kavanagh quickly shifted her gaze to Charlotte. "Miss Brody, how are you today?"

"I'm well, thank you. And yourself?" Was she going to completely ignore Brigit? Charlotte glanced between the two women, wondering if it was their status that made this such an uncomfortable meeting.

"Quite well, thank you. But I'm in a bit of a hurry," she said apologetically. "If you'll excuse me."

Mrs. Kavanagh swept past, her hurried boot steps thumping on the walk. Charlotte and Brigit watched her depart. Brigit's face registered nothing, not anger or disappointment. While Charlotte hadn't expected the two women to greet each other with friendship, the absolute coldness of Mrs. Kavanagh's reaction seemed extreme.

"Do you know her at all?" Charlotte asked.

Brigit shook her head. She faced Charlotte, a small, tense smile curving her lips. "I'm afraid I have to get inside. Let me know if there's anything else we can do."

Charlotte wanted to ask if Brigit had known about Darcy's delicate condition, or about the money and papers sewn into the coat, but she couldn't. Not yet. It was information and evidence that needed to be kept mum for now. "I will. Thank you."

They headed in opposite directions, but Brigit stopped her before Charlotte got more than two steps away.

"I'm two girls down now that Marie is gone." She gave Charlotte an appraising look, but there was amusement in her dark eyes. "Could use a pretty blonde like you."

Charlotte grinned. She liked this woman and her wicked

sense of humor. "Thanks, but Toliver already beat you to it. If that doesn't pan out, I'll let you know," she said with a wink.

Hunching her shoulders against the rain, Charlotte hurried to James's office with Brigit's laughter echoing behind her.

Charlotte walked into the marshal's office just as James was leading a disheveled man toward the side door marked JAIL. Marshal Blaine sat at the deputy's desk, writing in a large ledger. A second man sat on the hard wooden chair in front of the desk, elbows on his knees and holding his head in his hands.

"Have you got the fifty dollars or not, Rawlins?" Blaine asked.

"Nah," Rawlins drawled. "Who has that kinda money all at once?"

"Not the likes of you," Blaine said, not unkindly. "So maybe you better consider that next time you and Carter decide to fire up your still and try to sell hooch, eh?"

Rawlins nodded, and the marshal went back to writing in the book. When he was finished, he stood and smiled at Charlotte.

"Miss Brody. A pleasure to see you again. What can I do for you?" He came around the desk and grabbed the other man's arm, assisting him to his feet. Rawlins stood, wavering slightly.

"I don't mean to interrupt police business, Marshal." Though the information she had, scant that it was, qualified. "Is the deputy available?"

Blaine narrowed his gaze, holding Rawlins still as he regarded her. "He'll be back in a minute. Why don't you have a seat here while I deal with this?"

Charlotte moved forward as Blaine escorted his charge through the same side door James had gone through earlier. She sat, removed her hat, and couldn't help glancing at the ledger. Though it was upside down, she easily read Blaine's neat block writing that filled the last line. Rawlins, John had been arrested for violating the Alaska dry law and was charged fifty dollars in fines and fees. It appeared his friend was in trouble for the same crime.

"Miss Brody." James's voice behind her set Charlotte's heart racing. He'd caught her snooping.

"Deputy. I was wondering if you had a minute."

He stood beside her, but glanced toward the hall to the jail. Seeing if Blaine was near? "Is this about last night?" he asked quietly.

She nodded as the marshal strutted back into the front office. He eyed the two of them with curiosity bordering on suspicion. "You need me, Eddington?"

"No, sir."

Blaine took his hat and coat off the rack near the door. "Good. I'm going to the café." He gave them a significant look as he shrugged into his coat. "Anything important will be passed on to me."

It wasn't a question.

"Yes, sir," James said with a solemn nod. The marshal left the office, and James turned back to Charlotte. "Did you talk to Brigit?"

"I did, but she refused to name anyone." He scowled. "But," Charlotte said, laying a hand on his arm, "Charlie said someone had him pass a note to Darcy that night."

"Who? Why didn't he say anything when I was there?" James's anger and frustration blazed in his eyes and darkened his cheeks beneath the shade of whiskers. He was intimidating, even when the look wasn't aimed at her.

Charlotte squeezed his arm. "Maybe because you scare the hell out of him?"

His frown deepened. "Kids love me." She couldn't help but laugh, and James smiled. "So what did you manage to get out of him, oh charmer of children?"

"Actually, Brigit was the one who got him to talk." Charlotte lowered her hand. "He'd been outside when he wasn't supposed to be, which is why he didn't say anything before. The man gave him the note and a couple of store tokens. I guess Charlie is used to being discreet and didn't think much of it."

"Who was it?"

"He couldn't tell," she said. Charlotte told James everything Charlie told her and Brigit. "It was dark, and the man kept his hat pulled down. Charlie only had a vague description of his height and build."

Charlie's comparing the man to Michael flashed through her mind again. How many others fit that description? Probably quite a few.

"Could've been anyone," James said, clearly disappointed, "and no way to know for certain if this man was responsible."

Charlotte rose and fiddled with the brim of her hat, working out what little they knew. "The timing is too close. That man had something to do with Darcy's death, I'm sure."

James stepped past her to open the door. "Your conviction is fine, but it won't get me my killer. We need facts and evidence, Charlotte."

We. She grinned up at him. He smiled back, and Charlotte's heart fluttered. Without a second thought, she rose up on her toes to peck him on the cheek. "Thanks for letting me stay on the case with you," she said. "And for backing me up last night with Michael."

James raised his hand to where the brim of his hat would have been in a gesture that was becoming quite familiar to Charlotte. "Any time, ma'am. Go settle things with your brother. I have those damn prisoners to process. Then I'll walk the path behind the buildings and down to the trees where Darcy was found, to see if I missed anything."

"I have the feeling your task will be more enjoyable than mine." Most would find retracing the steps of a murderer and his victim distasteful, but Charlotte didn't relish the idea of confronting Michael either. Still, it had to be done to mend the rift between them.

"It'll be better in the long run," James said. "Now scoot."

Charlotte sighed dramatically, smiling when he laughed, and headed out.

Chapter 12

Charlotte hurried across the street, reaching Michael's office as the skies opened and the rain fell as if blasted through a hose. At least it wasn't raining sideways this time.

She entered without knocking and pushed the door closed. No one waited in the visitor's chair, nor was Michael at his desk. Shaking most of the rain from her hat, she hung it and her coat on the rack behind the door. The exam room was empty as well. The stringent bite of carbolic acid used as a cleanser made her nose itch. She continued through to the door of his living quarters and knocked.

"Just a moment," he called out. Within a few seconds, Michael opened the door. His surprise at seeing her was obvious. "I didn't hear you come in."

Charlotte clasped her hands at her waist. "I should have knocked on the outer door, but it was raining pretty hard."

"No, no, that's fine," he said. "I leave it unlocked just for that reason."

The tension between them was too much. They were treating each other almost like strangers, and it made her heartsick. Had their bond finally snapped?

"Michael, I—"

"Charlotte, I'm sorry," he said, overriding her own apology. "I've been a complete ass about . . . everything."

She didn't try to hide her relief. "I'm glad you figured it out, because I wasn't quite sure how to say it." They both laughed, and some of the tension ebbed. "But I was a bit of an ass too. And I'm sorry. I think we've both been through some difficult times of late."

His blue eyes filled with understanding as well as curiosity. "Come inside and have something to eat. I was just heating some chicken soup Mrs. LeVoy gave me."

"Something else I need to apologize for," she said as she followed him into his quarters. "I was supposed to be cooking for you."

Michael shrugged. He grabbed another bowl from the stack beneath the sink, then filled it from a pot on the stove. "It's not a problem." She sat down, and he set the bowl in front of her along with a spoon and a linen napkin. "I think it's time we talked about what's been bothering us."

Her hands trembled at the thought, but the idea of the rift between them getting larger scared her more than sharing her secrets.

He sank onto his chair across from her, shoulders slumped. "Last night at Eddington's, I was trying to be the big brother after not being there for you the last several years." He reached across the table and covered her hand with his. "Alaska can be a hard environment for a woman, Charlotte, and I don't want to see you hurt."

She turned her hand so they were palm to palm and grasped his. "I know. In a way, I do appreciate it, but I'm a big girl, Michael. I've seen and . . . and done things that give me a little more experience and wisdom than you might expect."

He squeezed back, concern on his face. "Some of those things were rather painful, weren't they?"

Charlotte's throat tightened. She could only nod, unable to speak.

Michael drew in a long, slow breath, then let it out in a shaky exhalation. "I know how that feels. There's something I've needed to tell someone for a long time, and I just couldn't. I thought coming out here, finding some sort of normalcy away from all the reminders might help, but it hasn't. Not really."

His voice cracked, and when he continued, she saw such sorrow in his eyes she could have wept for him.

"While I was at the hospital," he said in a near whisper, "there was a soldier there. Private Isaac Barnes. He'd been wounded by a landmine in Germany and sent stateside after he'd recovered enough to travel." Michael let out a short bark of a scoffing laugh. "Recovered. The poor bastard had lost all his limbs and suffered a disfiguring head wound that caused seizures and fits of rage. He either slept or was agitated, with moments of brief lucidity between morphine doses."

Charlotte squeezed Michael's hand, not wanting to interrupt the horrific story he needed to get off his chest.

"His parents came to bring him home. We told them he'd require round-the-clock care—toilet, feeding, hygiene, and bathing—and that it was better for him to stay in a hospital permanently. They were older, you see, and we didn't think they'd be able to handle his needs. They didn't have much money to pay for such care. They'd sit at Isaac's bedside, talk about selling part of their land, their possessions. After they left for supper one evening, Isaac called me over. 'Don't let them,' he said. 'I'd rather die than see them go through that. Morphine. Something. Please, Doc. Please.' "

Michael focused on Charlotte, his face drawn. "He was asking me to put him out of his misery, to save his parents from heartache and debt. I started to argue with him, but he had a seizure. I was going to ignore his plea, then he asked me again two days later. After another seizure, one that required a nurse to help hold his thrashing body before it rendered him semicomatose, I made up my mind."

"Michael." Charlotte swallowed the lump that had risen in her throat. "Your oath."

"Do no harm." His eyes hardened. "Wasn't it more harmful to have Isaac and his family live that way for years, maybe decades? The least I could do was treat him better than we'd treat an animal."

He was on the defensive, but she hadn't meant to sound accusatory. She could only imagine the struggle he'd faced.

Michael shook his head and took another deep breath. "I prepped a syringe with digitalis, kept it in my coat pocket until he had another seizure. I didn't have to wait long. I had the nurse usher his parents out, then administered the dose. Once his heart rate had dropped, I called his parents in, told them the last seizure had been too much, that his heart hadn't been able to take it. He died with them crying on either side of him, their heads on each of his shoulders and their hands twisted in his pajama top."

Charlotte closed her eyes, her fingers wrapped around Michael's, tears trailing down her cheeks. How horrible to have your child die in your arms.

"'He's at peace,' his mother kept saying, 'He's at peace.' So it was the right thing to do, wasn't it?"

Charlotte was nodding before she even looked at him. His expression was defiant, but in his eyes there was the need to be told it was all right. "Yes. Yes, it was, Michael."

Relief washed over his face, and he bowed his head. "You have no idea what it's been like, living with this. Knowing I've taken a life, even if it was for the best."

Charlotte squeezed his hands as tightly as he squeezed hers. His fingers trembled. His jaw muscles stood out under the paleness of his skin. Finally, the trembling stopped, and his muscles relaxed. Michael drew in a long, slow breath and released it with a sigh. Confession was good for the soul, they said.

"I do know," she said, her voice catching in her throat.

Michael's head came up slowly, the question he hadn't voiced plain in his red-rimmed eyes.

"Guilt. I know the guilt you're suffering." Charlotte tried to moisten her lips with her parched tongue. She'd never spoken to anyone about her indiscretions. Only Kit and Richard knew, and Richard, the bastard, didn't matter. "I did something that I thought was for the best." The lump formed in her throat again. It took two hard swallows to clear it enough to be able to speak. "I still believe so, but maybe it was for a selfish reason."

His fingers tightened around her trembling hands.

She squeezed back, grateful to have him listening without judgment. At least not yet. "I'd been seeing Richard Hamilton. Going to dances and lectures, that sort of thing."

"I remember your mentioning him in a few letters," Michael said when she paused.

"We were friends, then things changed."

Tension vibrated through his hands, and he frowned. "Did he do something untoward?"

"He didn't. *We* did." Her face and body heated. She couldn't believe she was telling her brother about her love life. About this much of it. "We had relations. Intimate relations."

"Oh," he said, sounding relieved. "I mean, it's not something you want to think about involving your sister, but women nowadays are taking all sorts of aspects of their lives into their own hands." He stopped, reading the expression on her face. "There's more."

Her entire body felt cold, and she shivered. What was he going to say? What was he going to think? When she'd asked if Ruth was pregnant, he'd been shocked, practically insulted that Charlotte would ever think such a thing. Good girls didn't have sex. They didn't get pregnant. And they certainly didn't do what Charlotte had done.

"Charlotte?"

"I don't want you to hate me, Michael." She gripped his

hands so hard she thought she'd break his fingers, but he held on. "I couldn't stand it if you hated me."

"There is nothing you could ever do that would make me hate you." Tears filled his eyes. "You are my sister, and I love you more than anything in this world. Tell me, if you think it will make you feel better, but it's okay if you don't."

He was giving her an out, a way to avoid revealing herself at her worst. He'd confided in her, trusted her to hear his confession and relieve his conscience. Michael had set the ball rolling, and now her own guilt pushed against her skull and compressed her chest. She had to tell him or she'd shatter into countless pieces.

"A year ago, I got pregnant." She said it fast, the words tumbling out with barely enough pause to take a breath. "When I told Richard, he wanted me to marry him. But he didn't want me to keep working. Wife and mother only, no more articles or anything like that. I didn't love him, not enough to marry him. Not enough to lose everything I'd worked for. And to be honest—"

The next words stuck in her throat. They sounded so wrong, so selfish in her head. But they were the truth, her feelings then and her feelings now.

"I didn't want a baby, Michael," she managed to say. "I didn't want to be pregnant. I didn't want Richard. I had plans and ideas that didn't include any of that. So I—I got the name of a doctor in Buffalo, and Kit drove me up. We told everyone I was going for a long visit at her family's place to get over breaking it off with Richard."

Michael stared at Charlotte across the table, his jaw muscles tight. What was he thinking? She didn't want to know, not just yet. She had to finish this first.

"They were nice, really. Very understanding. It was well after regular hours, of course, and the shades and curtains were drawn."

The doctor's office had been above a drugstore on a dingy street. The nurse had her and Kit sit in a little room, separated from the two or three other women with appointments that night. Charlotte never saw anyone, but heard muffled voices and sobs. She'd always remember the antiseptic smell and the sobs.

"The nurse told us some of the women who came there were like me, unmarried girls 'in trouble' who didn't want a baby. Some had beaus who wouldn't marry them. Others already had families and were too poor or too sick to take care of another baby. We all had our reasons, and no one reason was better or worse than the other."

Richard's voice sounded in her head. *Abortions are for poor, desperate women. Not for women of our class.*

A cramp pinched Charlotte's hand, and she realized she was squeezing Michael's fingers hard enough to hurt herself. "Sorry," she said, loosening her grip.

He shook his head as he stood. For a moment, she thought he was going to walk away from her, and her heart sank to the pit of her stomach.

But he didn't. He came to her side of the table and knelt down. Michael wrapped his arms around her shoulders and drew her into a hug. Charlotte embraced him and started to tremble. He wasn't angry or disappointed. He understood. She'd lost over a year by keeping secrets, fearing he'd be disgusted with her.

Charlotte buried her face against her brother's neck, taking in the scent of starch and carbolic acid, as a sob ripped through her chest. Guilt and shame and anger, suppressed for so long except in the late-night darkness of her bedroom, finally found their way out. She tried to say more, to explain herself, but every time she opened her mouth, there was just more sobbing, more tears, more body-wracking shivers.

Wrung out, her limbs like water, Charlotte eased out of his

arms and slumped in the chair. Michael handed her a fresh handkerchief from his pocket. She wiped her eyes and blew her nose. He dried his own tears with his napkin.

"I wish I had been there for you," he said, his voice rough.

"I couldn't tell anyone." Her throat was raw, her voice scratchy and low. "I was so stupid. Richard was horrible, and I didn't want to admit I'd been fool enough to be with him like that. And I certainly didn't want to marry him."

"I'd like to punch him in the face," Michael said.

Charlotte managed a wry grin and cupped his cheek. "I know. Me too." They both laughed quietly. Then she took a deep breath, ready to tell him more. "But it wasn't all his fault. I made the ultimate decision. I didn't want a baby, not even to give it up later, because I had other plans for my life. I wasn't ready to be pregnant, let alone a mother. I don't regret my decision, but at the same time I feel terrible that I don't. Does that make any sense?"

"No one can blame you for your feelings, Charlotte." He tucked a damp tendril of her hair back behind her ear.

"I can blame me," she said. "Mother and Father would have had a fit if they'd known, but maybe telling them wouldn't have been so bad. I don't know. I'll never know."

Michael returned to his seat. "I think we've both learned valuable lessons here."

"For the guilty, there is no peace." She couldn't recall where she'd heard that before, but it was appropriate.

He fiddled with his spoon. "I was thinking more along the lines of don't underestimate the power of your sibling's love and concern for your well-being." Their eyes met over the table. "We can help each other find peace now, Charlie. Can't we?"

Another knot tightened her throat. She reached across the table and held his hand again. "We will."

Chapter 13

After helping Michael tidy up, Charlotte headed back to Sullivan's, and he hurried to keep an appointment with a homebound patient. The rain chilled her, seemed to seep into her bones even through her coat and heavy boots, but also soothed her both physically and emotionally. She stopped, eyes closed, and just breathed. She had no idea how long it would take for her to completely get over what she'd done. Maybe she never would. She had to accept that the decision she'd made was best for her at the time.

There was no way to change the past, and no way to say whether she'd do the same or different if the situation were to repeat itself. The best thing to do was avoid another chance of its happening entirely.

In the meantime, she'd work through and around what she'd done. Focus on Darcy's case. If she could help bring the murderer to justice, perhaps Charlotte would feel her decision had been meaningful. Ending her unwanted pregnancy, in order to continue to help women achieve the freedom to make the same choice, would do more good than harm. Maybe it was a selfish straw to grasp, but it was the only one within reach. She'd hold on to it and do her damnedest.

Charlotte opened her eyes, ready to start off again. The sign for the First Federal Bank caught her attention, and the chance meeting between Tess Kavanagh and Brigit replayed in Charlotte's head. Not a word had passed between them, but the tension had been palpable. There had been an immediate sense that neither woman particularly cared for the other. Why? Their social status? Some previous encounter? While it would have been unusual for the two to be bosom buddies, Charlotte had expected some acknowledgment of each other's existence at the very least. Yet there had been nothing of the sort.

Something niggled in Charlotte's brain. There was a connection there; she was sure of it. But what? The two women shared a few physical features—hair and eye color, most notably—but also a confidence and bearing that made them stand out. Seeing them on separate occasions, Charlotte might have unconsciously noted their similarities, but now that she thought about it, she realized there was more. Not only did they share the same coloring, but the same high cheekbones and small clefts in their chins. And each woman's surprise at seeing the other on the street had revealed unguarded expressions that were too much alike for coincidence.

With the suspicion that Brigit was one of the women in the newspaper clipping Darcy had secreted away, Charlotte now wondered if the other woman was Tess Kavanagh. Were Brigit and Tess actually the Jensen sisters? Had they and John Kincaid changed their names and made their way to Cordova after avoiding criminal charges in Fairbanks?

"But how to prove it?"

"Beg pardon, miss?"

Charlotte jumped, startled by the voice. A thin man with graying brown hair stood beside her. His brown suit was dappled with rain, and he held a wrapped bundle beneath his arm.

"Were you needing something, miss? Are you lost?"

"No, not lost, thank you," she said, offering him a reassuring smile. He nodded and started to move past her. "Oh, but could you tell me, perhaps, where the Kavanaghs live?" If she wanted to get answers from Tess Kavanagh, she'd have to start asking questions.

The man gave her a quizzical look. "You mean the mayor and his wife? Why, they're in the big gray house up Council Avenue, way at the top. Can't miss it."

Charlotte thanked him and hurried back to her room to pick up her notebook, pen, and a few cards she'd had printed before leaving New York. Locking her door behind her, she headed out again. The trek up Council took her past Second Street and The Wild Rose, the restaurant James had taken her to the other night.

She shook her head and pushed the memory of dinner and the kiss aside. She definitely needed to avoid making another mistake with a man. Even if that man were James Eddington. Discretion was the better part of valor when it came to relationships.

Charlotte found the Kavanaghs' home exactly where the man had said, up the road, beyond the businesses and homes that crowded the slope down to the sea. James's cabin was among those buildings, nestled between two modest houses. The Kavanaghs' home was on par with the Bartletts', well kept but not so grand as to indicate the mayor lived here. Neatly trimmed shrubs and flower beds surrounded the house. Even the poorer neighborhoods seemed to take pride in their tended yards and gardens. The wilds of Alaska? Not quite, but pretty flowers and well-kept yards didn't hide the fact that bad things happened in small towns.

She stepped up onto the wooden planks of the walk from the road to the front door, the first flutter of nerves tickling her stomach. Dropping in on Mrs. Kavanagh was a breach in social protocol, but she'd rather keep the woman slightly off balance by a surprise visit than give her a chance to plan and control the conversation. It was an interview technique that often resulted in more honest responses.

Charlotte lifted the simple iron knocker and rapped on the door. While she waited for a response, she smoothed her hair as best she could. At the first sound of the latch being turned, she affected what she hoped was a charming smile.

An older woman of forty or so in a simple black dress, her dark hair in a neat bun, answered. "Yes, may I help you?"

Charlotte withdrew a card from her coat pocket. "Good afternoon. My name is Charlotte Brody. I met Mrs. Kavanagh at the mayor's party and again at Reverend Bartlett's home. I was hoping Mrs. Kavanagh was available for a short interview."

The housekeeper took the card and gave it, and Charlotte, a dubious look. Would Charlotte's association with *Modern Woman* and previous meetings with the mayor's wife be enough to sway? "I haven't seen one of these in a few years."

Charlotte wasn't sure if the woman was impressed or amused.

"My mother still swears by visitor cards," Charlotte said, "and insisted I get something printed up." She'd tried to explain to Mother that fancy personal cards were a bit out of fashion, and settled on a business card with elegant script rather than argue over the matter. Business card. Visitor's card. If the housekeeper was impressed enough to let her in, Charlotte didn't care what anyone called the piece of card stock.

The older woman smiled. "Wait here in the foyer, and I'll see if Mrs. Kavanagh is taking visitors."

Charlotte unbuttoned her coat, and the housekeeper headed up the carpeted stairs. The house was eerily quiet, with only the occasional clatter from the back. Kitchen, more than likely.

She gave herself another quick check, brushed a bit of mud from her skirt, and smoothed her wrinkled blouse. Perhaps she wasn't dressed for a formal visit, but she was neat and clean for the most part.

After several minutes, the woman returned. "Mrs. Kavanagh

will be down in a minute. She asked that you wait in the parlor. May I take your hat and coat?"

Charlotte retrieved her notebook and pen from her coat pocket, gave the garments to the housekeeper, and entered the parlor. The scent of linseed oil barely covered the lingering aroma of the mayor's favorite cigars. A vase of wildflowers on the table in front of an armless couch added bright color to the understated room.

"May I offer you some tea, Miss Brody?"

"That would be wonderful. Thank you."

The woman nodded, then crossed the room to a door that likely led to the kitchen. Charlotte took the opportunity to wander the room, getting a sense of the Kavanaghs. Or rather, the people who called themselves Frank and Tess Kavanagh.

Don't jump to conclusions, she admonished herself. *Speculation isn't proof.*

No, but gut instinct and recent actions and reactions of people made her feel she was onto something worth pursuing. If it could shed light on Darcy's murderer, so much the better.

There was nothing among the knickknacks and glassware on display that suggested the Kavanaghs were anything but what they appeared to be. But Charlotte knew how well someone could hide a cruel streak behind a façade of fine manners and clothes. Richard had fooled her for months, his easy smile and openness making her think he'd be supportive when the time came. Far from it, she'd discovered.

When they'd first met, they'd talked for hours about politics and books, ethics, and basic human rights. Their rapport had grown into friendship, friendship into desire. His views were so modern and refreshing, it was no wonder she'd fallen for him. They'd had fun in and out of bed, but when fun turned into a serious personal situation, he'd shown his true colors. Funny how a bit of pressure could reveal so much.

"Miss Brody, how nice to see you again."

Charlotte shook off the distraction of her past and concentrated on her current task. She smiled at Mrs. Kavanagh and crossed the room. "Please forgive the intrusion, but I got it in my head that I just *had* to interview you, so here I am."

The mayor's wife, dressed in a dark brown suit and matching shoes, took Charlotte's offered hand and clasped it with both of hers. The more delicate bones of the smaller woman held Charlotte in cool, friendly firmness. "No trouble at all. And please, call me Tess."

She gestured for Charlotte to have a seat. They each chose a spot near the ends of the couch and sat, half-turned to face each other across the short expanse of brocade. The housekeeper returned with a sleek wooden tray and a silver tea service. She set the tray on the table.

"Thank you, Mrs. Popovich," Tess said. "I'll serve Miss Brody. We'd like a bit of privacy, please." Mrs. Popovich nodded, smiled at Charlotte, and left the parlor, sliding the pocket door behind her. The mayor's wife poured out two cups of tea into delicate chinaware and offered Charlotte cream and sugar. "Now, tell me what this interview is about."

"It's quite exciting," Charlotte said with true enthusiasm. "The readers of *Modern Woman* will get an in-depth look at life in the wilds of Alaska."

Tess laughed. "I wouldn't call Cordova the wilds. We try to be civilized when we can."

"I have to admit, I'm a bit sorry to say that's all too true," Charlotte said with a playful sigh of disappointment. Tess laughed again. "I want to particularly focus on the women who make their way up here. It takes a certain sort, don't you think?"

"I suppose." Tess sipped her tea, watching Charlotte over the rim with bright brown eyes.

Why didn't I notice how similar they are to Brigit's?

"For instance," Charlotte said, "Mrs. Sullivan told me of her growing up in Canada and following her second husband to Dawson City. Such adventure and heartbreak for her over the years, marrying a couple of times, losing a child, but she made her way in Cordova and is now a successful businesswoman. Her story will enthrall readers." Charlotte opened her notebook, set it on her knee, and readied her pen. "What brought you to Alaska, Tess?"

"Clams. Not as exciting as gold, I'm afraid." Tess smiled, teacup and saucer in hand. "The clam canneries were growing, and Frank partnered with a couple of business associates. They couldn't stay to oversee the operation, so here we are. I followed my husband, like many women."

"I understand you were in Virginia before this." Charlotte had learned as much from her research at the newspaper office. "Is that where you're from originally?"

"No, I'm from Ohio, a small town west of Cleveland. A tiny place without much going for it other than being outside of Cleveland."

Charlotte chuckled along with Tess, but her mind whirled. Brigit had said the same thing, almost to the word. Coincidence? Not likely. Charlotte would bet her bottom dollar that Tess Kavanagh and Brigit O'Brien were sisters.

"I met Frank in Virginia," Tess continued, setting her cup and saucer on the table. "I was going to nursing school, and he was working in his family's business doing the accounting."

Charlotte remembered she was supposed to be taking notes and jotted the information down. Most of what Tess had said was in the Toliver interview from several years before. "After you were married, you stayed in Virginia until his partnership brought you here?"

"That's right."

"Did you come through Canada? Dawson City, perhaps?" Charlotte kept her pen poised over the paper, but she held the other woman's gaze. "Have you been to other towns in the territory, like Sitka or Fairbanks?"

Tess's smile faltered, and a wariness darkened her eyes. She folded her hands in her lap, right over left, rubbing her gold wedding band. "No, nowhere else. We came right here on the steamer."

Time to ease up a little, Charlotte decided. "This must have been quite a change for you after being in Ohio and Virginia. What sorts of challenges did you face when you first arrived?"

Tess's shoulders dropped a little, and the tension lines in her face smoothed out. She told Charlotte of the things she found to be different in Cordova compared to the States. Charlotte dutifully took notes. Tess's story, completely true or not, was interesting, and Charlotte hoped she could use it in her series. For several minutes, Charlotte prompted Tess to expand on certain aspects of life on the frontier. Then she asked her next question.

"And how do you know Brigit O'Brien?"

Tess blinked at her, her cheeks pale. After a few seconds, she drew in a deep breath and gave Charlotte a tight smile. "I don't."

"Funny, she said the same thing this morning after we all bumped into each other at the bank." Charlotte set her pen and notebook aside. "But you do know her."

It wasn't a question this time, and Charlotte's heart raced with her audacity. A journalist had to know when to ask and when to put forth statements. She wasn't afraid of Tess Kavanagh's getting mad at her, though that could happen. No, she was more afraid that the mayor's wife would stop talking.

"Of course I know *who* she is, but I don't know her socially." Tess's voice cracked in the middle of the last word, and she had to clear her throat. "We've been in Cordova long enough to recognize most everyone."

"That's not what I meant," Charlotte said. "I think you and your husband know her quite well. I think someone else knew this too, and it became a problem."

Tess's concern or anger—perhaps it was a mix of the two—became confusion. "A problem? What are you talking about?"

Then something dawned in her dark eyes. She rose abruptly. "I'm not feeling well, Miss Brody. I think I need to lie down."

I'll bet you do.

Charlotte stood, her notebook clasped tightly. "Whatever you, your husband, and Brigit have schemed, it wasn't worth a girl's life."

It was a risk to say so much, but if Tess, Frank, and Brigit were responsible for Darcy's murder, they needed to know they wouldn't get away with it.

The other woman's mouth dropped open. Her face turned red. "Mrs. Popovich! Miss Brody is ready to leave."

The housekeeper must have been standing at the kitchen door, awaiting her mistress's summons, because she hurried in, smiling, until she saw the distress on Tess's face. The smile fell, and Mrs. Popovich gestured for Charlotte to precede her to the foyer.

Tess glared at her. "I don't appreciate your accusations, Miss Brody. You're wrong, and if you print a single word otherwise, I'll sue you and your magazine."

"I assure you, Mrs. Kavanagh, when my article comes out, there will be only the truth of this ugly matter."

Chapter 14

James was going to kill her.

The thought looped through her brain as Charlotte trekked down the hill toward Sullivan's. She had no proof that Tess and Brigit knew each other, except for gut instinct and a few facts that could be mere coincidence. Based on that alone, she'd accused the mayor's wife of deceit and murder. A brutal murder, at that.

Yep, he was going to kill her.

Charlotte entered Sullivan's, wiped her feet on the provided mat, and continued on to her room. She opened the door, half expecting another note, but found nothing. She removed her coat and gently shook off the rain before hanging it to dry. Slipping off her boots, she turned on the table lamp. The yellow glow helped brighten the gloom of the room, if not her attitude. That would require something else.

My gut's usually on target, she assured herself. At least with things she wasn't personally involved with. The Kavanaghs and Brigit were hiding something, and Darcy had known it. Charlotte was sure of that much.

But murder? There was motivation, of course, but that was a

huge conclusion to jump to without solid evidence. There might have been others who wanted Darcy dead for completely different reasons. If so, who and why?

In Charlotte's experience, the "why" was usually the key to the "who."

"The baby," Charlotte said to the empty room. She opened the valve on the radiator and held her chilled hands out. Deep in the wall, pipes pinged and moaned as steam circulated. "Or the blackmail?"

She sat down and jotted all she knew of the Kavanaghs, Brigit, Darcy, and the newspaper articles. The timeline of the murder came next. There were still many questions and blanks, of course.

Just after five, Charlotte perused the pages she'd written that afternoon. She didn't dare tell Michael what she was doing when he came to collect her for an evening at the Empress Theater. The antics of the comedic acts and toe-tapping music helped distract her, but thoughts of the case were never far from her mind.

Even as she fell asleep that evening, possibilities of who might have wanted Darcy Dugan dead and why swirled in her brain.

A loud crash and sudden pain woke Charlotte. She bolted upright in bed, her hand to her face. She felt sticky blood as the papers on the table and a few that had scattered onto the floor went up in a rush of flames.

The acrid stench of gasoline and alcohol seared her nostrils. She scrambled out of bed, snatching the blanket as she set her bare feet on the floor. Sharp points of pain in her right foot made her yelp and lift her foot. Broken glass. The window had been smashed, and her room was on fire.

Fear and pain gripped Charlotte, twisting her stomach and tightening her chest. She grabbed for the pitcher on the table. Too light. She hadn't filled it before bed.

Oh, God! Now what?

Move! Better a few cuts than to die here.

Favoring her injured foot, Charlotte swept the floor in front of her with the blanket, clearing away glass as she made a path to the door. The pages on the table burned. Glowing bits floated on the breeze from the broken window. One touched near her ear. She jerked away, slapping at the heat and pain.

A second bottle through the window crashed at her feet. Charlotte screamed. The blanket caught fire. Flames licked at her nightgown.

She tossed the fiery blanket into the room and yanked the door open. "Fire! Fire!" She pounded on the door across the hall. "Fire!"

Her heart beat loud in her head, and smoke filled her lungs. Beating on doors, coughing and yelling, she took the stairs as fast as her injured foot would allow. Doors slammed open as the women who lived on the ground floor scrambled out. The light in the upstairs hall showed several sleepy men staring at her from their doorways.

"Fire!" She yelled again. "Get everyone out!"

She didn't wait to see if they'd move, but hobbled back down the stairs. Her bloody foot slipped. Charlotte cried out as pain radiated from her sole to her ankle.

Go, go, go! Make sure Mrs. Sullivan gets out!

The main floor was filling with smoke drifting through the hall to the open door. Shouts of "Fire!" sounded outside.

Coughing, her eyes watering, Charlotte pounded on the landlady's door. "Mrs. Sullivan! Mrs. Sullivan!"

She turned the knob. Inside, the cozy room was dark. Charlotte plowed into a low table, sending knickknacks crashing to the floor. She stumbled to the bedroom door and threw it open. Faint light through a single window allowed her to see Mrs. Sullivan sitting up in bed.

"What is it? What's wrong?" Her voice was high with fear.

"Fire. Come on."

Charlotte hoisted the older woman up by the arm, dragged

the blanket off the bed to wrap around her, and half carried her out of the building. People were running to the nearby laundry with buckets. Bells clanged down the street.

Rain and wind whooshed up the street, drenching them. Charlotte crossed the road to the front of McGruder's store where another older woman stood under the awning. She held her arms out to Mrs. Sullivan.

"Thank goodness you're safe, Alice."

Charlotte let Mrs. McGruder take the landlady in hand. She looked back at the rooming house. In the early glow of dawn, she saw thick, black smoke billowing from the building. A bucket brigade had started to set up from the laundry to the back of the house.

"Is everyone out?" she asked as she started forward.

A strong hand grabbed her arm. "Stay put."

She tried to pull out of James's grasp, but he held tight. "There may be some who—"

"I'll go. You're barefoot." He glanced down. When he brought his gaze back up to her face, there was concern in his eyes. "And bleeding."

Charlotte looked at her foot. After the initial pain, adrenaline must have taken over, for the most part, allowing her to function without feeling the wound. But now it started to hurt. Another gust of autumnal wind and rain set her to shivering.

James whipped off his coat and draped it around her shoulders. He reached into the side pocket, withdrawing a flashlight. "Stay here," he said, pointing the device at her.

He bolted toward the burning building, leaving no room for argument.

She drew his jacket closer, feeling his warmth as she watched the smoke thicken. Several dozen people were gathered in front of the burning building while a bucket brigade handed water down the line until the fire truck could arrive.

Flames flickered over the roof at the back of the rooming house. Beside her, Mrs. Sullivan gasped.

Finally, a clatter of hooves and shouting came from up the street. A team of six horses drew the tank cart in front of the building, snorting and stamping as the driver reined them in. Another carriage with four horses, its bell clanging and men atop it yelling, came up behind the first. Eight men scrambled to the pumping lever, four to a side. Two men attached the hose from the pump to the tank. Several other men unwound a hose coiled on the pump truck and hauled it to the back of the rooming house.

"Ready!" shouted one of the men at the tank.

"Ready!" replied someone on the hose.

The four men on one side of the pump pulled down while the others pushed up. The alternating action drew water from the tank and sent it into the hose. The line of the brigade continued passing sloshing buckets of water to the fire and empty ones back to the laundry.

Shivering, Charlotte leaned against the wall of McGruder's store, slid down onto her backside, and drew her knees up to her chest. From the front, Sullivan's looked intact. The fire seemed to have been contained at the rear. For now.

A few of Sullivan's residents watched in glassy-eyed shock. Did everyone get out? God, she hoped so. She glanced at Mrs. Sullivan and Mrs. McGruder. The landlady's face was drawn with fear and sorrow.

I should go over to Mrs. Sullivan, Charlotte thought, but she wasn't sure her shaky legs would hold her.

The sound of shattering glass made her jump.

"My God, Charlotte, are you hurt?" Michael knelt beside her, his black leather doctor's bag in hand. Gently, he held her chin and angled the left side of her face toward the light. "That doesn't look too deep."

She'd forgotten about the cut on her cheek. "I'm fine," she said, her voice rough. "Just a little smoke. And my foot."

Michael squinted at her foot in the poor light, touching the wound with the tip of his finger. Pain burned through her sole.

Charlotte sucked in a breath and winced, jerking her foot out of his hand.

"Sorry. That piece is in pretty deep. I'll need better light to get it out and to clean the wound properly."

James crossed the street, his soaked shirt clinging to his body and his hair plastered to his face. Soot streaked his clothing and cheeks. "Fire's under control. Back rooms are pretty bad."

"Anyone else hurt?" Michael asked, rising.

The deputy shook his head. "A few minor cuts and scrapes, but nothing serious. Everyone got out." He squatted down on the other side of Charlotte. "I think you got the worst of it. How's your foot?"

"She'll need stitches," Michael said. "I have to get her to my office."

James helped her to her feet. He held her arm, and, though she was feeling steady enough, she didn't mind having him there to lean on. "You can't walk. I can carry you."

"Deputy," someone called. "We need to move these people out of here."

He shot the man—the head fireman by his leather helmet—a glare.

"I can get her to my place," Michael said.

Charlotte swallowed hard and touched James's arm, stopping him before he went back to work. "How bad is it? The building?"

"The fire spread pretty quick. Would have jumped to the neighboring buildings if we hadn't had so much rain. We'll take a look when it's light, but I think you'll need to get some new clothes."

"And my typewriter?" She'd had a few pages of her manuscript on the table. Those were gone. Luckily, she'd sent off the bulk of the story several days before.

James's features softened. "We'll have to see."

"Do you know how it started?" Michael asked.

"Someone threw something through the window," she said,

reciting the facts. Somewhere in the back of her mind, Charlotte knew she should be more emotional than her words portrayed. Shock. The force of what happened would hit her later. "That's what woke me up. The crash, and glass hitting my face." She shook her head. "Why would someone risk the lives of everyone in the house just to get to me?"

James leaned closer, his voice low. "Because anyone willing to kill a pregnant girl probably doesn't have much regard for anyone who might be in the way." He glanced at Michael. "I'll be by later to talk to you, Charlotte." She started to shrug off his coat. He laid a hand on her shoulder. "Hang on to that."

Her face and body warmed despite the cold seeping into her nightgown. But the effect didn't last long, and she started shivering again. Michael put his arm around her shoulder.

"Send anyone with injuries down to me. I'll be up for a while."

"Will do." James touched his fingers to his forehead in his typical salute, then strode off, calling for people to clear the area.

"I need to talk to Mrs. Sullivan before we go."

Michael leaned closer, whispering in her ear. "Don't mention anything about someone threatening you. Not yet. It'll only scare her."

She had been ready to apologize to the poor woman, but he had a point. When Charlotte reached Mrs. Sullivan, leaning on Michael to walk, she took the landlady's cold hands in her own. "Are you all right? I'm so sorry this happened."

From the corner of her eye, she saw Michael's worried face, but he didn't say anything.

"Oh, my dear, such a terrible thing. Thank you so very much for waking me. I'd have been dead otherwise." Mrs. Sullivan squeezed her fingers. "Mrs. McGruder here will take me in for now, and I think the others have places to stay. Will you be all right?"

Charlotte nodded. "I'll be at my brother's."

"All our things . . ." Mrs. Sullivan's voice trailed off, and she gazed sadly at her business. Her home.

"I'll come back as soon as I can to help clean up," Charlotte said. "I just hope the damage is limited and the building is safe."

"There's a builder or two in town who can inspect it," Mrs. McGruder said. She was no taller than Mrs. Sullivan, but thin as a rail. "Come on, Alice. Let's get you inside and out of this rain."

The older women entered the store. The McGruders lived above it, if the lights burning in the windows on the second floor were any indication.

"All right, let's go." Michael turned his back to Charlotte and crouched down a bit. "Get on."

"Michael, we'll look silly." What a thing for the townspeople to see, their up-and-coming doctor carrying his sister piggyback. What would Ruth think? Charlotte covered her mouth to stifle the laugh that threatened. Good Lord, she was near hysterical from the morning's excitement. That had to be it.

"Better silly than you trying to walk three blocks on an injured foot," he said over his shoulder. "I'd never hear the end of *that,* for sure. Now get on."

She climbed on his back and wrapped her arms around his neck and legs around his waist. Michael hooked his arms under her legs and hoisted her into a more comfortable position.

"Tally-ho!" Charlotte said, gently tapping his thigh with her uninjured heel.

"Ruth's right." He grunted when he shifted her weight again. "You are such a card."

She hugged him tighter, and off they went.

Charlotte pulled on a pair of Michael's canvas trousers, tucked in the worn cotton shirt he'd lent her, and decided she needed a belt. The clothes were roomy and comfortable, and part of her envied men for the privilege of wearing pants in public. Women here learned the impracticality of wearing a dress or a skirt while doing physical labor. And trousers were considerably warmer. She'd been known to wear pants beneath her skirt on particularly cold days back in New York, but her mother would have been appalled to see Charlotte outside the house in them alone.

Luckily, Mother wasn't here. Besides, with Charlotte's own clothes destroyed in the fire and the pending mess of cleanup, trousers were the best choice for the time being.

She didn't want to think about what she'd find at Sullivan's. Not yet. Her nose scrunched with the acrid scent that still burned in her nostrils, even after several hours and a washup with Michael's strong antiseptic soap. The movement pulled at the drying plaster and bandage on her cheek. Reopening the cut might cause a larger scar than she suspected she'd have anyway, so she set her features to be as neutral as she could manage.

Hitching the pants up by the waistband, Charlotte limped to the other side of Michael's living quarters to the chest of drawers against the wall to search for a belt. She was able to put a little weight on the side of her foot with the cushioning from the wrap and a pair of thick socks. Michael had cleaned and stitched the wound, then wrapped it in a thick layer of bandages. Removing the piece of glass had hurt more than the stitches. The shard had felt like a knife blade, but was no larger than the pearl in one of her earrings.

She pulled open the top drawer. Socks, underwear, and long johns were stuffed inside. Charlotte searched for a tell-tale coil of leather. Her hand touched something crinkly. Several somethings, in fact. Curiosity getting the better of her, she pulled one out of the drawer and unfolded it. As she made out the obvious shape of a prophylactic, Michael came in from the exam room.

"Charlotte, Eddington's here to—" He stopped short, looking at what was in her hand. His face turned crimson, and he stiffly walked over to take the condom from her. "Do you mind?"

"I was looking for a belt, I swear. Not snooping." His lips pressed together; he didn't believe her. "I wouldn't do that, Michael. Besides, what does it matter? You and Ruth are adults who are soon to be married." Charlotte could scarcely believe her future sister-in-law would agree to get a jump on the honeymoon. By the deepening color on Michael's face and the way his gaze dropped, maybe she hadn't. "You're not using them with Ruth, are you?"

He stuffed the packets back under his clothing, focusing on the placement of socks and garters. "No," he said, his voice rough. His admission stunned her. Michael was cheating on his fiancée. Having relations with another woman. The world had surely gone insane. "A man has needs."

Shock changed to scorn. "Oh, please, Michael. Not that pathetic argument."

Though she couldn't fathom how he and Ruth had become a couple, let alone engaged, she couldn't condone infidelity.

"She knew."

Charlotte blinked up at her brother. "And she was fine with it?" That was not the Ruth she would have expected. "Wait, you said she knew, not she knows. Have you stopped seeing this other woman?"

Michael drew a hand over his face, smoothing his moustache, and looked her straight in the eye. "It was Darcy."

"What?" Charlotte couldn't have been more stunned if he'd named Tess Kavanagh or Mrs. Sullivan.

He glared at her, then hurried to shut the door. "Quiet," he admonished. "Eddington is in the office."

"Michael, how could you? She was—"

"A prostitute?" He said it in a harsh tone, but Charlotte wasn't sure if the harshness was meant for her or himself.

"Your patient." She couldn't help the sharpness in her voice.

His bravado didn't last long, and Michael's shoulders sagged. "I know. I shouldn't have started anything. But she was so sweet, so understanding of my . . . frustrations."

Charlotte almost blurted out that understanding the needs and frustrations of men had been Darcy's job, but she saw something in Michael's eyes she'd never seen before. Not even with Ruth. "My God, Michael. Did you love her?"

He pinched the bridge of his nose, his face contorted as if in pain. "I don't know. She was so easy to talk to." He looked at Charlotte. "I know. It was wrong to see her, to even imagine something like a normal life with her. That never would have happened. We knew it wouldn't go beyond what it was, but at the very least we were friends."

"And Ruth knew this." Charlotte still found that hard to believe.

"I was discreet and didn't speak of it. I only went into Brigit's for health checks. I left Darcy notes when I went to the house with times and dates I wanted to see her." He sat on the edge of the bed, elbows on knees, rubbing his cheeks. "Ruth didn't approve, of course, but, as long as I was careful, she agreed to look the other way."

Charlotte sat beside him. She didn't want to ask the next question, but had to. "Was the baby yours?"

Despite the evidence and claims of his caution, Michael didn't immediately deny the possibility. Charlotte's heart ached for him, but something approaching fear twisted in her stomach.

"I don't know," he said quietly, shaking his head. "We were careful, but condoms aren't infallible."

How well she knew that.

"But you didn't know she was pregnant until the autopsy, did you?"

His head came up. "No, of course not. I was as surprised as you. It made me sick to think someone purposely—" His eyes widened with shock and hurt. "Wait. Did you think *I* might have killed her?"

For a fleeting moment, she had, but she wasn't about to admit that to him. "Of course not." Charlotte gathered his hands in hers. "Michael, you have to tell James before someone else does."

"No one else knows. Darcy wouldn't have said anything. She never spoke about her . . . her other relations. I'm sure she didn't tell anyone about me."

Brigit had said she prided herself on her girls' discretion. But how good were they, really, at keeping their client lists to themselves?

"Maybe so, but if anyone ever saw her going to you or suspected anything, they might say as much to James." She couldn't believe she was having this conversation with her brother. "He's already considering that one of her customers might have killed her. You were there with us, talking about that very thing that night." Was that why Michael had seemed so on edge? "If your name comes from anywhere else, you'll be questioned. Better to come clean with him right away, don't you think?"

Michael's sideways glance told her that no, he didn't think it was better. But after a few moments he sighed and nodded. "I guess so. Come on, he's waiting in the office."

They both stood, and the trousers slid down Charlotte's hips. "I still need a belt."

Michael shook his head, retrieved one from the second drawer for her, then led the way into the other room while she threaded the belt through the loops.

It didn't take long for James to take her statement. There wasn't much to add to what she'd already told him about the firebombs breaking through her window. He finished writing her account in a small book with a decisive tap of pen on page.

"And you have no idea who might have done this?" he asked yet again. One dark eyebrow was raised. Of course he suspected she'd said or done something to someone that had instigated a more forceful warning than a note. She couldn't blame him, though that might have been due to her own guilt over riling Tess Kavanagh.

"I didn't see anyone."

"That's not what I asked." James narrowed his gaze and leaned forward on the desk. "We talked about this just the other night, Charlotte. How you're not supposed to be doing your own investigation. Remember?"

She crossed her arms. "Of course I remember. I'm not senile."

"No, but you are stubborn," he said, flipping the book closed. "Could someone have learned you had been given Darcy's coat and the contents?"

Charlotte shifted in the hard chair. She didn't say anything and found it difficult to maintain eye contact with the deputy. He was going to be angry.

Michael, leaning against the wall behind her, said, "Charlotte, tell the nice policeman what you did."

"I spoke to Tess Kavanagh yesterday."

James's scowl brought out his dimple. "What did you say to her?"

"I'd walked with Brigit to the bank, and we met Tess as she was leaving. They gave each other such cold looks, at first I thought it was a social differentiation thing." Charlotte knew she was rambling, delaying the inevitable, but she needed to explain herself. Not that it would likely help much. "I also noticed how very much alike they look. Like they could be sisters."

James straightened at that. "Sisters?" He thought about it for a few moments, then nodded. "All right. I can see the resemblance. They're rarely at the same events, as far as I know. But what did you say to Mrs. Kavanagh?"

"Nothing then," she said. "But I went to her home later and asked for an interview for my *Modern Woman* piece."

"And?" He drew the word out, clearly suspicious of Charlotte's actions.

"They had both given me very similar answers to questions about where they're from. I also asked if they'd ever been to Fairbanks, and both were hesitant about responding. I think that pretty much confirms our conclusion that they're the women in the photograph, don't you?"

Even if James agreed, Charlotte was also pretty sure he'd be upset.

James closed his eyes, his lips moving silently, as if in prayer. When he looked at her again, she resisted the instinct to scoot back on the chair. They needed to know for sure who was in the article Darcy had hidden. Now they did. "So now both Tess and Brigit know you think they had something to do with the crimes in Fairbanks a decade ago."

"No, they don't," she said, splitting hairs with her next words. "Only Tess does."

The deputy threw his hands up and rose from the seat. He turned his back to her, grumbling something about damned meddling reporters.

"Maybe it's not so bad," Michael said. He stood beside her, hand on her shoulder in support. "Maybe this will be too much for them and one of them will confess."

James spun on his heel and glared at both of them. "Maybe. And maybe they'll hare off on the next steamer before I can get solid *proof*," he said while pinning Charlotte with his hard gaze, "that either of them actually killed her."

"I took a chance, I know," she admitted. "But I don't think Brigit killed her, and if Tess is involved, it's not directly."

Chapter 15

"What are you talking about?" Michael asked. "Why confront Tess if you don't think she was involved?"

"I needed to see her reaction for myself." Charlotte got up. Putting pressure on her injured foot made her wince, but moving helped her think. She paced gingerly between the two men. "Brigit's desire to learn who killed Darcy feels too real to me. She's not just putting on a show. And Tess was appalled when I suggested she had a hand in the murder."

"They're living lies," James said, "so their acting abilities are probably well beyond casual observation."

She faced him. They were close enough that she had to look up into his eyes. "Agreed, but that lie is in regard to their past in Fairbanks. To possible involvement with a man's death, true, but I never mentioned him. I think they're guilty of trying to reinvent themselves here, and had to pay Darcy to keep the secret. But I don't think either of those women killed her."

"Then who?" Michael asked. He came alongside her and gently took her arm. "Sit down, Charlotte, before you tear open those stitches."

She did as he instructed, tapping on the desk since she

couldn't pace. "You saw the condition of Darcy's body. The blows were concentrated at her stomach. Whoever killed her was furious over her pregnancy."

"Couldn't Brigit have been angry over it?" James suggested. He sat on the corner of the desk.

Charlotte shook her head. "I don't think so. She has a son, so she knows pregnancy is a risk in her business."

"The father of the child." Michael stared hard at her. She wanted him to tell James about his relationship with Darcy, and he didn't like it.

"More likely," she said. "Someone important. Maybe even the mayor."

"The mayor?" James and Michael said simultaneously.

"Are you out of your mind?" Michael asked.

"What in the name of God makes you suspect the mayor?" James stared at her as if a third eye had grown in her forehead. "There are plenty of men who could have been the father."

Charlotte and Michael locked gazes. "It's just an idea. Until we know for sure, it could be anyone. Right?"

No one spoke for several seconds. Though she couldn't see his face, Charlotte suspected James was frowning at them.

"Is there something someone wants to tell me?" he asked. "Charlotte? Doc?"

Michael flinched first. "Damn it. Fine." He looked at James. "I was seeing Darcy."

The deputy's lips pressed together. There wasn't anger so much as irritation in his expression. "And you chose not to tell me because you didn't want to be under suspicion."

"He had nothing to do with her death," Charlotte said. "Michael wants to be up-front, that's all."

"You knew this." James took a step forward, hands clenched, then stopped. Visibly calming himself, James drew in a deep breath. "You knew he was seeing her, and you were protecting him. I get it."

"She just found out, Eddington," Michael said. "Charlotte

convinced me it was best to give you all the information. Yes, so I could be ruled out as a suspect."

"Where were you that night, Doc?" James's tone was 100-percent deputy. Such doggedness pushed the boundaries of trust between the three of them. Yet, Charlotte admired his professionalism even as it annoyed her.

But Michael didn't blink. "At a city council meeting until nearly midnight. We were discussing land purchases."

"Was the mayor there?" Charlotte asked.

"For a little while," Michael said. "He left at ten or so."

She gave James a significant look. "Giving him time to go to Brigit's."

James crossed his arms. "Charlie said the man who gave him the note was built more like your brother, not the mayor."

Damn. She'd forgotten that. "Unless the mayor had someone else deliver it. He'd be very conspicuous and wouldn't want to be seen anywhere near Brigit's if he wanted to meet with Darcy." It was a bit of a stretch, but not a completely insane supposition. "Perhaps the man delivered the note, then Darcy met Kavanagh outside. She tells him she's pregnant. Between that and the blackmail, he goes off the deep end and kills her."

Silence hung between them as they considered such a scenario. The more she thought about it, the more it made sense to Charlotte. Frank Kavanagh certainly had the physical strength to subdue a smaller woman like Darcy. He had the motive to shut her up about his past, even if he wasn't the father of her baby. And he had opportunity to get to Brigit's that night.

"It's a decent line of thought," James said, surprising her, "but I need proof or a witness."

"That is a bit of a sticking point," Michael quipped.

James scratched the scruff on his jaw. "Yeah. And I can't focus solely on Kavanagh to the exclusion of all other possibilities. As far as real evidence goes, anyone could have killed Darcy." He narrowed his eyes at Michael as if imagining her brother doing something so heinous. Before she or Michael could challenge him, the deputy seemed to shake off the thought. "I need something solid. I searched the probable path from Brigit's to the railroad tracks again. Found a cigar stub, a shoe, and a button."

"Those could belong to anyone," Michael said. "If it makes you feel better, I don't smoke cigars and have all my shoes and buttons."

A wry smile quirked James's mouth, and he gave a humorless grunt.

"The mayor smokes cigars," Charlotte reminded them.

"So do half the men in town," Michael said.

"We'll figure it out." She'd ease up on the line of thought pointing to the mayor for now, but he was her prime suspect. "Can I look at your findings?"

James's intense gaze shot straight to her. "You've been involved more than necessary, and obviously you're getting under someone's skin."

A bubble of pride formed in her chest, but Charlotte could tell by his demeanor that he wasn't praising her efforts. Not in the least.

"With threats and now an attempt on your life, you will not make a move without consulting me. As I asked you before." He leaned over her, bracing himself on the arms of the chair and bringing his face within inches of hers. The smell of burned building emanated from his clothing. "If you do anything—anything at all—without talking to me, I will arrest you for obstruction. Is that clear, Miss Brody?"

The back of her neck prickled. Part of her understood James was trying to keep her safe, but there was an overwhelming desire to shove him aside and tell him she could look out for herself. Physically, she knew she would never be able to move him. So she resorted to her preferred method of dealing with an overactive sense of control.

"I understand," she said, acknowledging his threat, but not agreeing to the conditions. She wouldn't withhold evidence or information, but she wasn't about to ask anyone's permission to do her job either.

James stared at her for a moment longer. Surely he felt the tension vibrating between them, as she did, and realized she hadn't conceded. Before he could say more, someone opened the outer door.

"Oh. Sorry to interrupt," a male voice said. James straightened and stepped away from her. A man of forty or so stood in the doorway. "Deputy, the marshal was asking for you."

James reached for his coat hanging on the back of the chair. "I'll be right there." The man departed with a nod to each of them. James shrugged into his mackinaw, the one he'd lent her just hours before. "The rooming house won't be safe to live in."

"There's a smaller hotel closer to the railroad yard," Michael said.

"The Lakeview," James acknowledged. "It's a bit more expensive than Sullivan's, but cheaper than the Windsor. They might have a room available."

"Thank you for the information, Deputy."

He frowned at her use of his title rather than his name. "Come by later to look at what I found, but I don't know what good it'll do."

Shoving his hat on his head, James touched the brim then strode out.

"What's going on between you two?" Michael asked.

Charlotte stood. "Nothing. Nothing at all. I'll need one of your spare jackets and pairs of boots so we can go see what's left of my things."

Nothing. There was nothing left of Charlotte's belongings except for the metal workings of her Royal typewriter among the scorched bits and burnt wood of the carrying case. Darcy's coat had been destroyed as well, but luckily James had taken possession of the newspaper clippings and money as evidence.

Charlotte and Michael stood at the back of Sullivan's, peering into the dark, smoldering space that had been her room through the huge hole in the wall. Several rooms above and around hers had suffered similar damage. The rest of the rooming house had filled with smoke and then been drenched in water. The rain had stifled the spread of the fire to other buildings and allowed the exterior to remain somewhat intact. Thankfully, no one had been hurt, but the interior, and much of what was in it, was destroyed.

Poor Mrs. Sullivan had lost almost everything, and it was Charlotte's fault.

The weight of anger, fear, and guilt pressed in on Charlotte, making it difficult to breathe. Michael's arm settled around her shoulders.

"We'll replace your things eventually," he said, reassuring her with a kiss to the top of her head.

It wasn't the loss of material goods that bothered her so much, though her favorite books had gone up in flames. No, it was the idea that someone had wanted her hurt—possibly dead—for what she knew, and was willing to endanger others for it. Even if she didn't really know anything.

"Maybe James is right," she said, sniffing. The stench of burned wood and other material made her eyes water. She'd left Yonkers because of broken windows and angry letters. This was worse. Much worse. "I should just forget the whole thing before someone else is killed."

At Michael's office, she'd instinctively wanted to oppose James, to do anything she had to in order to get to the bottom of the case. But now, standing outside the ruins of her room, the ruins of other people's lives, she knew she couldn't risk it.

Michael squeezed her tight against him, but didn't argue. He agreed with the deputy. She'd gone too far. Charlotte wiped her eyes and nose. She'd find a new place to live and go to work for Mr. Toliver reporting on the happenings in Cordova's social circles, perhaps the odd burglary or accident. She'd need to do something to make enough money to get back to the States. Alaska might not be her refuge after all.

"Charlotte?" Brigit picked her way along the debris-filled path beside the building. She lifted her dark skirt away from charred boards. Her plain hat and coat made her look like any other woman in town, her typical daytime persona. "Are you all right?"

Michael lowered his arm. "I'll go check on Mrs. Sullivan. Will you be okay here?"

Charlotte nodded, feeling the tension between Michael and Brigit as they eyed one another. Surely Brigit knew he'd been seeing Darcy. Was that part of the reason for their strife? Brigit had said something about Darcy's needing him at her funeral. Did Brigit know there might have been more between Michael and the young lady of the evening?

Did she know about Charlotte's chat with Tess? Probably not. Or at least not yet. And if Tess didn't tell Brigit, what did that mean? That Charlotte's assumption they were sisters was wrong? That her supposition that Brigit was innocent and Tess knew something was correct? Perhaps neither woman knew a damn thing, and Charlotte was dreadfully mistaken about everything.

After Michael was out of earshot, Brigit stepped closer. She took in the burned-out rooms and shook her head. "I'm so sorry. It's a miracle no one was badly hurt, or killed."

"Just a few minor injuries," Charlotte said. The cut on her cheek itched, and her foot started to throb as if in response.

Brigit glanced at the drying glob of plaster on Charlotte's face. "You poor dear. I have some dresses, skirts, blouses, that sort of thing, you can have to replace what you lost." She gave Charlotte's borrowed men's attire a quick perusal. A teasing smile curved her lips. "Though you look rather adorable in trousers. Fits right in here."

Charlotte smiled at the madam's attempt to brighten her

mood. "They're very comfortable. I may take to wearing them upon occasion." Both of them laughed. "But thank you. I appreciate the offer."

"I'd offer you a room at the house too," Brigit said, her grin turning wry, "but I don't think that would work well for you."

Charlotte could imagine the wagging tongues should she move into Brigit's house. Much of Cordova seemed to have the live-and-let-live sort of attitude she'd expected, but the push to make the town more civilized and proper meant behavior was keenly observed by some. For Michael's sake, she'd exercise some measure of care.

"I don't think it would work out for either of us. I told you before, I already have a job." Charlotte winked at the other woman, who laughed again.

She enjoyed the rapport with Brigit, and something that felt like friendship seemed to be forming between them. But if Tess was her sister, Brigit would soon learn that Charlotte suspected them of wrongdoing in Fairbanks a decade ago. That accusation alone could cause a rift. The thought of losing their tenuous relationship sent a pang of regret through Charlotte.

"I can bring some things around to your brother's for you later today," Brigit said. "And don't worry, they'll be quite appropriate."

"That would be great. Thank you so much." Charlotte laid a hand on Brigit's arm and gave it a light squeeze.

Brigit looked down at where they touched. She covered Charlotte's hand with hers, her grin wide as she raised her head. Her gaze flicked away, then back to Charlotte. "I have to get on with my errands. I just wanted to see how you were doing. See you later."

She made her way back toward Main Street, head high and back straight.

Charlotte watched until Brigit disappeared around the corner of the neighboring building. She could see them becoming friends, despite what societal boundaries might dictate. If they managed to get past the rough patch that was sure to come, Charlotte wouldn't give a fig what the rest of the townspeople thought. She liked Brigit and would cherish a friendship with her while she was in Cordova.

"Was that Brigit O'Brien?" Ruth asked. Her sudden appearance startled Charlotte. Ruth glared in the direction Brigit had gone, then her blue eyes zeroed in on Charlotte. "You shouldn't associate with her if at all possible, Charlotte. She's a wicked woman who perpetuates sin in our community."

Charlotte suppressed a sigh. Ruth's vehemence wasn't a surprise; she'd shown plenty of distain for Darcy at lunch the other day. "Brigit was offering her condolences over the fire and some clothing to replace what I lost."

"I'd go naked before accepting charity from the likes of that woman. I'm sure I have more appropriate clothing for you."

Charlotte tried to maintain a congenial smile. "Oh. Thank you."

"You were sounding quite chummy with her." With her stern gaze, Ruth looked a lot like her mother. Poor Michael. "People will get the wrong idea if you're seen with her. They'll assume you approve of her ways."

Charlotte shrugged. "I've told you, I have no problem with Brigit and her girls, as long as they aren't forced into doing anything they don't want to do."

Ruth's eyes blazed. "I can't believe you support their fornication, their sinning. They exert their wicked temptations on God-fearing men and spread disease like rats."

It probably wasn't the best time to remind Ruth that her fiancé was the one who kept the women healthy. Charlotte certainly wasn't going to bring up Michael's physical relationship with Darcy.

"Those filthy whores are a blight on our society," Ruth continued. "They need to be removed from this town one way or another."

"Does that include murdering them?"

The fire in Ruth's eyes didn't waver in the least. "They dance with the devil and get what they deserve. Every one of them. How could you defend them?"

"How could you condone killing a woman, no matter who she was?" Charlotte could understand Ruth's anger over Michael's affair with Darcy, but whatever happened to forgiveness? "She was a human being, Ruth. One of God's children, as your own father pointed out."

"She was a whore and a sinner. She and her bastard will rot in hell." Ruth spun on her heel and stomped back along the path around the opposite side of Sullivan's.

Charlotte stared after her for several moments, the woman's words echoing in her head. She'd heard plenty of rhetoric against sin in her time, but Ruth's rabid reaction to Darcy, Brigit, and the others seemed beyond the pale. Someone needed to stand up to the narrow-minded proselytizers of this town, to change views on the "lesser" women of Cordova. James would do his best to find Darcy's killer, but Charlotte would be the one to make the people care.

A steady rain began to fall. Charlotte cast a final glance at the ruins of her room, then went in search of Michael. She found him as he came out of McGruder's.

"Mrs. Sullivan seems to be holding her own," he said, flipping his collar up and tugging his hat down. "I have another patient to check on. Are you heading to the house?"

"I was going to have a cup of coffee at the café to wake myself up," she said. The early morning awakening was starting to catch up to her. "Then do some shopping here."

Michael reached into his pocket. He sorted out some notes and coins, then handed them to her. "Have McGruder's boy deliver the order. I don't want you putting any more strain on that foot."

Charlotte pocketed the money. "All right."

He laid a hand on her arm and searched her face. "You okay? Are you in pain?"

He meant the injury to her foot, but that didn't feel too terrible.

"I'm fine. Just tired." She attempted a smile. No reason to bother him about Ruth's latest rant.

He chucked her under the chin. "Take some aspirin and have a nap. I'll be out most of the afternoon. Lock the front door and put the 'Out of Office' sign up. No one will bother you."

He gave her a quick peck on the cheek, then headed to his next appointment.

Charlotte limped to the café. Inside, the air was heavily scented with coffee and bacon. Her stomach rumbled despite her not feeling hungry. She settled at a table where Henry took her order for coffee and a bacon and chicken sandwich.

Fatigue enveloped Charlotte. Once she ate, she hoped she'd have the energy to go to McGruder's. Her foot throbbed in time with a growing headache. Wonderful. Maybe shopping would have to wait. But she didn't want to walk back to Michael's then return to the store later. Might as well get the errand over with and get off her foot as soon as she could.

Henry delivered her food. The café wasn't crowded, and Charlotte appreciated the quiet while she ate. She was halfway through the sandwich when a flicker of shadow from the large window caught her attention. She looked up. Was that Michael staring in at her? He'd said he had appointments all afternoon, but maybe he needed to tell her something. Why didn't he just come inside?

She started toward the door. The figure outside dashed away.

Henry came up beside her, coffeepot in hand. "Was that Sam Bartlett again?"

"Sam? I thought it was my brother."

Henry shook his head. "Nah, it was Sam. I've seen him doing that a couple times lately. Though I can understand why you'd think so. They look a lot alike. More coffee, Miss Brody?"

Chapter 16

Charlotte placed her order with Mrs. McGruder, was assured the delivery would arrive that afternoon, then limped back to Michael's. Keeping her footing on the slick road as the wind whipped up the street made her foot ache and sapped her energy. By the time she set out the sign and locked the door, her head pounded as well. Some aspirin powder and a nap would do the trick.

But despite bone-weary tiredness, when she lay down on the bed, she couldn't sleep. When she closed her eyes, images of the fire and her ravaged room played like a film. Sometimes the roar of flames or her own shouts for the others to get out filled her ears, or the phantom bite of smoke filled her nostrils. Forcing those thoughts out of her head only replaced them with bits and pieces of earlier conversations.

I should just forget the whole thing. . . .

It's a miracle no one was badly hurt, or killed. She was a whore and a sinner. She and her bastard will rot in hell.

Charlotte's eyes flew open, and she sat up. *She and her bastard.* Ruth was referring to Darcy's baby. How had she known? Did Michael tell her? Ruth had likely been incensed enough about his relationship with Darcy. Revealing that the young prostitute was pregnant, possibly with his child, would have been foolish.

But how else could Ruth have found out? James certainly wouldn't have told her.

"It must have been Michael." Charlotte shook her head, befuddled by her brother's interpretation of honesty.

Perhaps he wanted a clean conscience going into the marriage. Or maybe by admitting his sins, and the possible paternity of Darcy's child, he was giving Ruth the option to call off the wedding. Considering his feelings for Darcy might have been stronger than those he had for Ruth, that would have been a safe route to take in seeking to end their relationship. He'd suffer humiliation for cheating on her, and Ruth's reputation would remain intact.

Charlotte heard the outer door open. She scrubbed her hands over her face, ignored the not-quite-gone headache, and rose to meet Michael as he came in.

"Oh, I thought you'd be asleep. Did you get some rest?"

Charlotte crossed the room to the sink and filled a pot with water. "A little. Do you want some tea?"

"Yes, thank you." He set his black bag on the floor against the wall, and hung up his coat and hat. "How's the foot?"

She shrugged. "Hurts a bit, but not too bad." Charlotte put the pot on the stove and added some coal to the firebox. "Michael, did you tell Ruth about Darcy's condition?"

He sat at the small table, pausing in the removal of a boot. "No, of course not. Why?"

"Are you sure?"

"Yes, I'm sure. It's something only you and I and Eddington know. Probably Blaine as well." He dropped the second boot to the floor. "It's not public knowledge."

Charlotte's stomach fluttered. "Ruth mentioned Darcy and her ba—her baby when I saw her this morning. Would she have spoken to Darcy at all?"

He scoffed. "No. Never."

"Then how would she have known?"

They stared silently at each other for several moments. As far as they knew, Darcy hadn't told anyone she was pregnant. No one knew, except perhaps her killer, considering the focus of the girl's injuries. There was only one conclusion, if that was the case, and it dawned in Michael's eyes just as Charlotte was about to say it.

"No," he said emphatically. "That's not possible. Ruth is a good person. She would never do anything so horrid."

"You didn't see or hear her talking about Darcy this morning." Charlotte couldn't believe she was considering the petite blonde as a suspect, but what else would explain her knowledge of the pregnancy? "She's disgusted by anything associated with Brigit or her girls and knew you were seeing Darcy."

"And she was willing to ignore it until the wedding." Michael's fists clenched in his lap. "Don't you think I know my fiancée well enough to determine if she's a killer?"

"Do you? People hide their true selves all the time, Michael."

From little white lies and minor denials to acting like a completely different person, only the rare few showed who they really were to the outside world. There was always something people kept to themselves, for one reason or another. She and Michael had secrets. Richard had pretended to be something he wasn't for as long as it served his purposes.

Michael stood and closed the short distance between them. "No. It wasn't her." His words were emphatic, but Charlotte saw the glimmer of doubt behind his need to believe Ruth would never do such a thing. "No," he said again, and walked away from Charlotte.

Of course he didn't want to believe, but it made sense to Charlotte.

"What about the mayor?" he asked. He kept his back to her as he prepared cups for tea. "That makes as much sense as anything, and Kavanagh certainly had as much to lose as far as reputation and finances were concerned. Either he'd be revealed as a fraud and possibly a murderer or he could slowly be bled dry."

She had to agree with him on that, especially since she'd been the one pointing to the mayor. But Ruth's words still niggled at her. "She knows more than she should."

Michael spun around, his face red. "Maybe you heard her wrong, Charlotte. Maybe you dislike her so much you want to pin this on her, despite lacking proof."

"I don't dislike her." The lie came easily, but they usually did when Michael confronted her about her feelings. She had to start being more honest with him. "And I didn't mishear her. She said something about Darcy's bastard. That was the word she used."

That made him hesitate for a moment, but then he shook his head, dismissing the notion again. "No. It's not enough to convince me the reverend's daughter is responsible for this."

"Because being religious automatically clears you of wrongdoing?"

He slammed his teacup down, sloshing hot water on the stove. "Enough. I won't have you maligning my fiancée and her values. Find some solid proof before you accuse people of murder."

He crossed to where he'd left his boots and yanked them on.

"Michael, wait." She started toward him, but he cast such an angry, hurtful glare at her that it stopped Charlotte in her tracks.

He snatched his coat and hat off the pegs and slammed the door behind him. The outer door slammed as well, rattling the cabin.

Heart pounding, Charlotte took a moment to catch her breath and calm down. Her questions about Ruth had hit him harder than she'd expected, but she shouldn't have been surprised. She'd accused his fiancée of murder. How much more upsetting a topic could there be?

But she couldn't ignore the gut feeling that told her she was on the right track. As painful as it might be, she'd get the proof Michael and James would need.

Charlotte donned her boots, coat, and hat. After she secured a messenger, she'd talk to James. And be prepared for his wrath.

James glanced up from papers on his desk. He started to grin when their eyes met, but his features quickly changed into a look of suspicion. "What did you do?"

Charlotte crossed to the desk and sat. She didn't like the fact he could read her so easily. "Something happened this morning, and I decided to go with my gut."

His frown deepened. "Without consulting me, like I asked you to."

"Yes, but let me explain." She told him about the conversation with Ruth. "I think she did it, James."

He crossed his arms. "No proof other than that? I can barely justify questioning her over what she said, let alone arrest her."

"I know there's no physical evidence."

He opened a lower drawer in his desk and withdrew a large brown envelope. He unwound the string that secured the flap. "Just this, and there's no telling who they belong to or how long they were out there."

James shook the contents onto his desk. A flattened shoe, a smaller envelope with something thick inside, and a wooden toggle button thudded on the surface. She opened the smaller envelope and shook out the cigar stub. It was damp, the paper band mostly torn. Was it the mayor's? She sniffed, but only smelled wet tobacco, not the burnt orange of Kavanagh's favorite brand.

She slid the cigar stub back into its envelope and laid the envelope beside the other items. So much for that idea.

"Sometimes a cigar's just a cigar, Charlotte."

She quirked an eyebrow at him. "And sometimes it isn't."

"It *could* be the mayor's," he conceded, "but he's not the

only one who smokes that brand. Nothing points anywhere near Ruth Bartlett either. No witnesses or suspicions other than yours." James cocked his head. "What does Michael think?"

Charlotte rose and started pacing. "That I hate her and would do anything to damage her reputation."

"Well, you certainly don't like her much."

She spun to face him. "How would you know?"

"I've seen you together," he said, "and when you talk about her, a wrinkle develops between your eyes. It's there now."

Charlotte touched a finger to the spot over her nose. He was right. "But I wouldn't suspect her if I didn't have reason."

"Like you have reason to suspect Mayor and Mrs. Kavanagh and Brigit O'Brien?"

"Their motivation is solid. You know that as well as I do."

James stood and stepped in front of her. "It is solid, and with some more questioning it may even be provable. But other than the mayor's leaving the council meeting early, there is nothing to put him anywhere near Darcy that night."

"No, a different man gave Charlie that note," Charlotte said. "A man who looked like Michael." She glanced down at the desk, and her gaze locked on the button. "Sam Bartlett's coat was missing a button the other night. And he's built a lot like Michael."

James's eyes widened. "You don't honestly believe—"

"Sam Bartlett looks enough like Michael that Charlie must have thought about Michael when he was describing the person." She watched James's expression change from shocked to thoughtful. Taking advantage, she pressed on with her theory. "What if Ruth was upset over Michael's relationship, and Sam used the note to lure Darcy out of Brigit's. Then Ruth killed her."

James shook his head. "She's a slip of a thing. Not strong enough to do that sort of damage."

"Maybe Sam did it. Or the two of them did it together."

"Sam Bartlett won't even look a person in the eye. You think he had the wherewithal to kill a woman?"

She'd sat across from Sam for over an hour, and the boy had hardly made a sound. He ran from her greeting on the street. The only thing that came close to Sam Bartlett's being any sort of threat was when he'd been behind her that night as she approached his family's home.

He was shy and skittish, but that didn't eliminate him as a suspect or an accessory.

"I guess we'll find out soon enough," she said, and took a deep breath. "I sent an anonymous note to Ruth telling her I knew what she'd done and was going to tell you if she didn't give me money to keep quiet."

James's expression darkened. "I should arrest you right this second."

She raised a hand as if that could stop him. "Hear me out. I told her to meet me at Nirvana Park tonight to discuss terms of payment. You go early and hide, then I'll get her to confess."

"That's the dumbest plan I've ever heard. And too dangerous. No."

Charlotte crossed her arms. Admittedly, it was pretty damn stupid, but what choice did they have? "Do you have a better way to get her to confess? We have nothing, James. I won't sleep until Darcy's killer is in jail, and I think you feel the same."

He rubbed his temples, his face a mask of irritation. "You're gonna be the death of me. Or yourself. What time is the meeting?"

The somewhat remote Nirvana Park northeast of the town proper was the perfect location for private, late-night meetings to discuss blackmail and murder. With only the small beam of a flashlight to guide her over the rough dirt road paralleling the lake, and the darkness pressing in around her, Charlotte was beginning to agree with James: This was the dumbest idea in the history of dumb ideas.

Two things kept her moving forward. She was determined to see Darcy's killer receive justice, and she wanted to prove herself to James. The former was more important than the latter, of course, but a little self-satisfaction would be nice.

She just hoped she was right.

The lights of the railroad yard to the right peeked through the spruce trees and willow brush. The buildings were too distant to offer adequate illumination anyway, and the smattering of homes along the road petered out not far from where she'd turned off Main Street. Cloud cover had kept the full moon hidden for most of the night. Charlotte soon reached the wider part of the road that indicated the entrance to Nirvana Park, her light playing over the carved wooden sign above the path leading deeper into the woods.

Were there bears in the park? Maybe so, but Charlotte was likely in more danger if Ruth waited for her.

When Charlotte had visited earlier in the day to familiarize herself with the layout, the glass and metal trinkets suspended from tree limbs by ropes and wires and the poles carved with fanciful figures had given the park a whimsical air. It was a popular location to relax and enjoy the peaceful surroundings along the lake, she'd been told. But by night, the chimes sounded dissonant, and shadows made the faces in the wood seem ominous and leering.

She suppressed a shudder and pressed onward.

In her note, Charlotte had instructed Ruth to meet at the bridge that crossed the creek running through the center of the park. James was hiding here somewhere. He had left over an hour before to find a place and wait, warning Charlotte that he wouldn't make himself known until Ruth gave her confession. It was reassuring to know he was around, but Charlotte still felt very much alone.

Her boot hit the edge of the first plank. The thud sounded

very loud in the deep darkness, louder than the slow-flowing water in the narrow creek. Charlotte scanned the ten-foot span of the bridge. Her beam of light fell upon a pair of heavy black shoes and the hem of a dress. Before she could bring the flashlight up, Ruth's beam caught her in the face. Charlotte squinted, trying to keep an eye on Ruth in the glare. How long had she been waiting there? Did she know James was nearby?

"I should have known it was you," Ruth said. "You've been a menace ever since you arrived."

Charlotte's eyes adjusted, and she focused on the woman across the bridge. "I'm not nearly the menace that other folks in this town are."

"We don't abide sinners here," she said. "That includes whores and blackmailers."

Charlotte gave her a knowing grin. "But at least I'm not a murderer."

"What makes you think I am?"

Clever. Ruth was trying to get Charlotte to tip her own hand first. Charlotte would give her brother's fiancée a hint. "You said something this morning that made me realize you knew more about Darcy than you should have."

In the glow of the flashlight, Ruth frowned. "What?"

"You said she and her bastard would rot in hell. How did you know Darcy was pregnant?" Charlotte watched Ruth's eyes narrow and her free hand clench. At least she didn't have a weapon. Not one she could access immediately, anyway. "No one but Michael, James Eddington, and I knew about that. And her killer, considering the condition of her body."

Ruth's features contorted into a mask of hatred, the indirect light making her appear demonic. "She was a filthy whore who deserved to die."

"She was a young woman, a human being," Charlotte said, anger rising at this woman who had decided to play judge, jury, and executioner. "She and Michael had intimate relations and you hated that, hated her, despite your supposed acceptance of his 'carnal needs.' It became too much to bear, didn't it, Ruth? What she was doing with him?"

"I wanted to talk to her. Tell her to leave Michael alone. I had Sam bring a note, like Michael said he did when he wanted her to meet him up at his room." Ruth shook her head, disgust on her face. "I told Sam the other night he had to go back and collect all of Michael's letters to her, but he didn't get the chance."

It must have been Sam and Ruth in the alley beside the Windsor the night of the mayor's party talking about the papers, not Tess and Frank referring to the articles Darcy had kept.

No one had mentioned finding notes from Michael in Darcy's room. Had she burned them, or hidden them somewhere, as she'd hidden the newspaper articles and money? Michael had mentioned getting word to Darcy about dates and times to meet. Surely he would have been smart enough to not explicitly request her in his private room or sign his name.

Ruth slammed her hand down on the bridge railing. "Only a wife should see to her husband's needs. None other. I told her to leave him alone, that tempting him during their health exams only added to her sins. But she laughed at me. Said Michael admitted he had more fun with her than he could ever have with me. And claimed that she and their baby would be his family."

Even in the low light, Charlotte saw Ruth shaking with rage. She'd been angry at Darcy, at Michael. Admitting she had spoken to the girl wasn't the same as confessing to murder.

"She was going to take Michael away from you," Charlotte said, "so you killed her."

Come on, come on. Say it.

"No." Ruth's fist clenched again. "I told the bitch she could have him. Then she opened her filthy mouth again."

"What did she say?"

"That maybe Sam was the father." Her lip curled into a sneer. "Or Michael. She wasn't sure. She ensnared my brother and my fiancé with her wicked ways. But she'd leave Michael alone and not tell everyone she was having *his* baby if we paid her."

If Darcy had been blackmailing the mayor and his wife, as well as her boss, why not extort even more money from the Bartletts? But it looked like Darcy might have gone a little too far. Maybe she hadn't expected the reverend's daughter to be so vengeful.

"She could claim Sam was the father even if she left Michael out of it. I had to protect my family from her. And now you're threatening me with the same thing?" Ruth leapt forward, flashlight raised over her head.

Charlotte stumbled back as the metal and light swept in front of her face. Her own beam jerked up into the trees, adding to the chaotic dance of light and shadow. She caught herself before she fell. Ruth brought her arm around in a backswing. Charlotte ducked, catching the blow on her right shoulder rather than in the face.

The pain would have been worse if she hadn't been wearing two heavy shirts and Michael's old winter coat, but it threw her off balance. Her retaliating swing missed Ruth's face and glanced off her arm.

Ruth grunted, slipped in the wet duff, and dropped her flashlight. Charlotte recovered her footing. She shoved Ruth and bolted in the opposite direction. Her own heavy breathing blotted out other sounds. Had James heard them? Where was he?

"James!"

Charlotte stopped to catch her breath and listen for him. To her right, she heard grunts and muffled shouts. The crack of a branch. Was James in trouble? She started toward the noise.

A blow to her lower back sent her sprawling. Still clutching the flashlight, she kept her face and head from hitting the ground, letting her arms and free hand take the brunt of the fall. The sting of scrapes and bruises would come later. Ruth's weight on her back pinned her down.

"You rotten bitch," Ruth yelled, yanking Charlotte's head back by a handful of hair. "You're just like her. You whore."

Sensing a blow coming, Charlotte turned her head away. Ruth didn't release her hold. Charlotte's scalp burned as hair was pulled from her head. The punch landed on her ear. Stars exploded in her ringing head, but Charlotte ignored them. With strength borne of desperation to escape, she pushed up onto her hands and knees and threw the smaller woman off her back.

Ruth didn't land far away. She started to rise. Charlotte braced her upper body and delivered a solid kick to the other woman's face. Ruth tumbled sideways, then lay still.

Charlotte scrambled to her feet. She could hear a second scuffle not far away and ran in that direction. The jumping flashlight beam created pockets of darkness, hiding roots and rocks that caught her feet. The knob of a root pressed into the wound on the bottom of her foot, shooting pain up her leg and making her stumble. She couldn't stop now. James might need her help.

She reached a small clearing where her light found Sam Bartlett straddling James's chest. James held the boy's wrists with both his hands, his face contorted in pain as he kept a pocketknife blade from plunging into his face. Sam's expression was murderous.

Charlotte darted forward and grabbed a short carved post that must have been knocked over during their fight. She cracked the heavy wood across Sam's head. He howled and fell to the side. James rolled away. He sprang to his feet, panting. Before Sam could recover, James snatched the knife from him and tossed it aside. He flipped the boy onto his stomach, securing his hands with a pair of metal cuffs from his coat pocket.

"Are you all right?" Charlotte knelt beside James and cupped his face in her hands. One eye was swollen and partially closed. His nose was bleeding, possibly broken for a second or even third time.

James's crooked grin made her smile despite the last few minutes of pain and panic. "I'll live. The little bastard caught me by surprise, and sure can fight."

She gently brushed his bloody lip with the pad of her thumb. "So can his sister."

James's head jerked up, and he scanned the area. "Where is she?"

"Near the bridge. I think she's unconscious, but I'm not sure."

James helped Charlotte to her feet. "If she isn't, she won't get far. I heard what she said just before Junior here jumped me."

Charlotte shook her head, a sudden sadness and pity wending through her. "Poor Ruth."

He gave her a startled look. "Poor Ruth? She killed a girl and tried to kill you. I don't think I'd be so charitable or forgiving under the circumstances."

"I don't know. I do feel sorry for her. She was willing to let Darcy go and put Michael out of her life until Darcy attempted to blackmail her. Sometimes we just don't know what will set someone off."

James draped his arm around Charlotte's shoulder. He kissed the top of her head. "You have an interesting way of seeing things. Come on. Let's find this 'poor soul' so I can arrest her and get her and her brother shipped the hell out of our town."

Chapter 17

Charlotte set another cup of coffee in front of Michael. He hadn't spoken for the hour she'd been there, explaining to him what had happened. He'd listened in complete silence, occasionally sipping his coffee, his face turning pale and eventually almost green.

Now, he sat there, staring down at the table. His clothes were askew, hastily donned when he'd answered her knocking at dawn.

"I'm sorry," she said quietly, sitting across from him. "Maybe I shouldn't have sent that note. Maybe I overstepped boundaries."

His head jerked up. Red-rimmed eyes held hers. "You did overstep."

Charlotte's heart sank. Damn it, she'd ripped open the tenuous healing of their relationship with her involvement. Would they relapse to strained conversations and secrets, ending up even worse off than before? She wouldn't be able to stand it if that were the case. In the back of her mind, she made a mental note to check the steamer office for the southbound schedule. Not that she currently had the funds for a ticket.

Michael's gaze dropped again. "But you were right about more than you were wrong."

"Barely." She'd thought Darcy's murder had been an impulsive act of passion, but both Ruth and Sam had proven capable of repeating the deed. That had almost been a fatal error, for both her and James.

"I can't believe I didn't see it in her," Michael said. "Maybe I just didn't want to."

Charlotte had wondered the same thing with Richard. Had there been earlier signs that he wasn't the type of man she'd thought he was? Had she fooled herself into ignoring the hints because otherwise being with him had been so interesting and fun?

She came around to Michael's side of the table. Much as he had done with her two days before, during their confessions, she wrapped her arms around his shoulders and rested her chin on his head. He pressed his face to her side as she tried to reassure him. "It's not your fault, you know."

"If I hadn't been seeing Darcy, Ruth wouldn't have been so angry at her."

Charlotte eased away to look at him. Tears welled in his eyes. "She was angry at Darcy for Sam as well. And Darcy was fool enough to think she could blackmail the Bartletts. Your seeing her wasn't the epitome of fidelity, but her death isn't your fault, Michael."

He grimaced, perhaps trying to believe it was so. Maybe he never would.

A heavy knock sounded on the door of Michael's living quarters. Charlotte stepped aside to allow him to answer. James Eddington held his hat, dark hair mussed and his freshly broken nose still looking painfully swollen.

"Doc." He nodded to Michael, then caught Charlotte's eye. "Miss Brody."

Michael returned to his seat. "You don't have to pretend to be so damn formal with her, Eddington. I think circumstances allow you to call my sister by her given name."

Charlotte and James exchanged glances.

"Fair enough," James said, shutting the door. "I know it's a difficult time for you, Doc. Sorry about all this."

Michael shrugged and shook his head, dismissing James's apology. "I feel worse for Reverend and Mrs. Bartlett. Have you spoken to them?"

James nodded. "First thing after we got Ruth and Sam squared away. They're with Blaine now."

"What happens next?" Charlotte asked.

"Considering Ruth's confession and all, I'll take them both to the federal court in Seattle with a female court officer out of Juneau. They'll stay at Morningside until their trial's set. The Bartletts will come along, I reckon. I'll need your written statement before we sail."

"Of course. I'll come down later." Though at the moment all Charlotte wanted was a hot bath and a long, dreamless sleep.

James glanced at Michael, then back to her. "We have Ruth's confession that she wrote the note to you, and that Sam threw the firebomb through your window, but you may need to bear witness in person at some point. You up for that?"

Charlotte met her brother's gaze. His lips were pressed tight. Surely he had expected she'd have to give her account to the federal court. He stared out the window over the sink. She hated seeing Michael like this, hated Ruth and Sam Bartlett for putting him through such a terrible time. And if truth be told, she also hated Darcy for being such a greedy little fool.

Had Darcy deserved to die? No, but the ramifications of her actions would be felt for a long time to come.

She faced James again. "Let me know when I need to be there."

"The court will send a summons." He put his hat on and tilted his head toward the outer door. "I'd best get back to the office."

Charlotte got the hint of his gesture. "I'll walk you out."

She closed the inner door firmly and followed James through the exam room. She shut that door behind them as well. Not that Michael would eavesdrop, but she wanted to maintain whatever privacy James sought. He waited for her at the front door.

"Is he going to be all right?" James looked at the exam-room door as if trying to see Michael through it. She followed his gaze, hoping the barriers between her and her brother weren't as solid as the doors and walls.

"It'll take some time," she said, "but I think so. There's a lot to sort through."

"Charlotte," James said, drawing her attention. "This isn't his fault, and it's not yours either. Ruth and Sam chose to take Darcy's life."

She gave him a wan smile. "I said the very same thing to Michael."

"You'll both get through this. Let me know if there's anything I can do." He glanced down at his boots, then back up at her again. Uncertainty filled his eyes, a rare thing indeed for the Deputy Eddington she knew. "I'll be gone for a bit to take the Bartletts to Seattle. Would it be too forward—" He cut himself off, grimacing.

"What?" she asked, her heart suddenly double-timing.

"Would it be too forward of me to ask you to look after the cat?"

Charlotte's shoulders slumped. The cat? "Oh. Sure."

It was better to have James as a friend who would support her and ask her to watch his cat, and nothing more.

Grinning in relief, he tapped the brim of his hat. "I'll see you down at the office later."

Charlotte shut and locked the door behind him. Unless there was an emergency, she didn't want Michael having unexpected visitors or people asking questions. Toliver would surely want to know the whole of the story for the newspaper. She'd convince him that she should be the one to write it, when all was said and done.

But for now, her biggest concern was her brother.

Charlotte brushed at the wrinkles in one of the skirts Brigit had donated to her. She hung it in the small closet in her room at the Lakeview beside the other items of clothing, including the trousers and heavy shirts she'd appropriated from Michael.

The hotel offered a fine view of Nirvana Park, but Charlotte rarely took the opportunity to appreciate it. Four days later was still a little too soon to put the encounter with Ruth and Sam far enough out of her mind to enjoy the sight.

The Lakeview wasn't as luxurious as the Windsor, but the room was larger than Charlotte's old room at Sullivan's, and more expensive too. She couldn't afford to stay at the hotel and replace her things, even with her income from *Modern Woman* and Michael's loan. She'd have to take Toliver up on his offer of a full-time job sooner rather than later and find a new place to live.

I guess that means I will be staying on past the spring.

Charlotte wasn't sure when, exactly, she'd decided that, but it felt right. Maybe it was after she realized James and Brigit and Michael would always be there for her. Or when she decided that finding peace for Darcy meant she could find peace for herself eventually. And this was the place to do it, to start over.

A quick double knock prompted her to close the closet door and cross the faded rug. She opened the door and smiled at Brigit. The woman was laden with more clothes. A carpetbag dangled from one arm.

"You're being far more generous than necessary," Charlotte said, taking the clothing to the bed.

"Not at all." Brigit closed the door behind her and set the bag on the floor. "Just a few more things, like nightclothes and undergarments. Shoes too. You can't go traipsing around in those god-awful boots all the time."

Charlotte couldn't argue there, though it was getting rainier and windier each day. The rubber boots seemed much more practical than the soft leather pair Brigit withdrew from the bag. "They're lovely. I can't thank you enough."

Brigit shrugged and sat on the edge of the bed. "You'll get more wear out of them than I will. With just the three of us in the house, I'll be on my back more than my feet."

She stuck her tongue out comically.

Charlotte laughed. "I'm sorry you're short a girl, but I'm still not interested in a job."

"Oh, I know," Brigit said, laughing along with her. "I'm just lamenting. I'd hoped at this point I'd be done with that end of the business."

Charlotte sat on the other side of the pile of clothes. "You could shut down the house."

The madam only shook her head. "And do what? I'm running a lucrative business, making money more often than not. It's just a momentary setback. Trust me, there will be some girls looking to get away from the canneries or domestic work sooner or later."

Probably sooner, thought Charlotte. At least at Brigit's they'd find a clean place to live, good food, and regular health care.

"Charlotte," Brigit said, suddenly serious. "I wanted to thank you."

"For what?" She couldn't think of anything she'd done that the woman could be grateful for. In fact, after Charlotte's accusing her and her sister of blackmail and murder, Brigit should be furious with her.

"Mary Theresa—I mean, Tess and I have been living this stupid lie for too long," she said. "It felt good to get it off our chests, even if it was only to you and Eddington."

Their meeting on the street the other day made sense now. The women weren't holding any hostility toward each other due to social status. They hadn't wanted Charlotte to learn they were sisters. With a little prompting from Charlotte, Brigit, Tess, and Frank Kavanagh had quietly approached James, the day after Ruth and Sam Bartlett had been arrested, to clear up the last few questions about Darcy and the contents of her coat.

Mary Theresa, or "Tess," and Elizabeth "Brigit" Jensen had changed their identities in an effort to start over after the trial in Fairbanks. John Francis Kincaid, aka Frank Kavanagh, had gone along with the sisters. They'd left Alaska, lived in Virginia for a time, then legitimately went into business with Kavanagh's cannery partners. By that time, Brigit had given birth to Charlie, but, she'd privately confessed later to Charlotte, she couldn't stand Kavanagh enough to even pretend marriage to him. Tess bit the bullet and actually married him before they all arrived in Cordova.

All three vehemently denied any involvement with the murder of Cecil Patterson. With no reason to question them, let alone hold them, James agreed not to reveal their true identities, but Mayor Kavanagh would have to withdraw from the upcoming election. The money Darcy had solicited from them would go into the new school being built. The Kavanaghs and Brigit O'Brien would be allowed to remain in Cordova as long as they followed territorial law from here on out.

"I'm glad you're done with it," Charlotte said, "but I still don't understand how Darcy knew who you really were."

"Her mother worked the Line with us up north, though I barely remember either of them. The trial in Fairbanks was a big deal. Darcy said she'd kept the clippings in a scrapbook because she was excited to know local 'celebrities.'" Brigit rolled her eyes at the younger woman's antics. "When she arrived down here and saw us, she got different ideas."

Darcy had been the daughter of a sporting woman. Was that why she had sought out similar work in Cordova, or had she learned who Brigit really was before meeting Marie? They'd never know.

Charlotte recalled her conversation with Marie at the Edgewater pool hall. "Ideas like blackmail being much easier on the back than cannery work or being a laundress or even working your house."

"Exactly," Brigit said. "Frank was looking forward to a political career. There's a long tradition of reinventing yourself in this part of the world, and we wanted to take advantage of it."

"I can understand that," Charlotte said. "But if you were acquitted and not involved with the death of Cecil Patterson, why worry about it at all?"

Brigit's expression hardened. She leaned closer, as if someone might overhear them. "To be honest, I'm not sure Frank is completely innocent in Patterson's death. Tess and I had nothing to do with it, I swear."

"He'd rather have paid the blackmail than have someone look too closely at the accident." Her view of Frank Kavanagh had already been skewed, but Charlotte's wariness now increased toward the otherwise genial lame-duck mayor.

What if he *had* been involved in the ten-year-old Patterson incident?

"Leave it be, Charlotte."

Bringing her thoughts back to the present, she focused on Brigit. "But—"

"Please." She reached out toward Charlotte. "As a friend, I'm asking you to leave it alone. We're happy here. I have my boy to think about. Tess and I don't want any more trouble, and there's no proof Frank had anything to do with that man's death."

Charlotte took her hand and gave it a light squeeze. "As your friend, I will leave it alone."

Relief softened the tension in Brigit's face. "Thank you," she said, squeezing back. "If there was anything more than my suspicions, I'd be happy to help put Frank away. There isn't, so it's not worth the trouble."

"You don't like him much, do you?" The trio had been partners in a suspected crime, but that didn't mean they got along.

The madam grimaced. "Let's just say we've had our differences and leave it at that."

Charlotte wondered why Brigit had traveled to Cordova with Frank and Tess, but didn't want to put more strain on their burgeoning friendship. Maybe Brigit would tell her someday. Maybe she wouldn't. It didn't matter.

Brigit stood to leave. "Come for tea tomorrow, won't you? Around two?"

Charlotte escorted her to the door. "I'd like that."

"You're not worried about what the rest of the town might say?" There was a glint of amusement in Brigit's eyes, but also a hint of worry.

"I'm not one to let others decide who my friends will be or what I do with them." Charlotte wrote of the need for change and acceptance; it was time to allow herself the same freedom, social "correctness" be damned. She opened the door, smiling. "See you tomorrow at two."

Brigit caught her up in a brief hug, then hurried down the hall.

Charlotte closed the door, smiling. Her new friendship with Brigit made her feel as at home as she'd felt in her family's or Kit's presence. And James Eddington made her feel . . . Well, that one remained to be seen. With Mr. Toliver's job offer, she could find a place to live, one she could make her own.

She sat at the small desk under the window and threaded a fresh sheet of paper around the platen of the now familiar Corona typewriter she'd borrowed from Toliver. Her first-person account of the story behind Darcy's murder in yesterday's *Cordova Daily Times* had been popular, even though she'd been forced to leave out certain details. Compromising the case, Marshal Blaine had warned her, could put Charlotte in the cell next to Ruth Bartlett down at Morningside prison. She didn't mention the Kavanaghs' or Brigit's past in the article either, or anything to do with their paying Darcy for the last year.

But Charlotte had to get the whole story out of her head before she burst. She'd write everything down in detail for her personal satisfaction, then modify a draft for a later installment of her *Modern Woman* series.

She ignored the rain spattering against the window, and her fingers flew over the enameled keys. *Death and Deception on the Last Frontier.*

Other than murder, blackmail, and copious amounts of wind, rain, and mud, Cordova wasn't such a bad town.

Please turn the page for an exciting sneak peek of
Cathy Pegau's next Charlotte Brody mystery

BORROWING DEATH

coming in July 2016!

Chapter 1

"How can we, as Americans, claim to support individual freedoms while advocating for such a restrictive amendment? Not to say overindulging isn't an issue, but even with current prohibition laws in some States and here in the Alaska Territory we have seen a rise in the illegal production and sale of alcohol and associated criminal behavior. There has also been an increase in wood alcohol deaths as the common man attempts to slake his thirst with his own poisonous concoctions. Is this the price we're willing to pay in what can only be a futile attempt at national sobriety?"

Charlotte Brody typed the final lines of her op-ed piece for the next day's edition of the *Cordova Daily Times*. She grinned as she swiped an errant strand of hair out of her eyes. "That'll put the ladies of the local Women's Temperance League in a tizzy."

She just hoped Andrew Toliver, the *Times'* owner and publisher, liked it. He was neutral on most major topics, at least as far as what he put in the paper, and it delighted him to have the town talking about what they found within its pages. This would get some tongues wagging, for better or worse.

With the twist of one of the linotype's several levers, she sent the sequence of steel mats to the molding mechanism. The machine clattered and whirred, the small motor by her left knee buzzing. In a minute or so, the new lead slug would be molded, dropped into place, and cool enough to handle.

How would Cordovans react to her take on national prohibition? A fairly even split, she reckoned. No matter what side they supported, she hoped it sold papers. Then again, as the only news source in a town full of folks who enjoyed a good debate, she was more than certain it would.

But that's not why she wrote the article. Increasing sales, while financially beneficial, wasn't her goal as a journalist. Seeking justice, informing the public, and getting them to talk about issues was what she loved about her calling.

Despite President Wilson's attempts to veto it—though not for the reasons she espoused—the Eighteenth Amendment would take effect in less than two months. Perhaps if enough people considered how ridiculous it was, and called for its repeal, this waste of time and energy would be a mere bump in history.

Charlotte slid the stool away from the massive linotype's keyboard and bent down to flick off the electric motor that ran the gears and chains of the machine. The buzz in her ears subsided. After three months as Mr. Toliver's assistant, she hardly noticed the tang of hot lead from the crucible anymore, but silencing the motor was always a relief. She felt her head clear, like cobwebs swept from rafters.

Now, the Nineteenth Amendment, *that* was a change that truly mattered and would have positive lasting effects. Nearly twenty states had ratified the voting amendment so far, and it looked like more were poised to join in. All the marching, protesting, and arrests of good women and men had made for a long, often painful journey, but it was worth it. Charlotte would never forget the stories of sacrifice and bravery that had paved the way, and couldn't wait to celebrate national suffrage someday soon.

Would she still be in Alaska when that happened? Hard to say. It would likely be spring or summer by the time ratification was complete, and she was looking forward to seeing the territory in more pleasant weather.

The late November wind rattled a loose panel of the metal roof of the *Times* office, reminding her pleasant weather was a long way away. It was probably snowing again.

Anxious to finish and get home before the streets were too terrible, Charlotte picked up the cooled lead slugs and aligned them in the frame on the proofing table. Seeing no obvious defects, she rolled ink onto the raised letters, then laid a fresh piece of newspaper over the frame. She used a second, clean roller to create a proof and lifted it carefully. With the eye of an editor, she searched for errors that would require retyping a corrected slug.

Satisfied, Charlotte put the rollers and ink away. Mr. Toliver would be in soon to run the large printing press across the room. First, they'd go over the next day's issue, making changes as necessary, then she'd go home while he stayed overnight to mind the machinery. He preferred working at night, he'd said when he hired her, listening to the rhythm of the press as he perused articles or created special advertisement pages.

The shared tasks suited Charlotte. She was able to write local stories, gather the social notices, tidbits, and comings and goings endemic to a small town paper during the day, and still work on her serialized account of women in Alaska for *The Modern Woman Review* in the evenings. What made for news in a remote Alaska town wasn't usually as exciting as back in New York, but you learned who threw the most popular dinner parties.

She closed the door of the press room behind her and entered the main office. It was much cooler away from the linotype, despite the coal stove in the corner. Quieter too, with only the tick-tock of the cuckoo clock to challenge the periodic howl of the wind. She checked the time as she sat at Toliver's messy desk. After eight already? He should be here soon.

Charlotte slid a piece of scratch paper under the circle of light made by the desk lamp and jotted a note about the thunking she'd heard earlier within the massive machine. Toliver had instilled in her the need to keep the linotype in tip-top shape, as it was their bread and butter.

Setting the note where he'd see it, or at least eventually find it, Charlotte was drawn to an article that had come in over the Associated Press teletype on coal miners threatening to strike down in the States. Goodness, what sort of things were happening to those poor people? She started to read, frowning at their plight.

A triple knock on the front door jerked Charlotte's eyes open. She'd only meant to rest them for a moment. Late nights and early mornings were starting to catch up to her.

All she could see through the frosted glass was a vague, dark figure. The streetlight must have gone out again. Who would be out on a night such as this? Toliver wouldn't have knocked, as he had his own key.

"Michael or James," she answered herself as she rose, her voice rough in her own ears.

Back in New York, she would have ignored a nighttime visitor. Or taken her brother's old baseball bat with her. Here, she was fairly confident the person outside wasn't going to hurt her. Besides, she'd left the bat at her parents' house.

She opened the door. A gust of cold, wet wind blew in, making her shiver.

Deputy Marshal James Eddington stood at the threshold, melting slush dripping off the brim of his hat. "You shouldn't be opening the door without asking who it is."

"Are you saying you're unable to keep the streets of Cordova safe enough for a woman to be at her own place of employment without worry?" She smiled as she said it, letting him know she was just teasing. James was a very good deputy, committed to his job, and most everyone in town knew he and Marshal Blaine weren't to be trifled with when it came to breaking the laws of the Territory.

His black eyebrows met in a scowl, but there was a glimmer of amusement in his eyes. "Common sense should come into play, even here. There are some unsavory elements about."

She'd certainly learned that in her three months in town.

"I'll be more careful from now on," she promised. "Come in and warm up. I'm almost done."

James slipped in when Charlotte stepped aside. She closed the door after him. He swept his hat from his head, shook off the excess water carefully to avoid wetting her, and hung it on a peg screwed into the wall alongside her own hat and coat.

"More snow since early evening. Cold and slick out there," he said as he unbuttoned his coat. "Wanted to make sure you get home okay."

Though warmed by his concern, Charlotte rubbed her chilled bare arms, her sleeves held up by an old pair of garters so they wouldn't get dirtied by the linotype. "That's very kind of you. Sit for a minute while I finish a few things. Mr. Toliver should be here soon. Would you like some tea? I think the water's still hot."

"Toliver doesn't have anything stronger stashed in his desk?" James asked with a sly smile.

He did, but friend or not, Charlotte wasn't about to admit it to a deputy who enforced Alaska's dry laws. "Just tea."

"Then tea'd be great, thanks." He sat on the straight-back chair on the other side of the desk while she went to the stove to check the kettle. Still hot enough to make a decent cup.

Charlotte prepared their tea and brought the cups to the desk. She sat in Toliver's padded chair, suddenly at a loss of what to say to James. They'd been friendly enough since she'd arrived in Cordova in August, and he was easy to talk to. They'd even gone to dinner, and another time a show at the Empress Theater with her brother and her friend Brigit. And they'd shared a kiss.

So why was she unable to come up with small talk now, as they sat in a dimly lit office while the wind blew outside?

"Anything exciting in tomorrow's paper?" He watched her over the rim of the cup as he sipped.

Relieved to have something to talk about, she passed him the originals of the articles she'd transcribed. "Mostly the usual, though there are a few that should get some attention."

How would Deputy Eddington and Marshal Blaine take her editorial? They already knew her personal stance on Prohibition, and Blaine had more or less agreed with her that enforcement was difficult. Putting it in print for all of Cordova to see was another matter.

He glanced through the drafts, stopping at a page and frowning. "This damn arsonist is driving us crazy."

"At least there hasn't been any serious damage or injury." Charlotte had written three pieces about fires set over the last month. Abandoned sheds and piles of brush seemed to be the arsonist's main source of entertainment.

"Not so far," James said, "but this is the third year he's done it. Sets a few fires, then stops. I'd rather not have this be an annual event."

"How unusual. Are you sure it's the same person?" There was no evidence pointing to anyone or any particular pattern other than the timing.

"Not really, but in a way, I hope so." He shook his head slowly. "We don't need a copycat—"

A muffled boom from somewhere not too distant cut him off, followed by three more smaller ones in quick succession. The explosions weren't loud, more like when she'd stood on the street in New York City for a parade and heard the bands' bass drums while they were still a couple of blocks away.

James set his tea cup down quickly, sloshing liquid onto the pages on the desk, and bolted from his seat. Charlotte followed him. Throwing open the door, he stood on the walk and looked up and down Main Street. His eyes widened as he faced west, toward the canneries. "It looks like Fiske's. Call the firehouse," he said, already running in that direction.

Charlotte took a quick look. Though she didn't see flames, there was an unnatural glow coming from two streets away. She about-faced, dashed back to the desk, and snatched up the candlestick phone. Placing the earpiece against her ear, she flicked the bracket several times.

After a few long moments, a drowsy voice answered. "Operator."

"There's been an explosion and a fire," Charlotte said. "At Fiske's Hardware."

"I'll call it in," the operator replied, perkier now. "Anyone hurt?"

"I don't know. Deputy Eddington went down there. Hurry."

Charlotte hung up before the operator. She grabbed her notepad and a pencil from the desk and practically broke her neck hopping one foot to the other as she pulled off her shoes. Thank goodness single buckles and slip-ons had replaced high-laced styles, but they weren't good in snow. She hurried to the door, shoved her feet into her heavy boots, on top of her wool socks stuffed inside, and yanked her hat and coat off their pegs.

Struggling to get her coat on while she slipped and slid in the slush, Charlotte made her way to the end of the street. By the time she turned toward Fiske's, fire licked at the side window of the building. Luckily, there was some distance between the hardware store and its nearest neighbor. The idea of a block-long inferno scared the hell out of her.

"James!"

He was nowhere in sight. The door was open and black smoke poured out, dimming the streetlight on the far corner. The acrid stench of burning chemicals made Charlotte's eyes water. The smell made her heart race and her palms sweat, despite the cold. She stepped back, rubbing the thin scar beneath her left eye. Not long ago, she'd been caught in a burning room, and the memory was too fresh to allow her to get any closer.

"James!" she called again, praying he hadn't gone inside.

The smoke was getting thicker, the flames growing larger and louder. The upper floor seemed untouched, for the moment, but that wouldn't last long.

Charlotte heard the bell clanging from the firehouse near the harbor. If any of the volunteers had spent the night there, they would be on the scene soon. But would it be soon enough?

She reached into her pocket for the notebook and pencil. Taking notes and focusing on the facts for the article she'd write kept her worry for James at bay, for the moment.

Several people joined her on the corner, some with coats pulled on over nightclothes.

"Anyone call the fire department?"

"I heard the bells going."

"What the hell happened? Anyone inside?"

Charlotte glanced up at the building as the flames snapped and flashed through the windows. God, she hoped the building had been empty. A shudder ran through her. She shoved her notebook into her pocket, buttoned her coat, and crossed her arms against the cold. Thank goodness she'd worn an old pair of long johns under her skirt.

By the time the sound of yelling and the clang of the fire engine bell came up the road, the fire had grown and smoke billowed out of the upper floor window. The four horse-drawn pump car with six men hanging on was followed by the six-horse tank. The firemen leaped off their carts before they came to a complete stop, boots squishing in the icy mud. Two men connected the tank hose to the pump. Others connected the fire hose to the other end of the pump and unrolled the rubberized canvas toward Fiske's.

Three men donned hard leather masks that covered their heads, the eye pieces giving them an insectoid appearance. Hopefully the air canisters attached to the backs of the masks would sustain them long enough to extinguish the flames. When their equipment was secure, they hurried to the hose.

"Ready!" came the muffled cry of the man at the front. He pointed the nozzle toward the open door. Four men operated the pump mechanism, two to a side. After a few pumps, water shot out of the nozzle. The man in the front slowly walked forward.

James came around from the back of the building, and Charlotte breathed a sigh of relief. He strode directly to Chief Parker, who wore a black, hardened leather helmet with a metal crest on the front, and began talking and gesturing. Charlotte couldn't hear what they were saying over the rush of water, the roar of flames, and the chatter of the men near her.

"Charlotte, are you all right?"

She turned toward her brother. Like some of the other men, Michael wore his mackinaw over a stripped pajama shirt and hastily donned trousers.

"I'm fine. Did you get a call? Is someone hurt?" Charlotte hadn't seen anyone come out of Fiske's with an injury. Maybe he'd been contacted as a precaution.

"No, I heard the commotion. But I have my bag, just in case." He held up his leather satchel, then turned his gaze to the building. "I pray I won't need it."

James nodded at something the chief said, then walked over to them. Melted snow plastered his hair to his head, but he didn't seem to be feeling the effects. "Doc," he said, greeting Michael. "Shouldn't have been anyone inside, but if you'll stick around to make sure the firemen are okay, I'd be obliged."

"Of course," Michael replied. "Has anyone gotten word to Fiske?"

"One of Parker's sons was sent to the house. He's not back yet."

The men manning the hose hadn't gone far beyond the front door. One inside shouted something. The men stepped back several steps as a loud crash sounded within the building. Black smoke billowed out of the windows and over their heads.

The onlookers startled and stepped back. Though they were far enough away to be safe from the flames, the chemical smell burned Charlotte's nose and eyes. Several men wiped sleeves across their faces.

"There's the chief's son," James said, nodding toward a lanky youth jogging down the road as fast as the slick surface allowed. He joined Parker, but the young man was shaking his head. James returned to Charlotte and Michael, his brow deeply furrowed. "Fiske wasn't at home. No one but the housekeeper was there."

"Caroline's out of town," Charlotte said. She recalled placing the travel announcement and Caroline Fiske's promise of a holiday party upon her return on the social page of the paper. "She gets back any day now."

"That's what the housekeeper told the kid. Helluva homecoming," James said.

All of them looked back at the building. Dread solidified in the pit of Charlotte's stomach.

"Maybe he's at one of the clubs or something," Michael suggested.

"I'll check around." James raked his fingers through his wet hair. "I need to catch that damn arsonist. This has gone too far."

It seemed like hours before the firemen trudged out of the building, smudged with soot and dripping. The outer walls of the hardware store had scorched, but remained intact from what Charlotte could see. Thank goodness they lived in such a wet environment. The interior, however, was likely a total loss.

The chief met with one man as he and his companions helped each other remove their masks, taking care with the air canisters. Charlotte couldn't hear their conversation, but the man gestured back to the building, curving his hand as if giving direction. Parker's frown deepened. Even from where she stood, Charlotte heard his emphatic "Son of a bitch."

He looked out toward the crowd, his gaze falling on James. "Deputy," he called, waving James over. "You too, Doc."

The three of them exchanged glances, and the dread in Charlotte's gut turned to a bilious cramping. There was only one reason to request Michael, the town's coroner, as well as one of its doctors.

"Damnation," James muttered, heading to the chief.

Michael and Charlotte followed. Both men stopped and turned to her.

"No," James said, holding up a hand. "This is no place for you."

Irritation bristled at the back of her neck. "I beg to differ, Deputy. As a journalist I have an obligation to report suspected crimes."

Michael rolled his eyes. "Here we go again."

She scowled at him.

"And as Deputy Marshal," James said, "my investigation into suspected crimes trumps your journalistic obligation. I'll relay any pertinent information to you, Miss Brody, but right now I'm ordering you to remain out here. If you don't, I'll handcuff you to the lightpost. Understood?"

He'd do it, too. Charlotte resisted her natural inclination to argue with anyone who told her she couldn't do this or that and gave him a curt nod. James nodded back. They'd known each other only a few short months and had quickly come to respect each other's duties. When James felt it was time to disclose information for public consumption and safety, he'd do it. Pushing him too far, too fast, would likely land her in one of his jail cells. Or cuffed to a post.

James and Michael made their way to the door of the hardware store with the chief. Two firemen loaned them their masks. The fire may have been out, but smoldering embers and toxic fumes from whatever chemicals Fiske had in his inventory could prove dangerous, if not outright fatal. The three men disappeared into the blackened store. Charlotte caught a few glimpses of smoky light from Parker's flashlight.

Worry gnawed around the edges of her irritation. What was inside the charred store? No amount of craning her neck allowed her to see past the front door.

"What's happening, Miss Brody?"

Charlotte gave Henry, one of her paper boys and a server at the café, a nod of greeting. What was he doing out so late? "The chief asked Deputy Eddington and Michael to look at something inside."

Under the wan electric streetlight, Henry's ruddy cheeks paled. "What would they need the doctor for? Someone inside get hurt?"

She wouldn't be the one to start rumors or set off wild speculation. James would never forgive her that transgression. "I couldn't say."

Henry stared at the front door and broken window leaking smoke, his expression the same as the few remaining gawkers who stayed to see what James and Michael might find. "It's not Mr. Fiske, is it? I mean, who else would be in his store at this hour?"

"We don't know what's what, Henry, so let's not jump to conclusions." She sounded a lot like James, but the words offered a small amount of hope that Lyle Fiske was all right.

"Even so," Henry said, "the store's a goner." He glanced at Charlotte. "Do they think the arsonist did it?"

Charlotte and others had entertained the same thought. "I'm sure the fire department and the marshal's office will investigate every possibility. But the three other fires were smaller, in places where no one was around. This seems like a jump in destructive intent to me."

Henry nodded, his attention back on the building and the firemen putting their equipment away.

Finally, Michael emerged from the hardware store. A fireman helped him with the mask. Michael took a deep breath of fresh air, but his face was drawn.

Charlotte started toward him. "Excuse me, Henry."

Her feet slid in the slushy road. It was particularly mucky where the water tank had been dripping, adding to the mess of the wet snow. As she reached Michael, James exited the building with the fire chief, the two of them talking low, their expressions similar to Michael's. James held something heavy wrapped in cloth and under his jacket to protect it from the snow.

"It's bad, isn't it?" Charlotte kept her voice low and her back turned so the onlookers wouldn't pick up on their conversation. No need to get rumors started. "Lyle Fiske?"

Michael nodded. "It looks like it. They'll bring the body over to the basement of the hospital. The new morgue is up and running. Just wish we didn't need it so damn soon."

"You'll confirm who it is and manner of death for an article, won't you?" Charlotte had no desire to attend this autopsy. One was enough for her lifetime.

"I don't want anything out about this yet," James said as he joined them. He looked cold and wet, his hair dripping. "There are circumstances that need clearing up."

"Like what?" she asked. "How the fire started? Do you think it was the arsonist?"

"Those questions, and who'd want Lyle Fiske dead."

"You're sure it was intentional?" What a terrible idea.

"The fire may not have been," James said, bringing the cloth-wrapped items out from under his coat, "but the knife and hammer near his body suggest his death was."

Charlotte shifted on the uncomfortable chair in Michael's outer office. Staying late at the *Times'* office, she'd typed up a short piece for the morning edition, just a few lines of facts and observations of the fire department's activities. Mr. Toliver had arrived by the time the fire department was finishing up. He manned the linotype, encouraging Charlotte to go home and get some rest.

Sleep had been nearly impossible. Speculation about how the fire had started, why, and the identity of the unfortunate victim were left out of the article, but not her thoughts. The discovery of a possible murder weapon contributed to theories about what had happened.

Poor Mr. Fiske. Charlotte hoped he was dead before the fire started. Awful as that sounded, she couldn't imagine the terror of being conscious while the building burned.

The outer door opened, and Michael came into the office, quickly closing out the cold and wind. Charlotte caught a whiff of burnt flesh under the "hospital" smell of carbolic acid and cleanser. Probably just her imagination, but she rose and cracked open the window for some fresh air despite the winter chill.

"How'd it go, Michael?"

He hung up his hat and mackinaw, then sat in the chair behind his desk. In his usual manner of preparing to deliver bad news, Michael straightened his tie and smoothed back his hair before meeting her gaze.

"I do believe it's Lyle Fiske," he said. "Build and clothing—what's left of it—are consistent with Fiske. His features had been damaged by flames, but not completely burned away. Still, since no one's been able to find Fiske in town, I believe it's him."

"Did the fire kill him?" She knew that often people were overcome by smoke before burned by the flames of a fire. With so many chemicals in the hardware store, it wouldn't have surprised her if toxic fumes had rendered him unconscious first. But unless he'd been asleep in his office, how had he not been capable of escaping? The presence of the knife and hammer became more than a little suspicious.

Michael scrubbed his palms over his face, the whiskers on his cheeks just long enough to become disheveled. She'd gotten used to the moustache he sported, but a beard was something else. Though understandable, given the climate. "I think he was dead before the fire."

Thank goodness for small favors, Charlotte thought. "Why do you say that?"

"His clothes and skin were burned, and he smelled of chemicals as if he'd been doused with paint thinner or something. That obliterated any obvious wounds on his front. I think the debris that fell on him after the explosion smothered the flames, essentially preserving the rest of the body. The clothing and skin on his back was relatively unscathed. But when I opened him up—"

Her stomach flipped. Images of Darcy Dugan's autopsy three months ago flashed through her mind like a jittery nickelodeon. How Michael managed to distance himself from such gruesome things astounded her. It must have been difficult, especially in a small town where he was familiar with the victims. On the one hand, she knew he was sympathetic to his patients' conditions. On the other, he managed to dictate graphic details of injury and illness with nary a hitch in his voice.

"—blood in his chest cavity."

"Blood? How?"

"A slit in his heart's apex. There was an obvious cut on the inside of his thoracic cavity and into the heart muscle." Michael pointed at his own chest, just under his sternum. "The killer thrust upward. Not an easy task to avoid ribs, but the knife found was large enough to do the trick. Still, whoever killed Fiske was pretty strong, and either lucky or skilled."

A shudder ran through Charlotte. The idea of a "skilled" killer in Cordova brought to mind the terrors of a Jack the Ripper–type. *Let's not blow this out of proportion.*

"Why would someone kill him?"

"That's Eddington's job, not mine. All I can say is he was likely dead, or close to it, prior to the fire." Michael shrugged and slowly shook his head, looking weary. "Fiske was a decent sort, as far as I knew him. He and his wife were well liked."

"Not by everyone, perhaps." Charlotte had only met the couple a few times. Caroline was ten or so years older than she, and Lyle another ten years older than his wife. They were friendly enough, and Caroline seemed to enjoy being among Cordova's growing number of society matrons—wives of the more prominent and successful businessmen.

"Poor Caroline."

After checking back issues of the *Times* earlier, Charlotte had found the social page where Mrs. Fiske's travel plans had been mentioned. On a more practical note, the fact she was out of town meant she wasn't a suspect. Michael had said killing Fiske took some strength as well. That covered a number of men and women who lived in a place that required muscle and skill to survive.

"Eddington will be questioning the housekeeper and whoever else works for them to ask about her return plans. In the meantime, we'll have Fiske taken over to the funeral parlor. I don't envy them this preparation." Michael rose, stretched his back, and crossed to stand with her at the window. "I know that look in your eye, Charlotte. Keep your nose out of this and let Eddington do his job."

She held up her right hand in the Boy Scout salute. "I promise not to impede his investigation."

Michael squeezed her fingers. "That isn't the same thing as staying out of it."

Charlotte eased her hand out of his and rose up on her toes to peck him on the cheek. "I wouldn't want you to call me a liar. Let me know when you want me to type up your report for Juneau."

As his sometimes secretary, Charlotte helped keep his patient files and official reports organized. Sending copies to the Territorial capital was one of the tasks she helped with.

"Oh, about that," he said, cheeks pinkening under his new beard. "I'm getting someone to help me with paperwork and some interpretation issues."

Charlotte couldn't help the surprise widening her eyes. "You are? Since when?"

They saw each other every day, or just about, and he'd never mentioned getting help.

"Well, it's not official yet, but with more of the Natives coming into town for work and whatnot, I thought it would be a good idea to have someone with me who knew them better."

That made sense, but it didn't explain why he'd never mentioned it to her.

"And I've been busy with the newspaper and unavailable," she said.

Michael's mouth quirked into a crooked grin. "That too. But mostly because Mary can really help me communicate with her people. And she needs the job."

"Mary?" Charlotte wasn't nearly as familiar with the local Eyak population as he was.

"Mary Jenkov. You might have heard her called Old Creek Mary. She's worked at the grocer before."

"Oh, yes." Charlotte recalled a young Native woman stacking shelves or behind the counter at McGruder's. A lovely girl. Well, not a girl. She was probably the same age as Charlotte. "She has a couple of kids, doesn't she?"

"That's right. A boy and a girl, five and around three. The grandmother watches them when Mary's working." Michael returned to his seat at the desk. "Her husband died last spring."

"How terrible."

"It was. When she mentioned she was looking for something more challenging than stacking shelves, I sort of offered her a job." He winced. "You don't mind, do you?"

"Of course not. In fact, I'm looking forward to talking to her." Charlotte crossed the room and retrieved her coat and hat from the peg on the back of the door.

Just as she lifted the mackinaw, the door opened and she stepped out of the way to avoid getting hit.

James came in and shut the door behind him. Removing his hat, he said, "Shoulda known you'd be here before me."

Charlotte grinned. "Early bird gets the worm." The deputy shot a questioning look at Michael. "Don't worry, James, I promise not to write or say anything until you give me the go-ahead. I won't compromise your investigation. But you'll inform me of any developments, right?"

James and Michael exchanged glances. After the terrible situation with Darcy Dugan, they knew Charlotte couldn't help but get herself involved. But they could also trust her to keep her word and not spoil the case.

"You've told her how Fiske died?" James asked Michael. There was a hint of irritation in his voice.

"She's my current secretary of record," Michael said. "I trust her with keeping pertinent evidence and case information to herself."

He'd just told her that a different person would be performing that task, yet here he was, covering for her. Practically lying to James. Though it was possible Michael wouldn't want to frighten his soon-to-be assistant Mary with the horrible details of an autopsy.

Charlotte suppressed a grin of appreciation. Not only for him standing up for her, but for the renewed closeness they'd achieved since she arrived in Alaska. Terrible things had transpired for each of them, inspiring them to regain the relationship they'd shared as children. In a way, Charlotte was glad for the challenges and heartache they'd both endured. Without it, they may never have reconnected.

James shook his head, resigned for the moment. "Fine. Was there a stab wound, or was it the blow of the hammer?"

"Stab." Michael recapped his autopsy findings. "Any idea why someone would kill him?"

"Robbery. The till was open and empty."

Charlotte could see that scenario play out in her head. The thief broke into Fiske's store after hours, thinking it empty. Lyle happened to be there, working late while Caroline was out of town. Surprised, the thief killed Lyle, then set the fire to cover up the crime.

"Whoever did this is looking at a life sentence, if not worse," James said.

Robbery was bad enough, but compounding it with murder—intentional or not—was almost a sure-fire way for the culprit to get hanged or sent to the electric chair.

"Have you been able to contact Caroline?" Charlotte wasn't close to the woman, but couldn't imagine returning from holiday to this horrible news.

James rubbed the back of his neck. His eyes seemed sunken in with weariness. "Just talked to the housekeeper. She comes in on tomorrow's steamer. I'll get a message to the naval office outside town. They'll wire the ship to have everyone kept on board when they get in. Better she wonder about the delay than come down the gangplank to a dock full of gawkers."

Charlotte nodded, appreciating his sensitivity about the matter. "You may want to have a friend of hers or at least the housekeeper with you."

"Good idea." He eyed her warily. "And no, not you."

Indignation heated her face and neck. "I'm a journalist, not a ghoul, Deputy. The woman deserves her privacy at a time like this."

"I'm glad we agree on that." James set his hat on his head and touched the brim in his standard salute. "Get me a copy of the autopsy report as soon as you can, Doc."

"I'll do that, but I think a nap is in order first." Michael covered a yawn, as if the very idea of sleep made him more weary.

Charlotte buttoned her coat and donned her hat. "I think that's a fine idea. Walk me home, Deputy?"

James's eyes widened, but without pause he opened the door. "Of course, Miss Brody. See you later, Doc."

As she walked with James, Charlotte pulled on a pair of mittens she kept in her coat pocket. The colorful wool cheered her, and reminded her of her friend Kit, who'd sent them as an early Christmas present. The sun had supposedly risen an hour before, but thick, dark clouds made it feel much later. Few were out on the snowy street, though there was inviting light from within businesses.

The cold and wet of Cordova, Alaska, in late November wasn't any worse than she'd experienced back east; it just felt colder and wetter because of the shorter days. Lack of daylight sometimes made her want to hibernate along with the bears. Sunrise around nine or ten and near dark by four in the afternoon took some getting used to. Some people never got used to it. Add that to being cooped up when bad weather hit, further darkening the skies, and folks tended to get a little antsy.

Those who could stick it out loved it in the Great Land, and she enjoyed interviewing those folks and sharing their stories with *Modern Woman* readers. It was a matter of staying busy, she'd been told more than once. That explained the frequent turnover of shows at the Empress Theater and the weekly community dance or two. Keeping entertained and social was a good prescription for fending off cabin fever.

"I didn't mean to imply you'd harass Mrs. Fiske as soon as she got off the boat," James said as he took her arm and guided her around a large, slushy puddle. "If you weren't a journalist,

I'd have asked you to come with me. I just don't want her to feel overwhelmed."

"Apology accepted," she said. "Did you get much information from the Fiskes' housekeeper or employees? Was Fiske having trouble with anyone?"

James shook his head. "I spoke to Mrs. Munson, but she's only been working there a month and doesn't see Mr. Fiske all that often. Fiske had two men working with him at the store. I'll interview them later this morning."

"Michael said Fiske seemed like a decent sort." Charlotte watched him for a reaction. James tended to have a spot-on opinion of most people in town. They both knew a person's public life could conceal unpleasant private activity.

He flicked a glance her way and shrugged. "Nothing reported to us."

"But you have your suspicions." What could James think Fiske was up to?

"I'm suspicious of just about everyone, Charlotte. It's my job."

She grinned. "Mine too."

In about ten minutes, they'd navigated the slippery incline of a side street and were in front of the little green house where Charlotte was staying. The owners, Harold and Viola Gibbins, were in the States for the winter. Having Charlotte live there gave them peace of mind that their home would be cared for while they were away. And since the first place Charlotte had lived in had burned down in August, she now had a roof over her head.

The house, with its angled footings to compensate for the road, was large enough to provide plenty of room, but small enough to feel cozy. The woodstove heated the place quickly, which was appreciated each and every morning.

James held her elbow as they ascended the stairs. The staircase wobbled a bit, and Charlotte made a mental note to have it looked at. Standing in front of the shiny black door, James said, "All settled, are you?"

"I didn't have much to move in, thankfully, but yes." Her parents were shipping more of her things, but storms had delayed arrivals from Seattle.

She glanced up at the quaint little home and the neighbors' similar houses. She'd only briefly met the folks on either side, but felt comfortable here, like she belonged. "I'll need to find another place before Mr. and Mrs. Gibbins return in March. It'll have to be bigger than a room at a boardinghouse, though. I rather like having the space to move about."

She tended to pace and putter about while mulling her writing, a challenge in a single room.

"So you're staying past spring."

Charlotte eyed him curiously. Was he asking or concluding? "That's my current plan."

James nodded. "Good. That's good."

"I'm glad you approve." She poured as much sarcasm into the words as she could while grinning.

He startled at her tone. "I'm not approving anything." She laughed, and his face pinked beneath his dark beard. "What I mean is, you don't need my approval or anyone else's. I'm glad you're staying. If you are."

The urge to tease him diminished, but only a little. "Even if I'm bothersome?"

"I'm hoping you'll grow out of that," he said with a mock scowl.

Charlotte laughed again. "Don't count on it." She unlocked the door and glanced over her shoulder. "Thank you for walking me home."

James put his hand on the doorframe, leaning slightly toward her. "Why did you ask me to, Charlotte?"

She turned and stared at him, her body suddenly tense, aware of his proximity. Why *had* she asked? Honesty seemed the best course with James Eddington. Even if he did seem to tie her tongue at times. "Because I enjoy your company."

The smile he gave her brought out the dimple in his cheek. "The feeling's mutual, Miss Brody." He tugged the brim of his hat. "Good morning."

"Good morning, Deputy," she said, more breathlessly than intended.

He made his way down the stairs and strode back toward Main Street. As she watched him turn the corner, Charlotte wondered for the umpteenth time if she'd ever be able to let herself truly relax around him.